LOVE IS ALL YOU NEED

LOVE IS ALL YOU NEED

Regina Burch

The Chapel Hill Press

Printed in the United States of America

Published by:
The Chapel Hill Press
100 Eastwood Lake Road
Chapel Hill, NC 27514
919/942-8389
919/968-3274 (fax)
www.chapelhillpress.com

ISBN: 1-880849-10-0

Acknowledgments

The creation of this book has depended upon the unwavering dedication, sacrifice, and loyalty of my husband and children. To Michael, Kitt, and Brian, thank you for all the times you understood when Mom was too busy for household duty. Thanks also for being supportive when I needed to bounce ideas off someone or needed your technical expertise on the computer. By helping me complete this book, a creative dream has come true.

I would like to thank the all the people who allowed me to interview them in preparation for this book: Special thanks to Joyce Gardner, Cindy Crabtree, and J. B. Shelton who provided editing and advice which made this novel possible.

Cover design by J. Brian Burch.

Back cover photo by Regina Burch

Photo on front cover taken by and used by permission of David Gray

INTRODUCTION

The Beatles were and are the most singularly powerful influence on the world of music. I was instantly hooked that Sunday evening when The Beatles made their first performance on American soil for the Ed Sullivan show. I have memories of being in suspended animation, staring at these exciting, handsome, and energetic singers on a black and white portable television. In the background, my alarmed Mother droned on about how shameful their long hair looked. The reaction of both females in my family was normal for our respective generations at the time. But after the Beatles have created huge quantities of memorable and inspiring music with innovative techniques, all generations now respect their valuable contributions to society and to music.

Please note that although this work is fictional, there are notations throughout the book designed to acquaint the reader with some facts about the real group, The Beatles. This effort is to give direction to interested readers so that they may do more study about this extremely interesting phenomenon.

I DO NOT BELIEVE PAUL IS DEAD! But my imagination said to me, "What if...?" and I listened. The goal of this novel is not to convince the reader that any of the events occurred. I hope that each reader will enjoy the fantasy, which is interwoven with historical facts. Ah...if I could have been a hair on Paul's head, what stories I could tell! But I wasn't. "Just gimme some truth!" John sings, but what I hope to give you is inspiration and entertainment.

Happy reading!

Regina Burch

NEW YORK

Geoff gasped as a solid blow connected with his shoulder, propelling him backward to sprawl his 6' 3" frame onto the royal blue training mat. Swiftly grabbing the slender ankle near his waist with both hands, he jerked, sending his opponent reeling to the floor beside him. Squinting blue eyes met startled green ones at close range for a moment as both bodies rolled and rose to circle threateningly, waiting for the next opportunity to attack. The lull was momentary. With blinding speed the petite green-eyed blonde in front of him sent a linen-clad leg slicing through the air to once again hurl him with a resounding thud to the floor.

The gong echoed through the studio freezing white uniformed bodies everywhere. The exercise was over. Bow to your partner, Geoff fumed to himself as he gritted his teeth. It was too early for this. Last night's party had barely ended. He could really use a few more hours sleep instead of this stupid waste of time. His hand reached up to swipe the wavy blonde hair from his face. His partner's long lush brown lashes swept up to reveal her green eyes glittering up at him. "Pay attention," she growled as she rose from bowing to him. "You're going to be black and blue before this is over if you don't wake up." Geoff grinned tauntingly at the beautiful but frowning face in front of him.

"I'm just simply overwhelmed at your beauty, love, that's all," he whispered back.

Tossing her blonde braid back over a slender shoulder, Alexandria Carmen Feldon, affectionately known as Tres by the young man she was sparring with, stepped to the right to meet her next opponent. Geoff, on the outer circle of participants, stood still to meet his next assailant rotating from the left. The new bowing ritual over with, Geoff resignedly prepared to meet the floor again. The hairy bastard across from him would no doubt take pleasure in crushing his head, which was already pounding steadily. "Begin!" commanded the master. Muscles tensed all around the small gym and the agonizing session resumed.

Geoff sighed inwardly. It was going to be a long morning.

CALIFORNIA

Candles lit the elegantly appointed tables in the rose garden and pool area, flickering over sterling silver, crystal and fine linens. Guests mingled, laughing and whispering in hushed tones, dressed in evening clothes. It was an elegant affair. With fountains dripping the finest champagne and expensive imported caviar served by uniformed waiters, they had spared no expense. Yes, the Bentleys knew how to entertain.

Geoffrey Van Heusen VI mused about the details of the party as he gazed at the pool sparkling in the moonlight. One could enjoy this, he thought dolefully if only it weren't so boring. The private moment ended abruptly as he felt two arms envelop his waist. A brush of a sweet smelling mane of hair was on his cheek as a feminine voice whispered tensely in his ear, "We gotta go..." The playful nature of her approach hid the strictly business message. Geoff turned to face the blonde. His eyes narrowed in concentration over the meaning of her next whispered words. "It's Crown. I saw someone go into the library. We've got him!"

The two entwined arms to project their facade as lovers as they slipped leisurely behind hedges bordering the pool. "Let's go!" he said as soon as they were hidden. They raced to the back of the mansion and through the trellis of the rose garden being careful to stay hidden by the shrubs. As they rounded the corner, both froze as they heard the unmistakable sound of helicopter blades slicing the summer air. A hooded figure bounded from the dark recesses of the mansion and leaped through the whirlybird's door as it swooped toward the ground. Just as quickly, it was off...bearing its mysterious passenger away East toward the mountains of California.

"Yes!" Geoff hissed as he triumphantly folded his arms and leaned against the latticework behind him. This was proof positive: the man who had emerged and was so swiftly borne off was working for Crown. Simon Crown had finally played out his hand in full view. Geoff turned to glance at his partner, Tres. Her satisfied gaze at the disappearing lights of the helicopter made her beautiful face light up even in the shadows of the surrounding foliage. When she turned to urge, "Let's go check the trap!" he admired the way the moonlight played on her satiny skin. The pair slipped through the doorway where the fleeing figure had exited. As they hurried to reach the library where their evidence awaited, Geoff's mind wandered.

They had lived together for six months now as partners in the espionage game that filled their every waking moment. To the world they were a happily married couple, with the "right" connections who attended the "right" functions made possible by his family's social ties. You had to be one of the accepted crowd to find out the inner workings, the secrets of what truly made the powerful what they were. Geoff had spent years as a jet setter until he had become very bored with the shipping empire his father had left him and the money inherited from generations of inherited wealth. He discovered that he craved more than the decadent lifestyle to satisfy him. He needed the excitement of the chase that being a spy offered. Geoff now owned the family homes in London, Paris, New York, and Vail—all the "right" places which enabled them to attend the gala gatherings that held the pipeline to the power in the underworld. Geoff and his partner's mission was to be in place when they were called upon to infiltrate and spoil plots by these rich jet setters who dealt in illegal trade.

Tres had the natural background for her role too. Alexandria, affectionately known as "Tres", learned as a young girl that to make it in a man's world you had to work hard and be tough. She had all the opportunities a young American girl could want—ballet, private schools, music lessons, cotillion dances, but she excelled in science. She was often teased about doing so well in class. Many times as a teen, she suffered humiliation as she was referred to by the "in" crowd as 'Alex the Great'.

Alexandria studied pre-med in college. She could not be intimidated by all the young men around her. The persistent girl was inwardly driven not be outdone. Success in her studies was her way to prove her worth! During her graduate school years, weekends were spent as a lab assistant to one of the outstanding researchers where she would often be found asleep at the lab table at the end of an arduous weekend. "Tsk, tsk, tsk" he would scold, "Hey, Alexandria, you'd better get some sleep. We're not going to be able to use our findings if you're not awake to note the results in our timed tests. Embarrassed, Alexandria would trudge home to the bare dorm room to heat up a can of soup and crash for a few hours. Right back at work she'd be before noon, measuring, making notes, examining samples to further the research.

This levelheaded young lady was very serious about her studies, although she was considered a little odd and anti-social sometimes. Many doctoral candidates didn't make it that year—too much partying, family problems, and illegal temptations due to the intense pressure and proximity of easily obtained drugs. These things were present all around Alexandria and yet she saw none of it. Her eyes were always on her goal. When she finally did become a doctor, her parents were delighted because they assumed a husband and children would be her next goal.

But she brushed off their broad hints about making a family. Yes, a new goal was needed, she admitted. How could she use this doctorate she had earned? She enjoyed the exhilarating feeling she got when she finally won the challenge in her research projects, but somehow research just wasn't what she wanted to do. She would soon have an unusual option open to her.

Geoff remembered the first time he had met "Tres". She was known as Alexandria then. Huge green eyes and long sweeping lashes stared up at him in surprise when the two of them were closed in a capsule. It was part of a research experiment they had both been invited to take part in. By the shocked look on her face, he knew immediately she had no idea of what she was getting into. She had stuttered, "I...I...thought I would be with another doctor in the capsule to do this research project. I was told I could meet other researchers... but it's nice to meet you," she hurriedly added.

"But we haven't met," Geoff chuckled. "Allow me to introduce myself. I'm Geoffrey Van Heusen VI," he murmured silkily as he bent to kiss her hand. He expected her to swoon and gasp as women did to his tactics, but she sounded genuinely distressed. "What a waste...I am so disappointed...I thought I would at least be working with someone I could learn something from." The words rushed out before Alexandria thought about how they would sound.

It was Geoff's turn to be surprised. He straightened to stare into the lovely face before him. "I beg your pardon. What makes you think you couldn't learn something from me?" His facial expression clearly gave a sensual meaning to his words, but the slender blonde woman backed away to stare down at the charts in her hand, ignoring his clear implication.

"I only meant...well, we need to get on with this task. Let's check the gauges and see if we have the correct readings to sustain our support systems. That was something both of them could share to end the awkwardness, so they began adjusting the climate for assorted specimens stored in the capsule. Maintaining optimum conditions was very demanding, and it was even more stressful to share the limited working space for five hours straight.

After an hour of frantic positioning of dials and setting up the data on the charts so they could monitor their task, a pause came. Geoff off-handedly stated to the wall he faced, "You owe me."

"What?" came her startled reply. She whirled her swivel stool to stare at the well-muscled back. Slowly he turned and smiled slyly at Alexandria. He had her attention now and that's what he wanted.

"You learned something from me and I need to learn something from you."

"What?" came her strangled reply.

This man was not at all making sense. The two young adults stared into each other's faces determinedly. Alexandria was searching for his meaning. What did she owe him? What had she learned from him?

As Alexandria stared at Geoff, he said softly "Your name...this whole time we have worked together, you've known my name...I haven't learned yours yet, he added teasingly. He had caught her off-guard. The tense silence was broken by her sudden burst of laughter. She had taken the whole situation too seriously.

"Alexandria," she sputtered, "Alexandria...Alexandria."

"Oh," he said solemnly. "Then I shall call you "Tres" which as I'm sure you know is Spanish for three. So unusual to have the **same name** three times." He turned his head and peered at her sideways. She stared exasperated at him, but then slowly smiled, feeling suddenly very comfortable with him. She understood the joke; for once a male had outdone her in a nice sort of non-threatening way.

The name stuck. After being released from the capsule, Tres was recruited by the agency into espionage. She had looked for a way to use her knowledge, and she accepted this new challenge. The two were assigned as partners with the cover of married jet setters. He could use his inherited wealth and family connections to get her into all the places the agency needed her to go. She could get the forensic evidence needed to put away the international bad guys. It was a smart arrangement, and it gave them both what they needed. For him, it was excitement, for her it was the challenge.

The whole scientific experiment they had participated in had been contrived by Interpol to see how they could work together in demanding and uncomfortable conditions. Quite a neat experiment, Geoff thought. The agent who had recruited Tres to attend had made a wise choice. Tres made a very dependable partner. She was an expert at collecting and analyzing evidence from her extensive research experience. Yet with their cover as a married couple, they could hide their involvement in obtaining it.

* * * * * * * *

Geoff's memories abruptly came to an end when the passageway ended. This wing of the mansion was quiet, deathly quiet. Guests obviously were not allowed back here during the gala. Tres reached the sliding paneled door. First, she placed her ear briefly to it and then slid it open. Geoff was right behind her. Tres had been correct. The portrait was pulled out from the wall. The safe was open. Part of its contents were spewed over the rich oriental rug...papers, jewelry, and glittering stones lay in a trail across the mahogany floor. "Someone definitely wanted us to know they were here..." Tres' voice was excited. The scent of the chase never tired her. "Now," she huffed, "all I need is..." and she pulled her kit from her beaded evening bag and began dusting for prints. "Got some!" she whispered fiercely.

"Judging from the intentional mess and a robber who didn't wear gloves, it's Crown all right. He wants us to know his man was here. It was so nice of our hosts to allow us to store our valuables in their library safe this week. We must remember to thank them." Geoff drawled.

He recalled all the conversations he had with this man Crown over the past months about possible shipping dealings. This man knew his target. Geoff's reluctance to ship cocaine and heroin had prompted Crown to take the bait they had planted in their hosts' safe. This planted blackmail evidence would lull Crown into thinking he had the upper hand. This way he would 'force' Geoff into shipping the drugs for him and could be prosecuted for trafficking with no possibility of entrapment being claimed. The trap had been set. Now all they had to do was wait for Crown's next move.

"Be prepared to act threatened! He's got the 'goods' on you!" Tres grinned up at Geoff.

"Let's go mingle, my dear. We wouldn't want to miss the party!" he said as he gathered the strewn contents and put them back into the wall safe. He'll be watching to see if the theft is reported. Since it won't be, he'll think we're an easy mark for his blackmail to get us into his deal.

Geoff paused to glance around the paneled study before turning off the light. The other door to the study, their usual entrance had remained undisturbed as they had assessed the evidence. The room looked as neat as though nothing had happened that evening—a comfortable study, cheerfully lit.

As the pair slipped stealthily back down the hall and into the night air, both were elated. The game was going to really get interesting because they knew they were getting ready to be asked to play. The opportunity to participate in this caper was what they had trained so hard for. Tres shivered as a stiff breeze blew through the trees behind the mansion and Geoff offered his tuxedo jacket. "No thanks," she murmured, but he put his arm around her shoulders anyway. As they heard something rustling in the bushes, Geoff pulled Tres close as a cover for their being in this secluded location. They were so close he could feel her heart racing. The middle-aged couple that emerged from the swaying foliage had obviously had too much to drink. Geoff recognized an inebriated Senator and an unidentified redhead staggering and clutching at each other. The statesman had managed to unzip the woman's voile party gown and one shoulder of the hot pink material hung down past her waist. Her ample breasts bulged from the push up bra still clinging to her. Upon being revealed, the gray haired man exclaimed, "What are you doing here?"

"Just out for a walk. Ciao!" Geoff assured him happily as he and Tres disappeared down the path.

The evening had just begun, so Geoff and Tres danced a few times, ate from the lavish buffet tables, and thanked the Bentley's for their hospitality this week, as they were their houseguests.

"We'll be leaving tomorrow," Geoff informed his host.

"Nonsense, none of us will feel like doing a damn thing tomorrow." the older man replied. "Probably right, Leonard, but Tres and I have tickets to fly to London tomorrow evening. She wants to see the opening of a new play there. I have business in my London office that I really need to attend to. Come visit us as soon as you and Nan can get away."

"No chance in hell for that" Bentley complained good-naturedly. "She's so tied up in this charity thing here. We don't get to travel as much as I'd like."

Geoff was thankful to Leonard for his help over the years. The older man had been his mentor, as Geoff's parents had died young. As Geoff had gotten into scrapes, Leonard had 'taken him under his wing' and had taught him about the ways to survive in the jet-set world. He had come to his rescue more than once as young ladies vied for his attentions and his riches. Since his marriage to Nan, his fourth wife, Leonard had settled down to more of a domestic existence, but always as before, he had time for Geoff if he needed him.

When Geoff and Tres finally made it through the lingering guests to their room that evening, they were both heady with the excitement that their challenge had been met. Both wanted to talk to headquarters about the events, but it was too risky on an unsecured phone. When Tres picked up the receiver on the mini-bar, Geoff warned, "you'd better be calling your Mom 'cause you sure ain't calling who I think you are."

"Yeah, I know you're right. We'll wait 'til we get there tomorrow. Let's sit down and do some strategy."

"Nothing to do. We have to wait...wait for their move." Geoff had been in this line of work a lot longer and displayed more patience. "Let's settle for an old movie."

So the two of them pulled on sweats and snuggled under a blanket to watch The Sting. After about ten minutes he felt her go limp beside him. She seemed to be out for the night. Well, so much for companionship, he commiserated. He scooped Tres up gently. She sighed and put her arms around his neck. When he placed her on the queen-sized bed, she sighed and curled up. Geoff tucked her blanket around her securely and snapped off the light. A few minutes later he was snugly bedded down on the couch, stretching and yawning for sleep himself. What an evening, he thought. Their well-planned scheme might work out now. He relished the thought of nailing Crown and stopping his impending madness

LONDON

The blazing lights of Suite #1 high atop Interpol Head-quarters pierced through five layers of bulletproof glass across the darkness of the Thames River. The surrounding office buildings were dark silhouettes against a gray, foggy evening sky.

"Burning the midnight oil again," muttered Retired Colonel Royster Wellington, as he furiously rustled through the pile of papers on his desktop and top drawer. "Damn! I'll never get through with this case." He was frustrated. Too many details still to be settled. Finding the sheet he was looking for right on top of the stack, he sighed, took a sip of his strong sweet coffee, and leaned back to study the statistics on the memo.

He had briefed the six agents involved, Tres and Geoff among them, on the final plans for the smuggling deal fourteen days from now. The agency had originally set up this sting operation to stop heavy drug smuggling that Crown was doing; however, a recent astonishing revelation from well-placed sources in Russia and Cuba had caused the agency to work feverishly to alter their objective. The stakes were much higher now. The Russians were planning to ship nuclear warheads through Crown's estate to Cuba. These could be used to threaten any of the countries in the western hemisphere, but the United States in particular might be their target. It actually was a brilliant plan. Who would suspect such innocent trappings to mask such a potent threat? When drugs had been the original cargo in this case, the trap had been set, the bait had been taken, and then all the agents had to do was show up at Crown's house party and complete the deal without raising any suspicions. The planted information Crown had stolen from the Van Heusen's valuables gave Crown what he thought was black-mail information to make the shipping magnet part of his smuggling scheme. Now the risks were much higher because those nuclear warheads had to be intercepted. Crown's estate was the only location that sources could guarantee that the warheads could be found. What a lucky break to already have two agents poised to go into Crown's private estate, a compound well known for its invulnerability!

All of Wellington's elation at having the plan fall into place came crashing down with two coinciding pieces of information. At yesterday's briefing, the people doing the detailed background check on the scum named Crown had an illuminating and alarming tidbit of knowledge to help the agents prepare for their stay at Crown estate. Simon Crown was a voyeur. The only way he would trust people he was doing business with was if he could secretly tape their bedroom activities. This served dual purposes; firstly entertainment on his part; and secondly as valuable blackmail material should the business partnership ever sour. The man was a weirdo, but his quirky habits might be why he had survived in the drug cartel so long.

The second piece of information came in a private conference with Tres Van Heusen after all the other agents had adjourned. He was surprised when she had confided in him that she was a virgin and, therefore, would not participate in having sex in front of Crown's hidden cameras. Either one of the details above would have been inconsequential to the case, but together they created a huge problem that had put the mission on hold.

'Twenty five' he read from her personnel folder.

"Twenty five" he grumbled. How the hell did a woman twenty-five years old stay a virgin that long? Why, it was 1962, not the turn of the century! The sixty-three year old man was lost in thought. He stared into the night and thought about other times. There had always been peeping toms, but they'd go to peep shows or girlie shows in his day. All this technology was a dangerous mix with immorality, he thought. This world was going to hell!

Wellington had just come out of a well-earned retirement to head this bureau temporarily. His predecessor had passed away with a heart attack just two months ago. He was hoping for a calm, easy ride until they could get someone to take this job. "Just mind the store!" they told him when he reluctantly agreed to come back since they were in a bind. Yeah, right. He was just becoming adjusted to the

11

workings of the office and getting used to the people he was dealing with when all this came along! This case was a mess! At first everything was falling into place but now this field agent had to screw everything up! At that thought he suddenly laughed out loud. Well, actually, the problem was exactly the opposite; she hadn't "screwed" at all. Well, he thought as he rubbed sparse hair, she surely had complicated matters. What should he do, have the Van Heusens stage a "lover's spat" and separate or even get a quickie divorce and then go on with the plan? That would be the easy way out. The way she was trembling and turning red this afternoon when she told him meant that's what needed to happen. She'd never be able to handle going to bed with Van Heusen or even faking it for Crown's hidden cameras. Well, Wellington mused resignedly; they certainly couldn't risk her blowing their cover at Crown's estate and endanger this mission.

Wellington decided to check on what it was that had been planted in the Van Heusen's things for Crown to steal and use as "blackmail" so he'd think he had the upper hand. Then he could deal with damage control. "Oh, I hope this separation thing won't throw a monkey wrench in the deal. Crown may think Van Heusen's unstable right now, " he muttered aloud.

After pulling the file out and opening it, Wellington was immediately alarmed. "Holy cow! We can't ditch the girl!" he exclaimed. The items that had been placed in the safe were pictures of Geoff Van Heusen on intimate terms with several different women along with Geoff's Dad's will stating that his tremendous inheritance could only be his if he remained married for five years to the same woman. Wellington's eyes lingered hungrily for several minutes on the obvious pleasure all of the participants in the pictures before guiltily closing the file folder and dropping it on the desk. The only way the pictures would remain a threat to Van Heusen in Crown's mind would be for the couple to stay happily "married" for the entire world to see. That was the key.

What could he do now? This Van Heusen girl seemed so inexperienced with men. Staring aimlessly around the room as he mentally searched for the solution to his dilemma, his eyes fell upon one of the pictures on his desk. His niece, Sandy, nineteen, was so sweet and innocent. Just out of convent school. This Van Heusen girl reminded him of Sandy. He had tried hard to be more of a father than an uncle since his sister and brother-in-law died long ago. Sandy was so much like her mother, so feminine and petite. She had always needed to be sheltered because she suffered from syncope or fainting spells. Now she was all tied up with that longhaired guitar freak. What was his name, Paul something or other. He'd never make the kind of living she needed to continue riding those Arabian horses she loved. With that thought, Roy's brow knitted and he chewed on his pipe. He wished she wasn't so in love with that boy. He was in a band...what was the name of it? Oh, well, maybe the young fellow was serious about her. Even though he was from a scruffy working class background, maybe he would make her happy.

Now enough daydreaming, back to his problem. Maybe what these field agents needed was a good vacation, time on their hands, let nature take its course, that sort of thing. Yet, if they did become physically intimate with each other, it would mean separating them after the caper. You couldn't have two agents sleeping together and trying to accomplish further missions. It would distract them and damage their priorities. No, they'd have to go their separate ways afterwards. And yet, the Van Heusens did work well together. Oh, a pity. But he'd try it. Send 'em to Switzerland for a couple of weeks and book 'em a honeymoon suite with the trimmings. Have champagne delivered by room service. Maybe this young agent would get her experience in time to save the potential fiasco in a few weeks at Crown's estate. Roy smoked silently thinking that over. If that didn't work, there were other ways to encourage her to get experience. Maybe he could arrange some help for Geoff. Roy sat his niece's picture down on his huge oak desk very gently. That musician chap better watch himself with Sandy, he thought sternly.

* * * * * * * *

Geoff was amazed but pleased at the news that they were suddenly getting time for a vacation. "Ta da" he flourished the plane tickets and reservations to a startled Tres in the living room of their luxurious London flat. "Let's pack! I haven't had time to ski in ages!" Geoff was already running up the stairs when Tres caught him. "Why?" she asked.

"Why? Because we've been so damn tied up with all these stupid social engagements that's why!"

"What?" she looked puzzled.

"Well, make up your mind what you want to know, love," he retorted and continued bounding up the winding staircase. She caught up again.

"No, not why haven't we had time to ski! I know that. I want to know why we're going on vacation suddenly!" she explained.

"I don't know—something about keeping up our image of a fun lifestyle until the house party, Wellington said." Geoff called back to her.

"There wasn't anything only for me...a message...? " Geoff turned to look at her when he heard her hesitant tone.

"No, what's up?"

"Nothing, I'll talk to Wellington later myself." She sounded downhearted.

"What? You're not thrilled to get this chance to ski and have fun in the Alps? Come on, let's party!" Geoff sang out enthusiastically.

Tres shook her head at Geoff's enthusiasm. The eternal playboy. It's what he did best. She sighed and wondered why Wellington hadn't responded to her problem she had confided in him. Oh, well, he said he'd consider it and get back to me. I'll hear from him, she reassured herself, but if I don't, I'm in trouble. She dashed into their enormous walk-in closet to see huge cases out and already halfway full. "Alps, here we come!" she murmured.

SWITZERLAND

The next few days were a blur. Mornings were spent eating huge breakfasts complete with champagne delivered to their chalet by horse-drawn sled. Geoff would hurriedly roll up the pallet he slept on in front of the fire to hide it behind the couch when he heard the sleigh bells and hoof beats draw near. The matched pair of bay horses would blow their steamy breath and toss their heads while the huge trays of food were brought in. Geoff protested the first time it arrived. "We didn't order this!"

"Standing order for this suite, sir," the uniformed server nervously explained. The waiter looked genuinely relieved when Geoff pulled out a bill for him. "Thank You!" he exclaimed and was on his way carving a new path through the knee high snow. And so the pattern was repeated each day. Geoff had come to enjoy the ritual. Tres and he would leisurely feast on the wide variety of foods— waffles with whipped cream, strawberries, eggs fixed many ways, sausages and bacon, juices, and of course coffee— huge steaming turrets of it, rich and black, and croissants that would make a French baker jealous.

They would lounge until 10:00 or so talking over the world news from the papers and laughing about whatever struck them as amusing. Geoff felt so at home with Tres. They really enjoyed each other's company. They were a perfectly matched pair; best friends sitting by the roaring fire chatting and reading, and devouring the tasty treats that had been delivered to them.

The first morning when the huge meal arrived, Geoff stood staring at the silver tray after seeing out the waiters. Geoff's mouth was watering at the unexpected treasure before him.

Tres, fresh out of the shower wandered into the great room toweling her still damp golden hair. "What in the world!" she murmured as she froze beside Geoff. She sniffed the luscious aromas. "Am I dreaming? Whoa! You really took Wellington seriously about his offer to live it up, Geoff! Do you expect the agency to pay for this?"

"Oh, this wasn't my doing..." Geoff began seriously, but then he flashed Tres a heart-melting smile. "Apparently the old man's giving us our last meal in advance! He really meant it when he said we were on vacation, but he's really just fattening us up for the kill at Crown's estate."

Geoff grinned mischievously at his joke about the impending danger of their mission two weeks away, but Tres felt sick. She paled and gripped the chair in front of her with white knuckles. Geoff immediately became concerned about her reaction. Was she this afraid of the dangerous charade they would play at Crown's house party? They had trained long and hard for this, carefully setting up their cover story to give them this opportunity.

"What is it? Are you okay?" Geoff whispered hoarsely. He took Tres gently but firmly by the shoulders and helped her sit in the chair she had been gripping furiously a few moments before. She crumpled on the table and wept, her head in her arms. Geoff amazed at her reaction, sat beside her and stroked her hair. What could he do, he wondered, to help her face whatever was bothering her?

"It will be okay. Everything's in place and we're ready," he whispered into her thick sweet-smelling hair. His hand moved to her neck gently, kneading. Where his touch had always been welcome before, it suddenly felt intrusive. Her head came up abruptly and they faced each other, almost nose to nose. His face showed his obvious surprise. Tres wiped the tears away from her eyes angrily and pushed his hand away from her hair.

"You might be, but I'm not!" she declared hotly.

"What's the problem?" His question hung in the air.

Tres tried to speak. She wanted so desperately to spit out what was bothering her. How could she, though? You just didn't tell someone that you didn't know how to make love or even 'fake it' as he had so laughingly said in their meeting in London. He was so casual about it, she thought bitterly. Suddenly, she regretted all those evenings she had once thrived in, hunkered down with her chemistry textbooks and lab results. Tres remembered the delicious

16

smells in front of them and shook her head. "I'll be okay. Let's not waste this food!"

The subject had been dropped. Neither mentioned it again as they began their morning habit of relaxed abandon. Yet the question lingered in the air for Geoff. He couldn't ignore the reaction she had shown...something was terribly wrong with Tres. She had never been the hysterical type, always thinking, always matter-of-fact, and dealing with whatever obstacles came their way. He figured if he listened well these next two weeks, they could solve whatever problem was bothering her.

And so they lounged in their silk bathrobes each morning, watching the fluttering snowflakes fall, half-listening to this news show or that one. They could laugh and talk about what the entire world thought was important, but each felt discomfort knowing that there was something they couldn't talk about. Geoff knew he'd have to find a way to help her gain confidence about the mission or they could both be in danger.

Just as mornings were long and leisurely spent, the afternoons were wonderfully enjoyable, but in a different way. Tres and Geoff would suit up in their ski gear and try to conquer the mountains. They both loved to jump so they would choose some of the roughest courses available.

On the fourth day as they were boarding the helicopter to take them up to a particularly tough peak, Geoff noticed how attentive one of the accompanying ski guides was becoming to Tres. The tall Nordic looking Swede was constantly at her side, helping her check her bindings or giving her a wink over some comment he had made. The strikingly handsome guy gave Geoff the creeps. To be so obviously flirtatious with a wife wasn't unusual in Europe, but right in front of him, the husband was too much. This guy either mistakenly thought he was very subtle or he was crazy!

Geoff tried to ignore it. He always had his little flings. Tres had never objected when he would tell her he'd be in late and then not come in until the morning. He wondered how Tres felt about this strange situation with the ski guide. She was obviously not bothered by Sven's attentions. She would smile and accept his help each time he offered it.

17

Maybe this was what she wanted...a fling before the culmination of their mission. It made Geoff very uncomfortable. He resented this guy moving in on her. But why?, he asked himself. They were only partners in the job they did, unusual as it might be. Still he had to admit to himself that it definitely bothered him.

As he watched the two of them laughing in the snow where they had fallen, side by side, Geoff bit his lip and examined this stabbing feeling that had grown from a slight pinch to a full gut-wrenching pierce. Geoff stared at Tres struggling to stand up and realized for the first time that he didn't like seeing her with another man. Until he had seen someone else trying to become her lover, he had not realized the deep emotions he felt for his best friend and partner. He loved Tres, the one he had shared every waking moment for the last six months.

Geoff skied effortlessly over the laughing pair still vaguely struggling in the snow. He braced with his poles and reached down to pull up a blushing and breathless Tres. He pulled her quite close to him and whispered between clenched teeth, "You are making a fool of yourself, woman."

Tres blushed even more and glancing down at her partner in crime, she said loud enough for both men to hear, "Some people know how to enjoy themselves."

Geoff was puzzled with this coquettish side of Tres he had never seen before. He let her go abruptly and skied on down the embankment. Let her have this empty-headed model, he thought, it will serve her right.

As he slid through the powdery white drifts, he heard her call behind him, "Don't wait up. I'll be in late tonight!"

* * * * * * * *

Geoff stretched his long legs before the roaring fire in their chalet and sipped the rum slowly. His eyes narrowed on the dancing flames as he thought of Tres—off to 'God knows where' with that cad this evening. He'd have a word with her tomorrow about the appearance of fidelity if they were going to maintain their cover for the upcoming deal with Crown.

What was she thinking of? This guy was such a loser! A ski instructor! Well, he had to admit he knew that Sven had won several Olympic medals. That had been bragged about when the small group had been formed to ski the mountains together this week. The ski resort touted his medals like reasons to live.

Geoff took a deeper sip of his rum. Tres didn't belong with this Swede, not while they were this close to achieving their mission to incriminate Crown. Geoff gulped the rum. Hell, not ever! She belonged with him. Geoff finished off the liquor in one final gulp and set the glass down with a crash on the table. He'd find her and tell her she belonged with him! He'd find her right now.

Grabbing the goose down jacket off the chair near the door where he had angrily flung it earlier, Geoff was bounding down the chalet steps, into the frigid winter wasteland that separated Tres from him.

The tavern at the resort was dimly lit. Couples laughing and glasses tinkling met his ears as Geoff slipped through the huge entranceway from the mall. Could he find her— yes, he would, he knew, but in time? He didn't want that slimy Sven's hands on her, not on his Tres. He had to find her and tell her how he felt, now that he knew.

Ah, there she was. Tres was sitting alone, nursing a red wine obviously waiting for someone, for Sven, Geoff reasoned. She was glancing nervously around. It was not too late! He had to tell her, but that Swede might show up at any moment. No, he had to go to Sven. He had to tell him to stay away from Tres. They couldn't afford a scene here in this bistro where Crown's men might well be watching their every move. Crown was a cautious viper; he knew where all his "business associates" were all the time. No, they couldn't risk that.

He had to get to Sven. The Swede might be an empty-headed glamour boy, but he was no fool. If an angry husband showed up in earnest objecting to his designs on his wife, he'd back down. Sven would know Geoff could have his job, and he would assume it might even mean his life if he persisted.

Geoff burst back into the frigid night air. He'd wager dear old Sven would be cleaning up in the locker room following his day of work. Ski boys had to punch the clock after all.

Geoff heard male laughter, voices bragging about the evening's plans as he entered the staff locker room. He clearly picked out Sven's twang among the others. "Ya, sure, I've got me a gut von lined up zes evening! I'm gonna vork hard tonight so you guys cover fer me in za morning, okay, Erik?" Another man, also tall and blonde, popped Sven with the towel on the rear as Geoff rounded the corner of the lockers.

"Hey, save some of that for me, will ya, Sven?" joked the one addressed as Erik.

"Maybe we can do a threesome tomorrow night!" yelled one of the others. They all laughed uproariously.

Geoff cleared his throat and the others suddenly became aware of the fully dressed man in their midst.

"Excuse us, gentlemen," Geoff said softly as the others quickly exited toward the showers, leaving the two men alone staring stonily at each other.

Geoffrey Van Heusen VI hands in pockets stood eyeing the half-dressed Swede. After a few tense moments, the blonde's face relaxed, and he began once again packing items from his locker into his overnight bag. The gall of this guy, thought Geoff wildly, to act so normal when he was planning and bragging about screwing another man's wife tonight right in front of him. Geoff thought, I've got to end this; he's crazy.

Geoff pushed the man's shoulder so he would face him again. The Swede did, as Geoff wanted, he stopped his packing and met his eyes. But what Geoff saw there amazed him!

Sven's face looked friendly as he finally said, "Ya, watcha need, Geoff?"

This man was not taking him seriously. He must know what he wanted; he couldn't be that crazy!

"Stay away from my wife!" Geoff growled. He thrust his jaw out and glared at the clearly relaxed man before him. Sven's next words shocked Geoff even further!

"You can cut ze crap now, Van Heusen; ze others they have gone." the Swede leered. Geoff grabbed Sven by the T-shirt. "Ze season is changing."

When Sven spoke the last sentence, Geoff froze and his words caught in his throat. This can't be, he thought. Sven is an agent!

Sven pried Geoff's tightly clutching hand off his T-shirt as Geoff continued to stare at him. So this was why Sven wasn't alarmed when Geoff approached the group of teasing, bragging men. Now Geoff knew why Sven had been so bold as to flirt with Tres. This man knew their marriage wasn't real. Sven was taking a real chance blowing all their covers! But, how would Sven know he and Tres were agents. Why would he know their marriage of six months was a sham? That information was on a 'need to know only' basis. This man was part of their vacation; he didn't have any 'need to know'. He wasn't part of their pending operation, or was he?

Geoff got a ticklish feeling deep in his gut. What part did this man play in their mission? What had Wellington arranged...?

The Swede had finished packing. His muscles rippled as he slammed closed the shiny green door to his locker. He knew what Geoff was thinking. Wellington obviously hadn't briefed Geoff on the plans for this evening.

"Look, old man, I'm just doing my job" Sven said as he faced Geoff once again. Geoff stared at him, wanting to know more.

Geoff was finally able to speak; he had to overcome this horrible feeling of doom. What was Wellington trying to pull?

"And that is..." Geoff prompted.

"Look..." Sven began, his face thoughtful "some of us get jobs to do and some of us get ze pie jobs, cherry pie, zat is, " he said and laughed a deep chuckle as we winked at Geoff.

"What do you mean?" Geoff persisted.

Sven's brow furrowed slightly. Wellington had obviously not shared the state of affairs of his partner or he would have gotten the joke. I've got to spell it out, he thought. This guy seems really mad, and he's liable to punch me out unless he understands what needs to be done to keep this mission on track. No need to risk my face, he reasoned.

"Van Heusen, just relax. I'm just here to provide a necessary diversion for your —ah, —wife." And in a lower tone, he added as he leaned closer, "apparently agent Tres Van Heusen is unskilled in —shall we say —intimate affairs, and ze bureau sent me to provide ze service." Pleased with his delicate and yet clever explanation, the blonde Swede relaxed his back against the locker, arms folded over his chest.

Damn! thought Geoff. The agency — what? His fist caught the Swede in the stomach and bent him double. Geoff's knee came up and quickly ended all the Swede's amorous evening plans. Sven had been totally unprepared for this response, so Geoff was untouched in the scuffle. Geoff left him writhing in pain on the tile floor. He'll be all right by tomorrow, though Geoff, but Wellington won't be when I get my hands on him.

As Geoff approached Tres' table in the bar, a man slid in the opposite chair and grabbed her face for a long kiss. God, thought Geoff, has Wellington sent several men to seduce Tres? He panicked and froze and then his senses kicked in...it wasn't Tres at that table. The hair was too brownish, the clothes too bright.

Geoff turned and half-ran back into the mall to make his exit. He had to find her. Where had she gone? Could she have gone to the locker room? A quick look there proved fruitless. Apparently Sven's buddies had scraped him up off the floor and into a hot bath somewhere. In another bar? He checked all over—the gift shop?—it was getting late! He'd go back to the chalet.

As the massive door groaned open, Geoff heard her crying—"Tres!" She was here! Geoff was so glad. She was safe, back at the chalet where she belonged, out of that nasty Sven's reach. Doing his job indeed! Sven was no more than a whore and Wellington his pimp! Geoff swore softly as he purposefully strode to locate Tres.

The door to the bedroom was closed, and that's where the muffled sobs came from. Geoff knocked gently on the door. He had to clear things up. He knew now he wanted Tres to be his partner in every sense. 'Til death do us part, he thought tenderly, if she'll have me!

Tres lay curled up on the king-size bed; 115 pounds lost in its huge magnificence. Geoff sat down beside her. She seemed unaware of his presence. Tres continued to cry as Geoff wrapped his arms around her and held her head and shoulders on his lap. He rocked her gently and whispered "Shhh!" into the fragrant honey-colored hair. "It's okay. I'm here. I love you."

Tres hadn't heard him. She continued to sob and through the tears, she mumbled "He stood me up. I waited and waited for him, and he stood me up."

Poor thing! How much did she know about this scheme? Was she part of it? He couldn't believe that someone as intelligent as Tres would go along with such an insensitive approach to lovemaking. They were not horses or cattle to be mated! So she was inexperienced, he thought. Then it dawned on him, the realization of what had been casually discussed and joked about in their last meeting at headquarters in London. No wonder she had been so upset lately! Her comment at brunch about not being ready for the mission had been sincere. Of course! She had never made love and yet they all expected that she had and would be able to play along with him in front of any hidden cameras that sleaze Crown might hide in their bedroom. Oh, how did we get into this mess? Well, everyone had assumed a woman of twenty-five...and who would expect carnal knowledge to be a job requirement? In this case unfortunately, it was necessary training. A virgin couldn't be expected to know how to fake it in front of a perverted voyeur. Then the word virgin finally sunk into Geoff's brain. A virgin—Christ, Tres was a virgin! He had never had a virgin. It rather awed him.

Geoff held and hugged the girl in his arms until she was only able to make gasping hiccuping noises. Her crying ended; she stared blankly at the wall.

"Tres, I know you're embarrassed, love, but we've got to talk." She nodded silently, still snubbing slightly. "Let's go in the living room. I need a drink."

When they had settled in front of the fire with their liquor bottle and glasses, the talking began. The whole story of her frustration over the upcoming expectations of this mission poured out—how she had talked to Wellington. Geoff leaned close to her and looked closely at her facial expression. "What did he tell you, Tres?"

"Well, he said 'don't worry about it, he would consider what options were to be had'." Yeah, thought Geoff, he knew what they included—having Tres serviced like a mare in heat.

Geoff shuddered at the thought.

"You cold?" she inquired obviously noticing his flinch. Tres pulled a hand-woven blanket off the couch behind them and they both snuggled under it as they sat, backs against the couch, sitting on the floor, legs stretched toward the flickering flames, comfortable as always with each other.

"Thanks," Geoff responded. He had to know if Wellington had her consent for this arrangement with Sven. Was she a willing participant? He couldn't believe that someone who had remained virginal this long disregarded the importance of intimate relations. Could she be that jaded? Or was she lesbian? Had she no interest in having intercourse with a man? Maybe that would explain why she had stayed inexperienced at this age.

Their glasses refilled again and again as they talked, firelight bathed their features. They talked about her life and his and why she had never had time for boys and men. Her job as a student had always come first.

Finally Geoff just had to ask "Tres, did Wellington ask you to do anything to help you get ready for your role as wife on this mission." He leaned very close and said it softly. Tres shook her head.

"No, he did get back to me though after we had arrived here to say to be open to new experiences. He encouraged me to relax. I told him I'd try."

Geoff sat a long time staring at the fire. So she wasn't aware of the set-up. "And then Sven swept you off your feet."

"Well, not quite. But I have to admit; he was attractive and very interested in me. I thought he genuinely could love me. But I...guess not. What would a famous ski pro see in me?

Hours had passed. They had killed a whole bottle of Chivas Regal. Both of them were getting really drunk. "Enough serious talk" she said. She reached out to the heavens, with both arms and proclaimed, "I hereby declare I will cry no more about lost possibilities. Let's party!"

"Yeah!" yelled Geoff as he jumped to his feet. "I'm usually the party animal. Are you trying to outdo me?" He turned up the music on the stereo, slipped on a few more records, and grabbed Tres for a dance. They danced and shrieked and had fun imitating some of the singers.

Finally, staggering together in a slow dance, Geoff whispered in her hair, "I've got a new possibility for you. I love you." They stopped dancing and stared at each other.

"I've had too much to drink!" she said in a stage whisper, "I thought you said..."

"No, no, I know it. I realized it today. I love you. I really do." He grabbed her face with both hands and hungrily covered her mouth with his. As shocked as she was, the liquor had plied her, had made both of them able to at last express the feelings they had shared for so long. They had just never allowed these feelings to surface. They kissed gently at first and then more aggressively as he pushed her onto the couch and hovered over her on his knees. They were enjoying the freedom at last to give action to their long-hidden emotions.

His hands explored gently, caressing her shoulders, her breasts, and the smooth expanse of her flat stomach to her flaring hips. She was responding too. Her arms stretched up and embraced the solid rippling muscles in his shoulders; her fingers kneading his biceps just about drove him mad. Geoff was surprised when Tres abruptly pulled away from their kiss. "What's wrong?" Geoff asked worriedly because Sandy suddenly looked strange. She had rolled on her side and was trying desperately to get up. "Did I upset you?" Geoff asked as he helped her up.

But Sandy didn't answer. She staggered two or three steps before Geoff rushed to support her. "I'm going to be sick!" Tres gasped as she stumbled toward the bathroom.

"Okay, it's okay!" Geoff reassured her as he helped her to the toilet. Tres stood there unsteadily waiting to vomit, and Geoff moved once again to help hold her up.

After a few minutes of leaning expectantly over the toilet with no results, Tres sighed, "I just want to go to bed!" She sounded pitiful, so Geoff grinned and pulled her close to him. He was usually the one who felt miserable from overindulgence.

"Oh, that liquor was too much of a good thing, wasn't it? Okay, now, party girl I'll get you to bed. Just relax," he said to comfort her. Geoff scooped her up in his arms and carried her into the bedroom, a place they had never shared in their six months of marriage.

"I love you, Tres" Geoff whispered as he began to undress her in the soft light. She nestled her head against his neck. Her scent wafted up and his desire to make love to her almost conquered his good sense. Oh, no, he thought, she's so willing right now. But after so much liquor I don't want our union grounded on intoxication. "I want you so badly, Tres," he whispered to her. But it wouldn't be right to take advantage of you," He reasoned that in the morning, when sobriety hit, they could agree to truly become one. That would give her a choice and some dignity. Taking her now when she was vulnerable would be a mistake, he realized.

Rolling off the big plush bed was one of the hardest things he had ever had to do. Then he forced himself to take the coldest shower he had had in ten years.

Those cold showers he took when he was fifteen hadn't lasted long before the delectable Marietta, his family's upstairs maid, had become a valuable teacher. She welcomed his advances and taught him many of the skills a young man

26

of the world needed to know. Geoff, now tanned and muscular, thought back to that simple time when he was an adolescent, whose only interests in the buxom beauty had been pleasure and a very interesting education. He stared at himself in the mirror as he dried his hair thinking of his youth and the wonderful sensual experiences he had that now he could teach to Tres. He promised himself if she would accept his love, he would be as patient as he needed to be to teach her all the pleasures that flesh can bring.

* * * * * * * *

Tres groaned and grasped her head in both hands. "Oh..." the sound was almost a growl deep in her throat. The light streaming through the window was agony! She clutched the pillow beside her and shoved it over her face. She moaned again and stretched. Tres froze. Whose legs were intertwined with hers? Whose arms were wrapped around her waist? What had happened? Tentatively she shifted her weight and turned to meet Geoff nose to nose.

"Oh, my head," he voiced her feelings aloud. "How does yours feel?"

"Geoff, what happened? I mean..." Tres gasped and tried to pull away from him. She was suddenly aware of the sensation of his body against hers.

"Oh, no, you don't. You stay right where you are," he whispered threateningly.

"Geoff, did you...? Did we...?"

The handsome face smiled down at her charmingly. "This might be an appropriate time to offer the promise of marriage...if we weren't already married."

Tres stared at him solemnly, his meaning slowly sinking in. She blushed, eyes lowered, mind blank. Geoff bent down and began to kiss her shoulder gently, nibbling up her neck. The action caused an overpowering feeling in her, an unmistakable yearning from deep inside her. Geoff brushed the hair back off her forehead and began to kiss her face. "You don't remember?"

Tres murmured, "No....oh."

27

He laughed softly, put his forehead to hers and stared deeply into her green eyes. His arms slid up from her waist to hold her shoulders. "No, love, we just drank too much and kissed a little..." There was a pause. "But I meant all that I told you. You don't remember that?"

Tres searched her mind wildly. Yes, she did remember drinking a lot, she did remember talking and dancing. Sven had stood her up. And then **he had told her he loved her!** As soon as the last thought entered her brain, she muttered..."You said..."

"Yes, I told you I loved you."

"You don't have to say that to get me to...uh, feel better about this."

"Is that what you think? No, I mean it. I love you. I didn't realize it for a long time. But I am sincere. I'm not trying to manipulate you. You've got to believe me."

"Yes, Sven stood me up, but you don't need to pity me!" She tried to move away.

Geoff pulled her back. "Tres, it's really not that way. I want you. Let me tell you a secret." They stared seriously at each other at very close range. "Sven did not stand you up. I found out he had plans with you, and I had a little talk with him. I gave him a few good reasons to leave you alone," he said, holding up his fists and boxing the air.

"Geoff, my protector" she joked.

"Tres, I love you. I know we've just been partners in our jobs, but now I want you to be my lover. Do you want me?" His eyes searched her face briefly. He kissed her deeply, thoroughly. Tres felt herself responding to him. She wrapped her arms around his neck and kissed him back. She lost herself in the strong feelings they obviously shared.

"Is that a 'yes'?"

"Yes, Geoff."

"Our marriage of convenience is turning out to be very convenient. I need to make love to you. Now."

"I need you too..." Tres murmured against his shoulder.

His breath was ragged as he hugged and caressed her. He was trying to contain his excitement. He didn't want to scare her since this was her first time to make love. She shouldn't hate or regret their lovemaking.

He kissed her deeply as his hands gently explored her body His touch made her delicate skin alive with sensation. "I love you. Just relax. I'll be very gentle." Geoff continued his light kisses. He pulled a large towel off the nightstand and pushed it under her. "We don't want the cleaning crew to know how recently we consummated our marriage." They smiled slightly at each other.

Geoff was glad that he was experienced at sex so that he could be patient during their lovemaking. He wanted her to have pleasure as well as the initial pain. After making love, they lay as one for a while, both enjoying the closeness. "I could really kick myself for waiting six months for this...but the time wasn't right until now." Geoff said. "Tres," he looked into her eyes solemnly. "I want to spend the rest of my life with you."

She smiled and they kissed a gentle kiss. Geoff stroked her hair as they whispered together.

After a while, Geoff patted Tres' back. "Tres, take the towel with you to the bathroom to clean up. We'll cuddle when you get back."

"Okay," she looked at him gratefully. He was being so thoughtful. She had never been through this before. She was so glad he loved her!

Tres did as he said. She was amazed at the amount of blood, but bathing made her feel better. When she slipped on the white terrycloth robe in the bathroom, she caught a glimpse of herself in the mirror. Was this the same girl she had seen a million times? She looked the same but now it seemed she ought to look different, changed somehow by the wondrous experience Geoff had given her.

Slipping back into bed, Tres snuggled closely to Geoff. "There's something I need..." she whispered.

"What?"

"I need a kiss before I can sleep..." Tres whispered as she would each time they were ready for a good night's rest.

Geoff grinned, "That I can provide." Afterwards, entwined in each other's arms, they drifted off to sleep, happy they had consummated their love.

HAMBURG, GERMANY

The trip had been a rough one so far, and Paul was pretty bummed out. He and his three band mates had arrived in Hamburg that morning on a flight[1] constantly jarred by air turbulence. One of his bags had been lost, and now he had to survive the tedium of posing for a bloody camera! Brian Epstein, their newly acquired manager had arranged for some publicity photos to be taken on an estate of a friend. Paul fervently hoped he could just hold on until the afternoon. Then he would get some relief from all this tension; the singing group was getting a rare chance at a holiday, brief though it may be. They would each head out on their separate ways until Tuesday when they would meet in Hamburg for their gig at the Star Club.[2] Paul obediently lifted his chin when asked as the shutters clicked around them.

"Hey, let's have a break, boys," Brian called, and the four lean young men dressed in suits[3] huddled at the barn door to light cigarettes, their long dark hair blowing in the wind. Each member of the group had his own special appeal to the girls who had begun to follow them around. John, who liked to clown around and be sarcastic, was always ready with a clever reply or a pun. Paul had classic good looks, a baby face, and drove girls crazy with the romantic ballads he loved to sing. George, the lead guitarist, had a lean craggy face but had been nicknamed "the beautiful one"[4] by the Hamburg audiences. He always appeared to keep his distance and be at peace no matter what turmoil was going on around him. Ringo, the drummer among them, had been raised in the scruffiest low-class neighborhood. He had a gravelly voice, huge puppy dog eyes, and a slight build which made his fans feel protective of him. Since he was always by himself on a riser while he played, apart from the rest of the group, he seemed a loner, but he was really the heart of the group. He was well-respected by the others for his steady, even-tempered manner within their nest of raging egos. Ringo was new to the group, having replaced a drummer their new producer rejected.

"How much more of this shit should we take?" George, the youngest of the Liverpool singing group complained, blowing smoke into the brisk spring air. "This is quite a bloody bore. I want to pull some birds in Hamburg." He leaned against the barn door staring into the distance.

"Those bloody photographers are bound to have gotten enough of us by now!" John in his usual take-charge manner promptly responded. "Let's give it 'til afternoon tea break. They can photograph our 'arses' if they want as we leave."

"Come on, lads, the price of fame!" Ringo reminded them as he thrust his fist into the air.

"Huh, Ringo Starr," John snorted, "you're the new bloke...shut yer bloody yap", but he winked at him to soften his words.[5]

Paul didn't speak. He just turned slightly away from the others and watched his cigarette smoke curl up toward nearby tree limbs. His mind was on the news that they had just heard hours earlier. When they arrived in Hamburg, they had been told that Stu, one of their closest mates and ex-band member, in fact, had died quite suddenly.[6] He and Stu had been at odds at one time over who should play bass, and Paul now regretted his insensitivity toward Stu over his lack of skill. Stu had stayed here in Germany with his true love, Astrid,[7] to pursue his painting, leaving the bass spot to Paul. Somehow the disturbing news made this entire photo shoot nuisance seem even more trivial. He just had to get some time away to think.

John touched Paul lightly on the shoulder. The two were kindred spirits[8] as they had shared many tough times and had written many songs together. Consequently, John had sensed Paul's subdued mood. "You're too quiet, Paul. Are you sticking with the plans we made to 'have a go' at the St. Pauli district?" John, Paul, and George had performed previously in several clubs in this section of Hamburg when they had come to Germany before. They had never before had the time to enjoy the notorious pleasures of the strip clubs without having to work the next day. However, this trip they had a bit more money too as they had had some success playing some clubs in their native England. Their agreed-upon goal for this brief holiday was to pursue the diversions these clubs provided, such as scantily clad hostesses and women's mud wrestling events, to their fullest potential.[9] It was a holiday only dreamed by most poor Liverpool boys.

Paul smiled slightly and turned to look at his best friend. "I'm so bloody tired, John. I just want to sleep 'til Tuesday. I think I'll find a quiet inn and crash. It'll give me time to think about Stu and all. You three go ahead, and I'll meet you."

"I'll take notes for ya!" Ringo said brightly. Although he was the oldest of the group at 22, he had never been exposed to the raucous joys in Hamburg, and he was obviously looking forward to the experience.[10]

Just then, Brian left the photographers and joined the singing group at the barn door. "Well, lads, that wraps it up. The photographer has all he'll need. You did well. Now, do each of you have your passports...money... anything else you'll need? We'll meet at 10:00 A. M., sharp Tuesday, at the Star Club, 39 Grosse Freiheit,[11] understood? If you need me, I'll be here with Fritz. You can ring me. You've got the number?"

"Thanks, Eppie!" chorused the four musicians as the photographer's assistants began stripping down the light structures and camera fittings. These anxious young men were ready to start their holiday and needed no encouragement. Their gear was gathered quickly, and as cars began to leave the circular drive, Paul decided he wanted to spend a few minutes seeing the German countryside. He had always been shut up in the smoky; smelly Hamburg beat music clubs when they had come over here before. He was amazed at the scent of this German country air...so much cleaner than London and Liverpool with their shipyards and factories. And so he tossed his seaman style duffel bag and guitar over his shoulder and set off into the woods behind the barn. He could catch a car to Hamburg later, he reasoned.

As he rambled deeper into the forest, he saw squirrels and other woodland creatures. This was a whole new world! He decided he'd like to have an estate like this someday. He chided himself for such a dream because at present the band had made only one record. He had to remind himself that he was lucky to play in this band so he wouldn't have to get a real job. He crossed a shallow but quickly moving brook just before he came to a huge dense wall made of bushes. Pushing his way cautiously through a slight opening in the hedge, his ears were still listening to the rushing water when he was joined by nearby galloping hoof beats.

Glancing upward, he saw the most beautiful angelic face he had ever seen right above the startled face of a gray and black horse. The horse completed jumping the hedge, just missing Paul by a couple of feet, but it shied away to the left dumping its gorgeous rider unceremoniously on the grass. Paul was as shocked by the event as the horse. He stared at the girl lying on the ground in front of him. She was elegantly attired in snug buff-colored riding pants, a white turtleneck, a burgundy jacket, and black knee boots. Wisps of flaxen blonde hair drifted from under the black-velvet riding helmet she wore as she sprawled on the grass.

Paul knelt beside her, checking for a pulse. He looked down into her blue eyes as she stared up at his brown ones. Both felt the immediate connection. They stared silently at each other for several minutes before either spoke.

"Are you okay, love?" Paul asked.

Sandy, eyes still locked with this handsome stranger above her, began speaking rapidly in German.

"Oh, you're German!" Paul said.

"What do you **expect** to find in Germany!" Sandy answered tauntingly.

Both continued to examine each other's faces and then suddenly the tension was broken as their last comments registered in their minds. They both began to laugh. Paul helped Sandy up and dusted her off.

After exchanging names, Paul began, "I'm sorry I startled your horse..."

"That's all right. You didn't mean to. But what **are** you doing here?" Sandy said.

Paul began to explain that he and his friends were in a band that had played some clubs in Hamburg before, and they had returned for another gig. The pair walked down a trail and through the forest holding hands, Sandy's gray mare trailing behind them.

"Do you live close by?" Paul asked.

"Yes, just through the woods. When I was a baby, my parents were both killed in an auto accident. This is Uncle Roy's estate, and he's very kind to let me live here. Unfortunately, he's always quite busy with his job in London.

"You must have loved growing up in this country atmosphere. It's really gear."

"Gear?" Sandy looked puzzled.

"Fab...great, you know." Paul interpreted.

Sandy laughed. "You have such different words. Actually, my sister and I grew up in a convent. In the last month we left the order instead of taking vows to become nuns. We really never had a home like most people".

"And so where is your sister?"

"She's in London hoping to become a model. I'm not sure what I want to do yet, but I think I'll get more equestrian training. I'd like to show horses. My uncle has been so kind to see that I have a stable of horses and a full staff."

Paul's eyes devoured every detail of the flaxen-haired beauty who seemed so open and honest. He was instinctively drawn to her. She was unlike any girl he had ever met either in Liverpool or in the Hamburg strip club scene. Paul couldn't take his eyes off this gorgeous creature. He wanted to touch her so badly; he reached out to stroke her hair without thinking that it might upset her. She stopped talking for a minute and looked down at her hands and blushed. Then she continued talking and acted as if he hadn't done it. Her laugh was warm and vibrant. Paul found himself staring at her lips. They looked so inviting. Without thinking, Paul leaned forward and tried to kiss Sandy. She pulled back just before their lips met and inquired, "Are you going to try to kiss me? My uncle said never to do that, so please don't."

"Hey," laughed Paul "you wouldn't be trying to do a 'Brer Rabbit' on me, would you?"

Sandy looked confused. "A what?"

"You know, Brer Rabbit, like in the children's story..."

He saw her blank look and continued, "the fable...you've got to know about Brer Rabbit and the Tarbaby. Everyone heard that when they were little."

"Well, the nuns didn't exactly tell fables or any stories at all." Sandy insisted.

"You've been deprived!"

"So why don't you help me?"

"It would be my pleasure," Paul assured her, laughing.

So Paul and Sandy sat down facing each other under a huge oak tree, and he related the whole fable about Brer Rabbit and his sly dealings with the fox.

"You see, by asking me not to kiss you, I thought like Brer Rabbit you might have been really trying to get me to do it!" Paul explained with a grin.

Sandy obviously took him seriously because she insisted, quite earnestly, "I see, but that wasn't the case, I assure you."

"I believe you, but..." Paul stopped mid-sentence because Sandy had begun to rub the back of her head.

"Are you okay, love?" Paul said worriedly.

"My head hurts where I fell, but I'll be okay," Sandy said rubbing her crown and frowning.

"Here, let me help you," Paul offered as he took her shoulders, turned her around, and began to massage her neck and back. When he rubbed her head, he gently parted her hair in the back and kissed her neck. She jumped at first and giggled, but then Paul felt her relax. They spent the afternoon laughing and talking and sharing stories from their childhood. As dusk began to creep up on them, Sandy took Paul to the giant stone mansion she called home.

"Please stay the week. We have plenty of room. We have many people on staff who will chaperone us." Sandy implored.

Paul inwardly rolled his eyes at the suggestion of having to be watched over, but he honestly wondered how he could ever leave this wonderful girl now that he had found her. For the next five days, Paul and Sandy were inseparable during waking hours. They rode horses together, took long

walks, and had picnics in the meadow near the lake. He
even managed to give her a light kiss or two.

Paul's stunning good looks had always assured him success with members of the opposite sex. In Liverpool he had
girlfriends by the score and when he came to Hamburg basi-
cally an innocent, he was quickly introduced to pleasures of
the flesh by the strippers, whores, and groupies there.
George, John, and Paul along with two band members, who
were no longer with them, frequently participated in orgies.
Many nights they would share six or more girls among them
in their dark slum-like room behind the screen of a porno
theater.[12] So it was with some frustration that Paul courted
Sandy for those five days. People always surrounded them
so he never had a chance to stroke that lovely hair or touch
all those luscious curves her body offered. When they were
sitting in the flower garden, the gardeners were pruning the
roses. When they rode horses, a stable hand was always discreetly in the background, and when he played the guitar
and sang for her, there was always a housekeeper dusting or
polishing something nearby. The staff was careful to see
that Sandy had adequate chaperoning, but they tried not to
be too obtrusive. The amazing thing to Paul was that it
didn't bother him to the point that he wanted to leave. All
he cared about was being able to be with Sandy even if he
had to put up with all these people supervising him. This
was the only girl with whom Paul was satisfied to spend
time with in innocent ways. It was enough to hold her hand
or talk to her or just stare into her eyes. Just being near her
made him happy.

But when it was finally time to leave to meet the others
in Hamburg, Paul asked her to slip away for just a few minutes of privacy. "I need to see you alone. Please come with
me into the barn," he pleaded in a low whisper.

Sandy hesitated and then nodded. "You go in first, and
I'll be there in a few minutes. That way the servants won't
notice."

Paul's heart raced. He was glad that she trusted him
enough to be alone with him. He just had to tell her good-
bye in private. Paul was hidden in one of the box stalls at

36

the back of the massive barn. "Here I am!" he whispered as she walked around searching for him.

As Sandy followed the sound of his voice, a stall door suddenly swung open slightly, and Paul reached out and pulled her in quickly. Alone with Sandy for the first time in days, Paul was elated to finally be able to touch her. He wrapped his arms around her and held her close, relishing the sensual feel of her body against his. Sandy stared up at him with no fear in her eyes, which pleased him.

"Sandy, you are so special to me. I want you to know that I don't want to leave you. Could you come into Hamburg to see me?" Paul whispered. His huge hazel eyes, which usually looked so dreamy, were dark and intense.

Sandy frowned and shook her head. "Paul, I could not possibly go to the Reeperbaum in Hamburg. My uncle would be very angry! I could not go against him!"

Paul thought of the seedy characters, the crime, and the whores she would be exposed to there and nodded. "Your uncle is right, Sandy, you shouldn't come, but I want to see you soon. I'll think of you everyday until I see you again."

Sandy nodded, her waist length hair tickling Paul's hands. "I will think of you every day too." As he felt the swish of his hair on his wrists, Paul noticed how long her eyelashes were.

"Will you write me?" Paul asked.

"I promise I will. Will you write?" Sandy asked. She looked up shyly into his eyes.

"I will. Oh, God, you mean so much to me." Paul pulled her to him in a crushing hug. "May I kiss you good-bye?" Paul heard himself ask for a kiss and couldn't believe his ears. He had never done that before, but then again, he had never encountered a girl as innocent and sweet as this one. He was relieved and pleased when she nodded.

Paul kissed her tenderly on the lips, and then he deepened the kiss, grasping her head in his hands and pressuring with his tongue for her to open her lips. She complied, and Paul continued the kiss, feeling encouraged as she began to respond. Finally, Paul stopped the kiss, wrapped his arms around her, and held her against his chest, trying to get the courage to do what he knew he must.

"I have to go, but I'll see you again as soon as I can. Here's my manager's card. You can find out where I am by calling his offices in London. Come when you can. I'll be waiting to see you." Paul promised.

Sandy nodded. Paul saw the tears pooling in those beautiful blue eyes. He felt like he would choke as they walked hand in hand to her uncle's limousine waiting in the gravel driveway. His luggage had already been loaded, and now all that was left was for him to get in and ride away.

Paul bent down to give her a chaste kiss and forced himself to get in the car. He felt his heart was being ripped from his chest as the blonde girl waving to him appeared smaller and smaller through the rear window. Normally he would have felt excitement about the envy his friends would show when he pulled up in a sleek limo.[13] But all he felt was loneliness.

LONDON

John and Paul were taking a break on the steps at the Abbey Road Studio where the group was recording.

"Come on, Paul. There must be some bird other than this German one who can do it to you." John urged.

Paul shook his head, and blew cigarette smoke up as he leaned back on both hands. "It's not sex, that's not what it is."

"What in hell do you call it? Mooning over this girl to the point you can't bloody function! What do you need if it's not a bloody good shag?"

"I need to tell her how I feel about her. And know how she feels about me."

"Well, ring her up!" John suggested emphatically.

"What?"

"You heard me. Ring her up. You've got to get over this. We need you to play good bass again, son. Your lust is messing up your sound." John was adamant.

Paul shook his head and blew more smoke up in the air. He stretched his long legs out and crossed one booted foot over the other.

"I can't talk to Sandy about our feelings on the telephone."

"Well, son, you can't fly to Germany tonight, and if you don't get over your problem with this bird and get your head straight, the rest of us may murder you!"

Paul suddenly laughed. "Okay, when you put it that way...I'll think about it."

Neil,[14] their road manager, who had been in school with John years earlier, clumped down the iron steps toward them.

"Let's go, mates. Break's over. George wants you back in the studio." Neil announced. George Martin, their producer, was an avid taskmaster, as usual keeping them at their jobs when they would wander.[15]

Paul tried once again to put thoughts of Sandy's ivory skin, golden hair, and crystal blue eyes out of his mind as the three pairs of Cuban heels stomped up the steps to the studio.

* * * * * * * *

The practice session in the dank, sweaty cellar-like atmosphere of the Cavern Club[16] in Liverpool had not gone well once again. The rock group had run through their songs for their gig the next day, and Paul had messed up lines in just about every song. While packing up their equipment to be put on the van for the evening's gig, George's and Ringo's eyes met John's..."I'll talk to him" John whispered when Paul had stepped away for a moment to get a guitar case.

"What happened to you tonight, Macca?" John began. Paul just shook his head as both slumped on the overstuffed couch in the tiny dressing room behind the stage. "Well, I wouldn't worry, sometimes ya just hit a bloody dry spell...or is it that little German bird again?" he continued.

Paul let out a long sigh as he put his hands behind his head and stared up at the ceiling. He stretched out his long legs out on the coffee table.

"I'm distracted, John. I'm going mad. I can't think about anything but Sandy. I want to see her so bad."

"Oh, I knew it had to be the German bird you met on that last trip to Hamburg. You're still hung up on her. Did you ever ring her up?"

"I just couldn't tell her how I feel on the telephone. That just wouldn't be right. And she's not German. Actually she's American." Paul explained.

"How's that?" John inquired.

"She's told me her parents were American. Her uncle works for the government and is here in London, but she's been raised in a convent school in Germany. She had just left the convent and was visiting her uncle's estate when we ran into each other. I told ya about that, you know."

"Yeah," John agreed. He pushed his black frame glasses, which he never wore in public, back upon his nose as they had slid a little. He looked intently at Paul. "So, get her to come here for a visit. Her family's got money from the looks of that bloody limo that got you to the Star Club, so they could send her. Macca, you need to hump the lass and get her out of your system."

"John, I told you before, don't talk such bloody rubbish about Sandy that way. I have special feelings for her. She's the only girl who's ever made me feel this way."

"Oh? Well, whatever you want to call it, you need to get **laid** son. Your playing stunk tonight, and this gig tomorrow's important. There are going to be some music studio people here tomorrow. It would be a shame to blow our group's chance to make it big just because you're having trouble with your **zipper** being stuck".

"John, you know how you feel about Cynthia."[17]

"Yes, and I need a good fuck at times when she's not around like when we're touring.[18]

"I can't feel that way, John. I really think I love her."

"And I love Cyn but I don't let me music suffer. You got to put the music first, son. Go shag some bird, and you won't miss Sandy so much."

"Can't you see I just don't want to...."

"Well, I'm headin' home so I can get laid proper before we leave tomorrow. You go find some local talent. You never had trouble laying groupies before. Get you a good knee-shaker! It'll release your creative juices, son. You'll see..."

Paul sighed and rolled his eyes as he and John clomped up the steps to street level. Oh, how he'd love to see Sandy's big blue eyes laughing at him. It was going to be a long and restless night for him.

LANCASHIRE, ENGLAND

John pulled the two giggling teenage girls to his chest and kissed both foreheads. "Thanks, Mal," he whispered hoarsely to his roadie[19] before the theater exit door slammed shut. Hmmm...the buxom one smelled like cinnamon. Now, he thought, which one should he give to Paul? He wondered as he shepherded them down the dimly lit hotel corridor. Paul definitely needed a jump-start lately, but he hated to give up that cleavage on the redhead. What bloody fun they would have tonight, he thought.

Knocking a pattern of beats on the door, John whispered something to one of the girls who then giggled louder, and then he began kissing the other girl on the neck. The door came open a few inches to reveal George's lean craggy face.

"Hello" George greeted the girls as he eyed them appreciatively.

"Delivery for McCartney!" John chortled as the hotel suite door opened.

"Ooooo, local talent," crooned George, stroking the brunette's shoulder. He seemed quite fascinated with her blouse. She gaped in awe at him as their eyes locked and she realized who he was.

"Hey, Paul!" John's voice was barely above a croak now. He had ripped up his vocal chords with that last rendition of Twist and Shout at the concert a few minutes ago.[20]

41

Several men stood at the mini-bar mixing drinks. "Get your lazy 'arss' over here and meet our new friends."

One of the men sauntered over to George, John, and the girls and put out his hand. "Hello, I'm Paul. Pleased to meet you." Both girls fell silent, obviously spellbound by his classic features and huge brown eyes. He still wore the velvet-collared suit he'd worn for the concert.

"Paul," John continued, "this is Jane and Anna. They told Mal they wanted to meet us and they're both over eighteen."

"Oh, really?" said Neil. "Do you girls have some ID? I help with security, and it's my job to check visitor's IDs...a driver's license maybe?"

"Relax!" John grumbled, "Mal already checked."

"Oh, we don't mind" the red headed Jane gasped. She frantically searched her handbag and jerked out a card to show. Anna pulled her license from her pocket.

The older man nodded. "Glad you two ladies can visit us this evening. Their relieved giggles echoed around the living room area. "Would you like to join us for some rum and Coke?"

Noticing that Paul had edged away from the girls to the other side of the group gathered around the bar area, John sidled over to him. "Hey, come on, let's go get some"

Paul shook his head and whispered "No, John, I'm very tired. The gig lasted a long time tonight. Get someone else."

"Come **on**!" John whispered forcefully. "You haven't humped anyone since you came back from Hamburg, for Christ's sake!"

"I pass," Paul conveyed his annoyance with a sidelong warning glance.

"Look, everyone's noticed how tense you are. That's why we set you up tonight. You need a good shag! At least a blow job! You've got all day to sleep tomorrow. We don't play until tomorrow night, son"

"No," Paul shook his had and looked at his shuffling feet.

"Why?" John would not be dissuaded easily.

"Just no. What about Cynthia? Have you forgotten her?" Paul asked.

"She's not here." John stated simply.

John gave him an inquisitive last time expression to see if he would change his mind, but Paul just shook his head.

During John and Paul's conversation, the other men had entertained Jane and Anna with mixed drinks and conversation.

"Your drums are so big!" trilled Anna to Ringo. He threw back his head and shook his long dark locks as he laughed. It was apparent how enthralled the blonde was with him. Ringo was clearly enjoying himself.

John moved next to Ringo. "You want in?" he breathed in his ear. "Get this. Paul's too tired to shag this bird. The bugger..."

Ringo grinned and wrapped an arm around Anna's shoulder. "You want to see my drumsticks? They're in this other room..." As he led her off he turned to wink at Paul, but Paul had already turned away to go in the opposite direction to his bedroom.

John was staring down Jane's blouse at her ample cleavage. He spoke in a funny high voice, "Let's go find another room. We'll see Ringo and Anna later!" Jane stared starry-eyed at John as he led her away to his bedroom. He began to tickle her and she ran ahead of him. John began chasing the redhead with a comical leering look on his face.

George and Neil looked at each other and shrugged. "Flip you for the couch" the rejected roommates grumbled. "Let's push Brian to spring for individual rooms next hotel. These groupies..." both men laughed and shook their heads good-naturedly. They'd make sure Mal rounded up some pretty stacked ones for them tomorrow night.

LONDON

Paul sat at a table in the hotel's grand ballroom, putting the finishing strokes on an autograph for a blonde beauty named Gail. He admired the soft skin, curls that tickled across his hand as he gave her the picture he had signed. She giggled a thank you before she reluctantly turned away, but Paul continued to stare at the golden hair, so soft like...God!, he thought, I'm doing it again! I can't keep my mind off her. It seemed forever since he had sunk his hands in that deep golden mane and drawn her to him. Abruptly Paul came out of his daydream to find George waving his hand in front of his face. "Brian wants you...some sort of PR thingie."

"Where?"

"At the door..."

Paul put aside his thoughts and met the other band members and Brian just inside the huge red double doors to the meeting room. Brian looked excited, cheeks pink. "Lads, the signing went well. We got all fifteen fan club presidents through here. "Now something else has come up I didn't plan on." Everyone's attention centered on Brian, who not only fulfilled all their business affairs but was also their friend. He directed all their moves, from appearances to holiday plans. He wasn't usually flustered, but he appeared so now.

Impatiently, John spoke, "Well, what is it now, Eppie,[21] old man? I've got a wife upstairs with big plans for the evening."

Brian who never seemed at a loss for words was struggling now. "I'm not sure you should do this, boys. There's a girl up on a fire escape here at the hotel, and the bobbies can't get her to come down. They say she keeps shouting for the Beatles. I thought you might be able to help." Brian mopped his brow with a silk handkerchief and looked genuinely distressed.

"Oh how grotty!"[22] John snorted. Hands shoved in his pockets, he abruptly started toward the elevator, dismissing the whole situation as ludicrous. "My day's over and Cyn is waiting. I'll see you lads later," he said over his shoulder.

Brian surveyed the remaining band members. "Are you interested? They say she's 'in a state' and they're afraid she'll jump!" Brian bent conspiratorially toward his charges.

George and Ringo fidgeted uncomfortably and watched Paul for his reaction. Finally Paul nodded and let out a long breath. "Well, I'll try." He was known for being the most diplomatic of the four.

George eyed Ringo and then Paul and all of them nodded.

"Come 'head then!" Ringo added, and the four men walked toward the elevator.

* * * * * * * *

The group briskly proceeded down the 7th floor hall. "Ah, those dippy little birds, what they won't do to get to meet us..." Ringo grumbled.

"Yeah, we sure could use a little rest this evening. No telling **what** we're getting ourselves into." George added.

"She better be fab, Brian, or you've **had** it!" Paul retorted.

"Now, lads, this is public service," Brian began but was interrupted by George.

"This may set a trend. You see, shortly birds'll be climbing fire escapes and threatening to throw themselves off all over London!"

Two policemen stepping out to stop their progress down the hall abruptly halted the conversation. One of the officers greeted them, "Good evening. This part of the hotel is not in use at this time. Please return back down the hall."

Brian put out his hand confidently. "Hello, Officer, I am Brian Epstein, the Beatles' manager and these are some of the Beatles. An officer Dunhally told me earlier he'd appreciate the boys' help...a matter of a young lady who has been asking for them?" He nodded his head down the hall to where he imagined the girl probably was.

"We've just been told to stop all traffic through here." The policeman turned to his partner and suggested that he find out information on this. While his partner trudged away to find Officer Dunhally, the first policeman asked them to kindly wait just a few minutes.

The tall dark haired young men in their collarless suits leaned on the wall in a row, heads together, whispering, arms crossed. They were used to waiting in hallways to perform, and this just seemed like another gig. Brian, always the ambassador of good will, made small talk with the policeman.

The returned officer almost collided with the group as he slipped hastily to a halt. He had run the length of the hall and breathlessly announced, "Follow me, lads!"

"At last, some action" mumbled Ringo as he scuffled behind the others.

What greeted them at the end of the hall surprised all of them. The hotel room they were led to looked like the scene of a violent struggle...lamps turned over, broken mirrors, disheveled bed linens on the floor and blood. Paul, George, and Ringo stared around themselves in amazement as Brian whispered with several of a half dozen policemen in the corner of the room.

"Whoooo" whistled George softly, "something's gone on here."

"Wonder where the girl is. I don't think this is a simple fan 'thing'." Ringo whispered as they gawked at all the mess surrounding them.

"Yeah, John will be so mad he didn't come. I'm going to ring him up." Paul volunteered and went to use the phone beside the bed.

A nearby policeman stopped him as he reached for it. "Come with me. There's one in another room you can use. That could have evidence on it we'll need."

George and Ringo joined Brian and Officer Dunhally in their conversation. "Lads, this isn't pretty as you can see," the tall middle-aged policeman began, "you might want to change your minds and not get involved, but I hope not."

"Where's the bird?" interrupted Ringo.

Dunhally looked puzzled. "I beg your pardon?"

"The girl" Ringo said impatiently.

"Oh, yes. She's out on the fire escape," he said, indicating the windows to his left. "She's quite hysterical and apparently from the blood around and the way she looks, she's been hurt. We don't know of course how badly, because every time one of our men tries to go out after her, she gets closer to the rail. We don't want her going over the edge."

All four walked to the window to stare at a slight form huddled in the pouring rain. The officer put his hands on George and Ringo's shoulders. "How about you give it a go? My boys tell me she's been yelling for a Beatle."

"What do you want me to do?" George asked in a low voice. He looked about nervously.

"Well, one of you go out and get her to come in so we can send her to hospital." The two looked at each other and did some sort of brief hand game.

Ringo turned back to the officer and automatically said, "I'll go."

"Here," the officer handed a gray-green poncho to Ringo as he started to climb through the window opening. Paul arrived back with the group from calling John to see Ringo approach the drenched girl. She screamed and grasped the rail.

"Now, hold on, love, I'm Ringo. Come here and we'll talk!"

"Nine!" she screamed and then she began to yell in words from another language. Ringo stopped when she leaned over the rail. God, she looks desperate, he thought.

"Okay, okay!" he said as she backed away. As Ringo crawled back through the window, he told the people gathered to help him back in, "She's a nutter, that one! I thought she was going to jump for a minute. But I gave it a go..." Dripping on the carpet, he turned to his two friends. "Next..."

The room was quiet as everyone considered that their plan had failed. "Bloody hell!" Dunhally's voice boomed. "I thought you blokes told me she was yelling for this singing group staying at this hotel, the Beatles!" The angry man turned to the officer closest to him and stared accusingly.

"No, sir, she's been yelling for Paul McCartney, and he is *one* of the Beatles." the young man corrected his superior gravely. "There's a difference, sir."

George broke the tense atmosphere as he elbowed his friend; "The girls are always after you, aren't they? I used to mind it, you see...now you're welcome to it!" A collective murmur and smothered laughter passed through the room.

47

"What's so funny?" demanded John who strode through the door to his friends. Behind him tottered a slight elderly man with a black bag and a long black umbrella he was using as a cane.

"Ah, Dr. Campbell, glad you're here," Dunhally greeted the older man with a handshake.

"Where's my patient?" Dr. Campbell inquired peering upwards at the policeman.

"Well..." Dunhally began when he was interrupted by screams from the fire escape. Most of the words she was frantically yelling were indistinguishable. "Does anyone here know German?" Dunhally demanded.

Then came a plea they all understood. "Paul ... help me please!" she shrieked several times and then collapsed crying on the fire escape. All eyes went to Paul. Paul looked sober, thoughtful, and stunned.

"Come on," said Dunhally, pulling the wet slicker from Ringo and handing it to Paul.

"Now wait a minute..." Brian stepped between the two men. "Paul, this might be dangerous. You saw how she acted when Ringo went out. If I'd known how disturbed she was, I wouldn't have allowed Ringo to go. She could pull you over the rail with her or attack you. This isn't the situation I thought it was to begin with."

The scream came again. The girl was getting more desperate. She was completely drenched and hysterical. "We don't expect you to risk injury or your life" Brian intoned sternly. Paul stared out the window at the pitiful creature in the deluge of rain and spied a long flaxen lock dangling down her back almost to her waist. Something clicked in him. He had to do this. He had to try.

"Don't worry, Eppie. I'll be careful," he said earnestly to Brian. "I've got to help her. Or at least try." His eyes stared keenly at the girl on the drenched fire escape.

"Paul! Paul!" she shrieked again.

He slipped on the rain slicker and began to crawl through the window.

"Here," Dr. Campbell said as he handed Paul a thick wool blanket. "Put this around her. And take this," he said handing him his umbrella. "I'm worried about exposure."

Paul suddenly felt numb. What was he about to do? He wasn't Superman. He crawled through the window and opened the umbrella. When his eyes fell on the pitiful girl in front of him, he once again felt the sense of purpose he had earlier. Slow motion seemed to take over as he approached the girl. He heard her muffled crying which hadn't been audible in the hotel room. Something terrible must have happened to her.

"I'm coming. It's okay, love!" Paul said as he inched about three feet behind her. She spun around and tried to get up, but she slipped. She crawled from him frantically screaming German words until she was almost to the railing. "You've been calling for me, love! I'm Paul!" he shouted. He had to get through to her. Poor thing. He couldn't bear it if this poor girl threw herself over the railing. He had to try to save her. Pulling the hood of the slicker back so that his face and head were bare to the driving rain, he tried again. "It's me...Paul!" And then she faced him.

"Oh, my God!" Paul said in shock. "Sandy?" They stood motionless. It took a moment for each to absorb the other's identity. They were oblivious to the surrounding circumstances as their eyes connected. Paul threw the blanket around her, and they grabbed each other in a fierce hug. He lifted her and rocked her back and forth and whispered in her ear, "My God, Sandy, how did you get here? What happened to you? Are you all right?" His questions weren't answered though. She was so upset her words were still tumbling out in German. She babbled hysterically.

Inside the hotel room, the others waited tensely. "Why doesn't he get her over to the window?" worried Brian. The other three Beatles and policemen alike stood silently spellbound by the drama unfolding before them. John had an instinct about what was occurring on the fire escape outside. He and Paul often shared thoughts. Finally, John spoke, "Paul knows this girl. Remember the one he stayed with in Germany that last trip? You know, we were having those photos made at Brian's friend's place right before our holiday."

Brian, George, and Ringo stared at him. "Are you daft, John Lennon?" George accused.

"Yeah? Well, how'd she get here then?" Ringo challenged John's conjecture.

Looking out the windows, John pretended not to notice their reaction. He continued to nod knowingly, "Yes, he's quite hung up on her..." Suddenly shifting gears, John noticed the mess around them. "What happened here?" he looked inquisitively at Dunhally after surveying the disheveled hotel room.

"Well, we don't really know, of course, but from the looks of things and from the report of the lad in the next room, she didn't like his intentions and went a bit potty."

"Quite a bit potty, I'd say...." Looking around the disheveled room, he added approvingly, "She's got a lot of spunk. So you caught the bastard that done this to her, eh? He must be a sick bugger. Just couldn't take 'no', eh?"

"When we got a call about all the noise coming from this room and calls from neighbors seeing the girl on the fire escape, we got here in time to hold onto him. You might know him. He says he works in a band here in London. Colin Dodd, he's called."

All three band members and their manager looked at each other. "Wasn't he in the band with George just before we all got together?" John asked.

George nodded. "Yeah, that was a bad scene when he and the other two who were in the band with me had a tiff, and you and Paul stepped in to play with me that night at the Casbah Club. I think he's always carried a grudge against us."[23]

Interest sparked in Dunhally's eyes as the other men spoke. "When was the last time you saw him and what did he do?"

"I think he turned up at the Cavern when we were playing there a couple of months ago. The bouncer had to send the bugger off. He was drunk and loud...swearing something about he'd get the lot of us."

"Any other information you can gather about him will help us greatly." stated Officer Dunhally.

George shrugged. "I can tell you where his family lives. He's a rowdy bloke, angry at the world."

Paul had managed to calm Sandy as they huddled on the rain drenched fire escape. He put her down from their hug but stayed as close as possible. The umbrella overhead helped to grant a sense of privacy. Paul noticed when he released her and helped her secure the blanket a little tighter, that her clothes were torn. Not having heard the policeman's explanation of why she might be out here, he was very confused about what had happened.

"Sandy, relax, love... I'm here."

"Paul...Paul..." she said and then the rest of what she said was a string of German.

"Sandy, love, speak English." He tilted her chin so that their eyes connected. He had to bend a little but when their eyes locked, she seemed calmer.

"Now, look at me. Think about what I'm saying. Speak English."

Sandy struggled to get out a few English words. "Paul... don't... leave me."

"I never will," he promised.

"Paul, please don't leave me." She began to sob miserably.

"Listen," he said as he bent to look into her eyes. "Tell me what happened."

She shook her head and covered her eyes with her hands. "So scared..." He followed her eyes as she looked down at her torn blouse, ripped to the waist. She blushed and made an effort to clutch it together as tears once more began to spill down her face.

"It's going to be okay. We're together. I won't leave you. Let's get you inside so you can change and rest, okay?"

"Paul..." she looked relieved and suddenly exhausted. "I think I'm going to..."

"Faint," he finished her sentence as she collapsed. He dropped the umbrella to grab her with both arms. Holding her up in his arms, he braved the continuing downpour to get to the window where help was waiting. After handing her in to one of the waiting policemen and crawling through himself, he questioned Dunhally.

51

"What happened to her?" His eyes followed when the officer carried her to an adjoining room followed by the elderly doctor and a waddling nurse who had just arrived.

Dunhally, reading his thoughts, assured Paul, "Don't worry, the doctor wants to check her out. He will see if she needs hospital. We'll know more in a few minutes."

Dripping wet but not even noticing, Paul continued his questioning, "How did this happen?"

Dunhally said honestly, "We don't know. We'll know more after we question the young lady. Do you know her?"

"Yes," Paul pulled the poncho over his head.

"How well?"

Paul handed the poncho to a nearby policeman and looked at Dunhally. "We are very close, but I haven't seen her in several weeks. We spent some time together when we were playing in Germany last month. Who did this to her? Do you know?"

"We don't know for sure, but we are holding Colin Dodd who was in this room when we got here. I understand you know him and have had words with him before."

"Yes, I can't say I fancied him much. Rather sneaky, that one."

"When you and the young lady were out on the fire escape, did she indicate any clues as to what happened?"

Brian had joined the pair, as always wanting to be in the know so he could intervene if necessary. "No," Paul began, "but she did keep repeating one word over and over in German. I don't know what it means, but..." and Paul turned to glance at Brian, "don't you deal in German a bit?"

"Yes, what's the word, Paul? It may give us a clue." Brian said. So Paul repeated the word Sandy had chanted over and over as she cried earlier. Brian's face was very grim as he stated, "Why, Paul, that means 'rape'!" Everyone was silent.

A piercing scream came from the adjoining room, and Paul dashed to get to Sandy. Two policemen stepped between Paul and the closed door. Paul turned to Dunhally and gasped "Please let me in to see her. She's terrified. And she's awakened to find me gone. I promised I wouldn't leave her."

Dunhally nodded his men aside, stepped by Paul and knocked on the door. "Could we come in?" he asked. The screaming continued, but over it you could hear Dr. Campbell's reply, "Yes, that's fine."

Paul shoved the big policeman aside before he could move and burst into the room, with Dunhally closely following. Dunhally stopped to confer with the doctor as Paul dashed to Sandy who was cowering in the back corner of the bedroom. Her ripped and drenched clothes had been replaced with a bathrobe the nurse had apparently found in her luggage that was laying open nearby. She was shaking and mumbling hysterically as she cowered against the wall.

"Now, calm down, Sandy" he said reaching for her. She seemed frightened of him too. "It's Paul...Sandy, look at me," he commanded. Holding her by the shoulders, Paul bent to look her directly in the eyes. She still shook but a slight smile came to her trembling lips.

"Please don't leave me again..." she whispered.

"I'm sorry. You fainted and the doctor wanted to look at you. Please forgive me, love. Come here..." He hugged her close to him and stroked her long blonde hair, still wet from the rain. After a few minutes of snuggling on his shoulder, he felt her relax. She was still shaking, but at least she was improving, Paul thought. He leaned and kissed her gently on the back of her neck exactly the way he had the first afternoon he met her. She jumped much as she did that day in surprise, but this time her reaction was much more pronounced. She wrenched herself from Paul's arms and slammed back against the wall right behind her.

"I'm sorry, Sandy," he said immediately, " I didn't mean to scare you!"

Sandy's eyes were wide with terror as she slid away from him down the wall. "Please come back here, love!" Paul tried again. He held out his arms to her, but she spoke in German and shook her head frantically, obviously hysterical with fright.

Paul glanced around at Dunhally, Dr. Campbell, and the nurse who were whispering as they watched. The nurse just shook her head as she looked at the frightened girl. Dr. Campbell motioned for Paul to join them. "We must give

53

her a sedative so she can rest. She has some cuts on her arms that might worsen if she keeps thrashing about so. If we can get her calmed down, I don't think she'll need hospital. Can you help us get her sedated?"

Paul knew the elderly physician was right. "Will it be a pill or a shot?"

"A shot will work much faster."

"Right!" Paul grimaced as he raised his eyebrows. He hated shots himself. How in the world was he going to convince someone so terrified to accept it? Turning on his heel, he went to Sandy and whispered soothing thoughts in her ear until she finally sat on the bed with him. After a while, he had convinced her the shot would make her feel better. The doctor was right. Almost immediately she was drowsy, clinging to him. "Sandy, love," he whispered as he put his arms around her, "Why are you here?"

"Mmmm..." the groggy girl slurred, "to see you...had to see you."

"But how did you find me...?"

"Your manager's card...mmm...you gave it to me... remember...I called his office and they told me where you were. Sorry I caused you trouble, Paul."

"No, love, glad you're here." He bent and kissed the top of her head resting on his shoulder. In only a few more minutes, she was sleeping peacefully.

"Now, son, let Sadie and me finish our examination. We will be only a few minutes and then she will be all yours." Dr. Campbell patted Paul on the shoulder as he left the bedroom.

Paul closed the door behind him gently, but the thud it made tore into his heart. He felt so separated from Sandy. He didn't know what she had experienced or what she would face as she recovered. How did this happen to this wonderful sweet girl, he wondered.

The other Beatles, Brian, and Neil were sitting together in the living room. Most of the police were gone now.

"You all right, mate? You look like a bloody lorry ran you over." John quipped.

"I'm fine, but I'm worried about Sandy..."

"She's the bird you've told me about; you stayed with her in Germany," John said.

"Yes, do any of you know what has happened here?" Paul questioned the others.

George offered "Well, you might want to ask that scruffy Colin Dodd. He's in the next room, I've heard, and the police found him in here when your bird was on the ledge there."

"Bloody swine!" Ringo added.

The door to the next room opened and a disheveled dark-haired man flanked by policemen on either side floundered into the room on his way to the hallway. It was obvious that he was drunk as he slurred out, "Oh, McCartney, so glad you could make it. Too bad you weren't here earlier. We could've had a threesome! That pretty Sandy was a handful!" Paul angrily lunged for him shouting, "Don't even speak her name, you bloody bastard!" It took all three friends to grasp Paul and hold him back.

John cautioned, "Macca, the damn bugger's not worth it!"

"Yeah," George agreed, "he's fuckin' rubbish, Paul!" George tightened his grip on Paul's chest as Paul attempted another lunge at Dodd.

"You bloody swine!" Paul shouted as he struggled.

Dunhally entered the room in time to hear Dodd's next growled insult, "I'm the best she's had. She was bloody tight, but I opened her up. Now I know why you left her in Germany. But on second thought, **I'll bet you fit right in there, 'Little Paulie',**" Paul renewed his effort to reach Dodd, but the others had him firmly in their grip. The policeman's eyes narrowed. Apparently this attack on the girl wasn't just a whim. This Dodd seemed to want revenge.

"Take the bastard somewhere else!" Ringo urged the guards, and they tugged the offensive man out the door of the suite.

"Oh, my God, my poor Sandy! What has she been subjected to? I can't imagine her alone with him. There's no telling what he did to her!" Paul moaned. He sat with his head in his hands, distraught at the recent events, his imagination torturing him. An image of Dodd taking advantage of Sandy ravaged his brain. She was so sweet and innocent!

"Oh, Dodd's just full of shit!," George tried to comfort Paul.

Ringo, gazing around the room observed wryly, "Yes, well, **something** went on here, and from the **look** of things, it wasn't very pleasant."

Paul sat silently as in a trance. "I hope he didn't force himself on her. I don't think I could stand it."

John with his ever wry humor wisecracked, "Look, there'll be plenty of pie[24] left for you."

Paul took John by surprise with a right hook as both crashed to the floor.

"Look, mates, no!" shouted George, putting down his cigarette, "Enough of that!" as he and Ringo both grabbed Paul and pulled him off John.

Still on the floor, John rubbed his jaw appreciatively. "You've gotten better, Paul. Look," he added as he stood up, "This bird seems to mean a lot to you. I didn't mean to upset you, mate. Colin Dodd is a bloody bastard to do what he did."

Ringo spoke up, "Hey Paul, my cousin was raped and some people rejected the poor thing. Thought she was ruined. Don't hold it against Sandy like they did to her."

"Yeah, you ought to help her get over it instead of condemning her. I wouldn't want my sister treated like that." George stated.[25]

"No, it's not like that. What I'm saying is not about me or my pride. Sandy is...or was..or anyway...she's never been touched in a sexual way, and it was important to her. She has been innocent. She's lived in a convent for her whole life until now, you see." Paul explained.

"Oh..." said George. George, John, and Ringo all looked at each other. "A VIRGIN!" they chorused together.

"And she's HOW old, Paul?" John asked incredulously as he shoved his face near Paul's.

"I'm going to hit you again..." promised Paul, waving his fist at John. But the tension was broken, and the teasing was good-natured even though it had an edge to it.. All of them giggled a little at that last banter and then fell into silence as they each mulled over the situation.

Brian had joined the group in time to hear the last two comments. Always the voice of reason, Brian chided, "Now, lads, calm down. It's important we all pull together." Turning to Paul, he asked, "Do you want this young lady to join our entourage?"

"Yes, of course, Brian!" Paul replied immediately.

"Well, is she of age?"

Paul thought briefly and then answered, "Yes, she's nineteen, why?"

Brian frowned as he said, "Paul, I've contacted our attorney and he says she must be of adult age or there could be serious trouble. How about family? Is there anyone we need to notify?"

"I'll call her uncle. He's here in London." Paul offered.

"Good," Brian continued, "I'll make arrangements for Sandy to reside in the suite next to ours up on the 8th floor. There's a nurse who will come and stay with her for a few days until she's better."

"Thanks, Eppie!" Paul said gratefully. That was Brian, thought Paul, always thinking ahead and making life run smoothly for them.

"Hey, Eppie! Do you think you could get two more suites and set me and Ringo up with a few birds? We won't need the nurses!" George said as he and Ringo laughed boisterously.

"I'll take the extra nurses in with me and Cyn! I like them white uniforms!" John boasted in a silly voice. "Cyn won't mind. She has a lot of headaches...and a bloke needs his pie!"

Brian just shook his head at them and went back into conference with some men who had just arrived in the hotel room.

Bryan Sommerville,[26] the Beatles' press officer, stepped away from the group with whom he had been talking and motioned for Paul and Brian to join him by the window. "It is important that no one knows this girl is Paul's friend. She's got to remain anonymous." he said tersely.

Arms crossed as usual when he was tense, Epstein soberly nodded his acceptance.

Paul came out of his stunned silence. His dark eyes flashed as he stated, "I will not deny knowing Sandy. She's done nothing wrong!"

"Now, Paul," Bryan Sommerville turned to look the irate young man sternly in the eye. Sommerville always looked like he had swallowed a lemon and now Paul thought he looked even more sour, if that was possible. The tall blonde man let his breath out and his eyes softened, almost looking at Paul as an exasperated parent or grandfather would. "Paul, listen," he continued, "we're not doing any disservice to that young lady in there by keeping her name out of the press. Someday when she marries and has children, she'll be very thankful indeed that her name wasn't linked with this mess."

"I see," Paul nodded his agreement. "That makes sense."

Sommerville turned to Brian and the two whispered a few minutes. "I'll get the lawyers together tomorrow after we know how the girl is doing. We'll hash out a resolution to this," he stated to Paul. Paul with his hands on his hips, looked disgusted by Sommerville's last comment.

Paul waved his finger in the older man's face. "There's no way Dodd is getting out of paying for this."

"Paul, be reasonable. If the hotel presses charges for damages, that will punish this man. There's no reason to have your friend in court testifying over and over and having to relive this nightmare."

"Well, there's no way Dodd could be adequately punished for hurting Sandy the way he has. I know what I'd like to do to him, but I know I can't. But you're right about protecting Sandy from all the court proceedings. It will be much easier for her to not have to recite details in a court of law. I'll grant you that."

"Thank you for coming down, Sommerville" Epstein said as he shook hands with his old friend.

"That's what I'm here for, " he responded.

As he prepared to leave, the older man placed his hand on Paul's shoulder. "Take heart, lad. I hear she seems to be a strong one. We'll not let anyone else get to her."

* * * * * * * *

Paul felt relieved when he finally saw Sandy again. She was unconscious but at least he could hold her hand as the policemen carried her on a stretcher to the suite beside The Beatles. Brian had to leave, but Neil took over and made sure everything was available Sandy would need. John, George, and Ringo sat in the living room as the doctor and nurse were situating Sandy in her bedroom. Paul paced nervously, puffing on a cigarette.

"Don't worry, Paul, I'm sure they'll let you see her again after they get her settled in," George said in an effort to support Paul.

Paul nodded and blew out some smoke. "I plan to stay with her until she's awake and functioning. I can't leave her like this."

"We've got a show tomorrow night" reminded Ringo, "but if you can't go we'll just tell Brian to cancel the bloody thing." He eyed Paul as he continued to pace.

John chewed his gum and nodded. "Oh, Brian will have a fuckin' fit," he said. He had his guitar and was playing around with a melody. He looked up at the other three who were standing. "If Brian insists on playin' the gig, we'll all be sick. He'll have to cancel then, the bugger. Want me to talk to him about it, Macca?[27] I'll tell him what's what. Then you can be here in case she wakes up."

"Yeah. Good idea, thanks, Johnny." Paul nodded as he answered. He crushed his cigarette into an ashtray with a shaking hand.

The bedroom door opened and the doctor tottered out with his black bag in hand. "Take care of her, son. No excitement for a while..." he warned. He gave Paul a knowing look.

"Thanks!" Paul said as he strode past him on the way to Sandy's bedroom to start his vigil until she improved.

The nurse smiled at Paul. "She'll probably sleep quite a while, due to the sedation and her body's efforts to get over what happened to her."

"That's fine. I just want to be here," Paul assured her, taking off his suit jacket. He seated himself in a chair next to Sandy's bed and held her hand.

After a few minutes, the other three came to the door. They nodded politely to the nurse. John whispered to Paul across the room, "We're going on back to our suite. We'll check on you from time to time."

"Right. Thanks, mates." Paul answered and nodded to them, but his eyes immediately returned to Sandy's still form in the bed.

Every hour or so, George or John or Ringo or Neil or Mal would drop by to see how things were. Paul would doze for a while, but nothing changed with Sandy until the next morning.

Midmorning, Neil came over to sit with Paul and brought him some tea. As they munched on yolk butties,[28] Sandy began to make a few sounds and moved her arms on the covers. Paul immediately left his food and drink to take her hand and gaze closely into her face.

"Sandy?"

"Mmmmm..."

Sandy's eyes opened. She stared up at Paul and smiled. She was a beautiful sight to Paul.

"Hey, love, how do you feel?"

"Not so well..." she groaned. She frowned and tried to move slightly.

"I'm not surprised." Paul agreed.

The nurse came over and sat on the other side of the bed.

"Sandy," she asked soothingly, "do you know where you are?"

"No..." Sandy gazed around. "I imagine a hotel, but I don't know which one."

"Do you know who we are?" she asked as she waved her hand encompassing herself and the two men. She placed her hands in the pockets of her white uniform and waited patiently.

"You're a nurse, but I don't know your name. This is Paul and..." Sandy frowned, trying to figure out who Neil was.

"That's fine, dear." She was obviously pleased that Sandy wasn't disoriented.

Paul immediately introduced Neil, his road manager. Sandy managed a slight smile for Neil. A nice clean-cut fellow, Sandy thought as Neil said, "Glad to finally meet you, Sandy."

"I'm Mrs. Perkins, Sandy, and I'm here to take care of you. Let me know of anything you need," the nurse offered.

"I'm a little thirsty." Sandy whispered hoarsely.

"Good. You need lots of fluids. I'll get you some juice," the nurse said as she rose to get it.

Paul smiled and whispered "Welcome back. I've been worried about you!"

"Oh, my head hurts and I'm sore all over!" Sandy looked down in surprise at the bandages on her arms and hands.

"Do you remember what happened to you?" Paul asked.

Sandy hesitated, and then her eyes filled with tears. "Yes," she nodded.

"Do you want to talk about it?"

"No," Sandy reached to brush the tears away but Paul got there first with his handkerchief.

He smiled tenderly at her. "If and when you want to talk, I'll listen."

Neil spoke up then. "Hey, I wish he'd listen to me. He always ignores what I say. Tell me your secret, Sandy."

Sandy smiled but suddenly looked very tired. "You're weak, love, you need to rest." Paul said as he pulled the sheet up a little higher on her.

"No, Paul, I need to tell you something. I argued with my uncle and left without telling him where I would be. He'll worry. I should call him."

"I'll call him, Sandy. Don't worry. I'll let him know you're safe." Paul assured her.

Mrs. Perkins got back with the juice.

"You lads might want to give Miss Wellington a little time alone," she said in a grandmotherly way, "It's time for her bath."

"Yes, ma'am" both men spoke obediently, getting up and gathering their food trays.

"Paul!" Sandy suddenly looked panicked, and she reached out to Paul.

"Don't worry. Let the nurse have you for just a few minutes. I'm just going next door to shower and change. I promise I'll be right back. Okay?" Paul said as he bent to give her a light kiss.

"I'm relieved she's awake," he said to Neil as they started back to the group's suite.

Paul's devotion to Sandy was apparent as he stayed by her bedside every minute he could during the next few days. She was well enough for him to continue playing the gigs they had scheduled here in London, but he had very little time to spend with the other three band members otherwise.

"Hey, this is getting old," complained John as he threw a card down on the table after the third day of Paul's vigil with Sandy.

"Relax, it'll change. She'll be better soon and Paul will be back" encouraged George, studying his hand before playing a card. Ringo and Neil sat silently, looking over their cards too.[29]

"I guess if she has to stay in bed much longer, we can just all stay over there," mused Ringo, playing his card.

"Don't be so complaining!" scolded Neil. But he as well as everyone else around the table felt the group's bond being weakened by Paul's absence.

* * * * * * * * *

John lounged drowsily at one end of the couch occasionally putting down a card on the coffee table as he played solitaire. Ringo was reading the newspaper in the chair next to him. As Paul and Sandy entered the hotel suite, Ringo muttered "hullo." Both nodded to him. "Hello," Sandy said softly.

"Sit here. I'll be right back," Paul gestured to a chair nearby and quickly strode toward his bedroom. Ringo noticed that Sandy watched Paul until he disappeared and wondered idly why he had left her there. She looked a little lost, he thought. Not my business, he decided and went back to the article he was reading.

"Hey, where's Paul?" George asked as he walked in from his room strumming his guitar. The tune was a lively one.

"Eh?" John murmured.

"I think I've got a gear riff for the new song you're working on," George explained and played a series of chords that sounded pretty catchy.

"Oh, he's taking a bath..." Sandy spoke up. All three looked at her in surprise. She hadn't yet spoken out loud since she arrived a few days ago.

"Ah!" George remarked, as he looked toward the bathroom which the whole suite of rooms shared.

"In Germany we don't bathe more than once a day unless we are doing an activity that warrants it. I ride horses and I don't even bathe as much as Paul does. You English do like to bathe often," she continued, shaking her head.

"What's that?" John broke the stunned silence. He leaned forward, keenly interested. His eyes were bright with mischief. "You say Paul is bathing a lot?"

"Yes, I don't understand you English at all..." her voice trailed off as George began to giggle.

"George!" Ringo said sternly, but when his eyes met John's, both of them joined George in bursting out into uproarious laughter. The glances they exchanged were meaningful. They realized how frustrated Paul must be to be taking so many cold baths. They had shared their sexual exploits for a long time, and they knew what Paul was used to. This little chit was really making him miserable!

Sandy stared in confusion as George bent double over his guitar while John slid off the couch on his knees during their laughter. When they finally could control themselves

63

enough to stop laughing, John gasped, "How many times has he bathed today?"

Sandy was looking very uncomfortable and puzzled over their behavior. "Um, three times." She glanced nervously from one man to another.

"Three times?" John asked incredulously and started giggling again, this time pounding on the table as he laughed. George began to giggle too. Sandy looked as though she might cry.

"George! John!" Ringo said in his sternest voice. He felt sorry for this lovely girl. She clearly didn't understand the situation. He looked from one to the other warningly.

"I don't know how to speak English well. Did I say something wrong?" she asked timidly.

"No, no, love," Ringo assured her as he shook his head. "You didn't say anything wrong." His tone was soothing, and he smiled at her to make her feel better.

John decided to follow Ringo's lead and help Paul out. He was having trouble keeping a straight face because he loved to tease his mates, but he took a deep breath. "Uh, Sandy, maybe you'd like to meet my wife, Cyn. She could talk to you and help you understand some things about...uh." He burst out laughing but stifled it when Ringo glared at him. "uh...some things about Paul," he offered. He couldn't help but grin mischievously at the thought of what they would talk about.

"Yeah, good idea, John," Ringo agreed. "See if she can motor down from Liverpool tomorrow." He frowned at John and George who continued to try to stifle their giggles.

"Oh, thank you, " Sandy smiled warmly.

When Paul emerged a moment later from the bedroom, Ringo, John, and Sandy were listening to George's new guitar riffs. Winks and knowing looks were exchanged among the lads. Although they didn't embarrass the girl, they'd silently agreed that they would later tease him mercilessly about his need for so many baths.

* * * * * * * *

Cynthia Lennon slammed down the magazine that she had been reading. "No, John. I do NOT want to come all the bloody way down there to baby-sit Paul's bird! I have plans tonight!" the blonde shrieked into the phone. The volume rose as she talked.

"Fuck your bleedin' plans! You get yourself here, girl, by 2:00 P.M. so you can meet the posh bird before our interviews," John growled.

There was a long moment of silence on both ends of the phone. The only sound was the rhythmical popping of John's gum. "So...pretty Paulie's found someone who can say 'no' to him. If she's smart, she'll keep her legs closed tight if she wants to hold onto him!" Cynthia raged.

"Look, Cyn, he can't keep his mind off his John Thomas long enough to play 2 bars on the bloody bass. It's terrible, it is! Our sound stinks!"

"Well, just get Mal to get a bird or two from the audience. He'll forget her in a minute if he gets one with big enough tits! Look, Gail and I are going to the cinema and that's that!

"Cyn, we've tried that. The lad's bloody frozen up or something. He's so hung up on this bloody bird. Now, somebody's got to talk to her. Paul's screwing up every bloody song! You GOTTA get her to 'put out' and soon!"

"You act like Paul's going to spurt!" Cyn sighed in resignation. "Oh, right you are, I'll call Gail and break our movie date."

"And while you're here...hmm...I could use a little servicing, too! My John Thomas is lonely," John added.

"A cold day in hell, most likely" was the blonde's tart retort. But she smiled hearing the guffaws at the other end of the line.

John started at the sudden awareness of someone close by. Putting down the receiver, he swung around face to face with George.

"For Christ sakes, George! Yer liable to give a bloke a bloody heart attack, sneakin' up like that!"

"Thought I was Macca, huh?" George drawled. "Is she comin'?"

When John nodded, George added, "I hope she can talk some bloody sense into the bird. It's not natural, you see, this celibate business she's puttin' Paul through."

"Cyn will set her little cunt straight..." John couldn't help giggling as he thought of Cyn's reaction to the state of affairs. "She'll give the little twit bloody hell until Macca gets his flaming pie!" George and John roared with laughter as Paul, Ringo, and Neil came in the hotel room door.

* * * * * * * *

Cynthia glared at the back of the beautiful golden-haired girl who was whispering to Paul near the hotel window. Although John had had little time to tell her about Paul's newest conquest, she instinctively resented this creature who was everything she wasn't...naturally blonde, slender, and assertive. She frowned as she enviously assessed the girl.

"Cyn!" John leaned down to whisper urgently. "Mind your manners, love. Do what I told ya now...I'll take ya out for steak and chips when we're back."

Cyn rolled her eyes but nodded compliantly at John. He was an irresistible force. She always did what he said eventually. Ever since she met him, she believed she couldn't exist without him.[30] He was like air to her, always drawing her to him no matter how irreverent and wild his behavior was. John affected other people that way too. He was a born leader.

"The interviewers are waitin', lads. Let's have ya. Come 'head." Neil urged as he opened the suite door and waved them toward the corridor. All were dressed in crisply pressed suits and ties just as Brian had directed.

"It's bloody silly to have to wear this lot," complained John as he pulled on his tie. Leaning down to his pregnant wife, he gave her brief kiss, and joined the others in the hall.

66

The door closed. There was an awkward silence...a ticking clock...the blaring horn of a lorry careening around the corner...Cynthia cleared her throat.

"Come here, Sandy, and sit with me," Cynthia said sweetly, patting the couch next to her. "I'll ring for tea..." Sandy obligingly joined her on the couch as Cyn picked up the phone. Being even closer to the German beauty, Cyn noticed her smooth and unblemished complexion. She could see why Paul was going potty over her.

Silence once again filled the room. Awkward silence...the heavy tread of feet in the corridor, the rumble of a truck outside, the delivery of the tea tray. Grateful to break the stillness, Sandy eagerly accepted the cup of tea Cyn handed her.

"Mmmm..." Sandy murmured appreciatively as she tasted the warm tea.

Cyn, disgusted to be spending her afternoon this way, frowned at Sandy. She had decided to be blunt and end this charade quickly.

"You know, Paul has a lot of girls after him, don't you?"

Sandy's eyebrows went up over the teacup. "Mmmm, yes, yes, I found that out when I first came to see him. There always seems to be a group of girls hanging about wherever he is."

"And he's getting tired of waiting to get your knickers down."

"I beg your pardon?" Sandy looked properly shocked.

"If you won't do it, there are lots who will."

Sandy's teacup began rattling in its saucer. "Who will do what?" she gasped.

"IT!" Cyn exclaimed, throwing up her hands. When Sandy still looked puzzled, she repeated, "IT!" No recognition registered on the German girl's face, which frustrated Cyn even further. "You know, shagging...**sex**!" she fairly shouted. Cyn was totally exasperated. This girl was really good at playing stupid!

"Oh!" was all Sandy could manage to say. The teacup continued to rattle in her shaking hand and a bright pink blush was creeping up her neck.

Cyn was quite cross by now. "Come on! Quit acting thick about it. You know you're driving Paul potty!"

"I didn't know I was bothering Paul at all." Sandy shook her head. "John said he'd ask you to come here and help me understand him. You see the British are so different from the Germans. Paul takes *so* many baths every day..." Sandy's voice trailed off as her eyes met the meaningful gaze that Cyn directed at her. As Cyn began to laugh, Sandy looked more bewildered than ever. "Why does everyone laugh when I tell them about Paul taking lots of baths?"

Cyn made an effort to compose herself. "You really **don't** know, do you?" and when the other blonde shook her head, Cyn continued, rather sarcastically, "Where **have** you been all your life?"

Sandy didn't take the question as a rhetorical one. Instead, she began quite earnestly to relate how she had been raised in a convent school, isolated from the world.

Cyn stared at her in shock. It was Cyn's turn to murmur "Oh!" After a moment, Cyn continued, "You're joking aren't you?" Cyn frowned thinking it over.

"No, I'm not. My sister and I lived there until about six months ago. We both decided to leave and live in the world instead of taking the vows to marry the church and become nuns."

The ticking of the clock was all that was heard for a full minute until Sandy asked timidly, "Do these frequent baths have something to do with the sex you said Paul needs?" Her voice was barely a whisper, and when she said the word, sex, Cyn noticed that her face blushed a deep pink.

When Cyn saw how red the other girl had become, she realized she had misjudged her. John hadn't told her about Sandy's background, and she had assumed the girl was holding out on the sex in an effort to force a marriage with Paul. Touching her arm, Cyn said gently, "I'm sorry, Sandy, I didn't know. And the answer to your question is 'yes'. Chaps take cold baths when they want sex and can't have it. They get frustrated, you see."

"Oh!" Sandy covered her mouth with her free hand. "All Paul's friends knew that when I was talking to them about Paul's baths, didn't they!" Sandy looked horrified. "That's why they were laughing! I'm so embarrassed!"

"It's all right, Sandy. Listen, Paul really likes you and now that you know what he wants..."

"But I **don't** know, really. My sister was always slipping away from the nuns after we went to bed. She would come back smelling of ale and cigars before sunrise. She told me she had sex. She told me a little bit about it, but when the nuns found out she had been sneaking away, they wouldn't let me be alone with her anymore."

"What did she tell you about it?"

"Well, she said a man would lay on top of you. It would hurt the first time, but then it would feel really good after that. I heard the nuns talking about Candy. They said once you do it, you always want to do it some more. The nuns said it was sinful until you're married. I guess you and John have...oh, I'm sorry...I didn't mean to..."

Cyn smiled at the embarrassed girl.

"It's okay. Yes, John and I have sex, but so do lots of people who aren't married."

"Then I guess Paul has it, doesn't he?"

Cyn nodded. "Oh, yes. He is quite popular with the girls."

"Can I ask you what he wants me to do?" Sandy asked, but when she saw Cyn's impatient expression, she hurriedly added, "I've never had anyone tell me all about it. I just don't know what to do."

"Well, to start with, you and Paul need some time alone."

Sandy nodded eyes intently on Cynthia. She took a sip of her tea.

"He'll want to hug and kiss you."

Again Sandy nodded. Cyn took a deep breath and forged ahead, "Oh, then of course the clothes come off!" Cyn got up to pour herself another cup of tea as she heard Sandy gasp. She was embarrassed to have to tell someone else about the sex act. The teacup in Sandy's hand started rattling again, and Cyn heard her swallow pretty hard.

"And then?" Sandy's voice was no more than a squeak.

"Well, then lads like to touch and taste, you know."

69

Cyn glanced over at Sandy in time to see her turn
ashen just before she went limp and fell to the floor, hitting
the coffee table with her head.

"Oh, my sweet Lord!" yelped Cyn, jumping from the
tea tray to Sandy in one leap. A touch on the other girl's
shoulder brought no response. Wringing her hands, Cyn
spotted fresh blood oozing from a gash on her head. She
could see the broken porcelain teacup and saucer under
her hand, which was probably the cause of the blood that
was coming from under her body.

Grabbing the telephone in a panic, she dialed the number where John and the others would be for the interviews.

"Quickly, let me have John Lennon!" she fairly shouted
at the person who answered the phone.

"Who?" was the puzzled response.

"John Lennon of the Beatles!" Cyn tried again. Her
panic was obvious. The next voice she heard was Neil's.
"Neil, please get John." Cyn begged.

"Cyn, you know they're all doing interviews. We'll be
back in a bit," he answered curtly and hung up. Cynthia
stared fixedly at the still figure on the floor nearby. She realized that she was on her own to solve the present dilemma.
It was an occurrence that was to be repeated often in her
marriage with John, she assumed. Oh, well, she thought,
I've got to be strong and take care of this. "Why did I fall in
love with a musician? " Cyn muttered as she bathed Sandy's
face and neck with a damp cloth. She smiled at the groggy
girl as she helped her back on the couch. Sandy smiled back
weakly when their eyes met, and Cyn observed, "He's worth
fallin' for, Paul is. But you didn't have to hurt yourself!"
Sandy couldn't help but giggle in spite of the blood trick-
ling down her cheek. "Let's get you cleaned up now..." Cyn
clucked in a motherly manner, dabbing at Sandy's new
wounds.

* * * * * * * *

With a clean white bandage on one hand and one on
her temple, Sandy once again sat on the couch. "If I stay

here much longer, I may look like a mummy," she joked as she surveyed her new bandages and the old ones on her arms.

"Sandy, I'm so sorry I upset you with what I told you. I really didn't mean to." Cyn leaned forward to convey her sincerity.

Sandy nodded solemnly. "It is overwhelming. I'm glad you told me, though. I just didn't know."

"Sandy, there's more that I didn't tell you, but you'll just have to trust your man. Paul really likes you, and I know he'll make you enjoy it."

The door burst open just then, and Paul rushed to Sandy, kneeling in front of her. "I missed you," he reached up to give her a kiss. Paul surveyed the new bandages. "Are you okay, love? Neil didn't tell me Cyn had called until just before we got back to the hotel, and even then we didn't know what the problem was." Paul paused to give Neil a dirty look. "What happened?" and he looked from Sandy to Cynthia and back again. He gingerly fingered the new white gauze on her head.

John stood with his hands on his hips and stared accusingly at Cynthia as the others filed in, loosening their ties and removing their coats. Cynthia remembered their earlier conversation when she had resisted counseling Sandy and suddenly felt very ashamed of her reluctance to help.

Sandy noticed John's apparent anger and wondered why he would blame Cyn for her accident. Sandy glanced from John to Paul to Cynthia trying to understand the dynamics of the situation. She spoke quickly hoping to dispel John's obvious anger. "I'm fine, Paul. I just fainted and hit the table."

Paul examined the bandage on her hand. "And this...?"

"Oh, I shouldn't be trusted to hold teacups." Looking up at John, Sandy smiled in spite of his menacing demeanor and said, "Thank you, John, for sending for Cyn. We've had a wonderful chat, and she's answered a lot of questions for me."

John nodded and walked away to one of the bedrooms, leading Cyn by the hand. Sandy couldn't help but think about what might go on in that room.

"Love, you're shivering," Paul commented worriedly as he squeezed her unbandaged hand.

"I'm fine, Paul. I was just thinking of some things Cyn and I talked about."

* * * * * * * *

A few days later, Paul and Sandy were huddled together on the couch in the band's suite, whispering as they watched George and Ringo play cards.

"Hey, you lucky bastard!" Ringo complained. "You've got all the bloody face cards."

"Not luck, it's me overpowering skill at cards!" George bragged.

The bedroom door to their right burst open, and Cynthia closely followed by a wild-eyed John crashed into the room!

Sandy immediately froze, open-mouthed. Everyone else continued with their activities, including Paul who downed the rest of his drink calmly and made a comment to Ringo that George was bound to be cheating.

Cynthia succeeded in traveling the length of the wall before John caught her in the corner, arms on either side of her. Holding her against the wall, he began to kiss her neck. She struggled and lunged away, but he tackled her. They thrashed about before she once more escaped. This time rolling over and running back into the bedroom. A brief shriek and John's muffled raucous laughter was heard, as the door was slammed shut. Then rhythmic pounding began on the wall between the two rooms.

Paul turned to Sandy "I'm glad I'm not in this game..." he began. When he looked at her, he was shocked to see that the color had drained from her face and she was shaking. "Love, what's wrong?" He was concerned at this sudden change in her.

"Paul, you've got to stop him..." she uttered.

"Stop who?" He followed her wide eyes to the bedroom door. "Oh, you mean John, oh...Sandy, everything's okay."

"No!" Sandy said emphatically, rising from the couch. She moved away as soon as he reached for her. By now, Ringo and George were aware that something was going on with Sandy. They watched solemnly as Paul tried to put his arms around her, and she backed away.

"John and his mischief" muttered George. "He's spooked her. She's thinking about that swine that attacked her, poor thing." Ringo just shook his head.

Sandy darted for the door leading out of the suite, but she didn't make it. Paul managed to grab her around the waist and hauled her into George and Ringo's nearby bedroom. "Stop struggling, love, ...now what's wrong?" he whispered as he put her down. He held her close.

"It's Cynthia. I'm worried about her!" she gasped.

Paul stepped in front of the obviously distressed girl as she tried to leave the room. He firmly held her shoulders and looked steadily into her eyes. "Why?"

"John was hurting her..."

"No, it wasn't the same thing that happened to you." Paul shook his head.

"How do you know?" she questioned.

"Well, John just likes to play that little game when he makes love. He and Cindy are married, you know, and they do stuff like that all the time. They've been lovers for a long time, Sandy. It's part of their love-making ritual, I guess you could say."

"Oh," was her reply. She had turned very red and seemed to be thinking this new information over.

"Sandy, I need to talk to you about something really important," Paul said as he took both of her hands in his and looked into her eyes. "The first time I saw you I knew we were meant to be together. I think of you all the time. I can't get you out of my brain. I love you. I've never told that to a girl until now. I want you to be with me always." He bent to kiss her briefly on the lips. "Will you marry me?"

Paul felt very vulnerable, as the next few minutes seemed like a year. Her next words relieved his tension.

"Paul, I love you, and yes, I do want to marry you."

Paul wrapped his arms around Sandy and cheered, "That's fab!" Sandy giggled as his handsome face lit up with excitement. Her laughter was musical to Paul. He pulled out a small box from his pocket and knelt on one knee as he presented it to her. His face was tense as he watched her open it. Inside was a gold locket on a chain.

"How beautiful!" she exclaimed softly.

"I hope you like it," he said rising. "I've put our pictures in it, yours and mine. Will you wear it as an engagement token?"

"Yes, I love it. I will always cherish it, Paul. Thank you."

"I rang Brian and told him I was going to ask you today to marry me, and he told me we had to talk about something." Paul was concerned about what he was going to tell her, and she prepared herself for something dreadful. "You see, Brian thinks that if our fans know I'm married, it will hurt the band's chances to sell records. John and Cindy have been married for a few months, but no one's supposed to know, and they've got a baby on the way!"

Sandy nodded her understanding, sensing that he really dreaded having to ask what she knew was inevitable. She wanted to encourage him because she didn't mind keeping their engagement and marriage secret. "It's all right, Paul." she assured him. I understand that we too have to be discreet."

As he gently kissed her, he felt like the luckiest bloke in the world. She was his! Or would be...if he could get up the nerve to talk to her about a subject that was haunting him.

"Sandy, I'm worried about you. You've fainted three times this week. Do you have any idea why?"

Sandy frowned. "Well, I have had an ordeal, and I just need rest, I guess."

"Sandy, I hate to mention this, but is it possible that you're pregnant?"

When she stared at him, stunned with silence, he blundered on. "It's okay if you are. We could marry straightaway here in London in a private ceremony. Of course, you could invite your uncle and sister. I promise I would love the baby as my own."

Sandy finally got her voice back. "Paul, there is no way I'm pregnant. We haven't...well, you know," she hesitated, blushing, obviously embarrassed.

74

Paul continued, "I know, but think about what happened with Dodd..." Sandy interrupted him quickly, "No, Paul. Is that what you think happened between us? I fought him. I did not give up my virginity to him!"

Paul was immediately apologetic. "I'm so sorry, love. You kept saying something over and over in German the night of the assault, and Eppie thought the words you were saying meant rape. The attack was not your fault. Whatever happened in that hotel room, you were the innocent one."

Sandy smiled wryly. "He tried. He pawed and pushed but I got away. That's why I got cut up so much. He used a knife when I wouldn't submit willingly. So I assure you there's no rush to marry me to legitimize a child."

"Sandy, I want to marry you whenever you'll have me. You name the date and I'll be there. Marrying you has nothing to do with legitimizing a child. I love you more than life." Paul assured her.

"I love you more than life, Paul, I really do. I think Christmas would be nice for a wedding, but I imagine we'll have to go through your Eppie to see when you're available."

Paul laughed. "I can't wait. Christmas it is!"

Sandy said meaningfully, "Well, you'll have to...now tell me about this chasing thing married people do. I don't think I like it."

"Okay, if you'll explain something to satisfy my curiosity."

"Yes, what?" Sandy asked in surprise.

"How did Colin Dodd ever get hold of you in the first place?" Paul's voice sounded exasperated.

"After I had that argument with my uncle about coming to see you, I got on a plane and came anyway, getting the location from your manager's office. When I got to the hotel, there was a huge crowd and the police wouldn't let me in, but I happened to ask about you in front of Dodd. He told me he could get me in to see you if I came up with him to his room. After that, the nightmare began!" Sandy shuddered lightly and began to cry. Paul put his arms around her and kissed her tears.

"Shhh, love, it's over. I'm here." He rocked her gently until she stopped crying and her composure returned.

75

"Now, tell me about this chasing thing," she whispered.

Paul took a deep breath and began. "Some couples like John and Cindy like that sort of thing, but it's not for everyone. Lovers find their own pleasures. I can imagine being only tender and gentle with you."

Sandy closed her eyes and sighed. "Thank you for being honest with me. I am relieved. I know I'd be stunned if you prowled and hunted me like that. He looked so fierce."

"It's just John's personality, Sandy. He loves the chase. Now, you just relax. You can trust me." Paul said.

After a few minutes, Sandy ventured, "You've made love to many girls?"

Paul looked down not wanting to meet her innocent eyes. He thought of all the orgies he and the rest of the band had enjoyed in Hamburg last year and all the groupies that constantly offered themselves at him daily.[31] "Let's say that I've had sex with a few girls, but with you it will be truly making love for the first time. I feel so complete when I'm with you. You give me what I really need, Sandy. Their eyes made contact and they relished this quiet moment together.

Sandy's heart raced. It was a little scary, but very enticing to imagine Paul touching and exploring her in ways Cyn had described. Paul's arms were around her, and she snuggled close enjoying the strength of his body. She was surprised when he pulled away and bent to kiss the tip of her nose playfully.

"Let's get back to the mates," he suggested. "George and Ringo probably think you need a doctor again, and if we don't get back in there, they may call Brian."

That evening and throughout the rest of her visit, Sandy was surprised that their betrothal didn't increase their physical closeness. Cynthia had suggested Paul needed time alone with her to become intimate. But he seemed content to do things with the other band members. They were seldom alone. When her visit ended, and it was time to go back to Germany to resume her equestrian career, Sandy determined to be patient. With daily concerts, sometimes two a day, odd hours, lengthy rehearsals, and the traveling to performances, Paul was absorbed in his work. Eventually, she hoped, he'd want more of a physical relationship. At least that's what she envisioned. She wanted to be normal; to escape the cloistered sterile feeling that living in a convent had given her.

Paul gave her a list of their bookings, scheduled dates, and Brian's phone numbers so she could let him know when she would visit next. "I don't want you in danger as before. I want you safe from harm. I love you." Paul whispered as he kissed her good-bye. He brought her gold locket to his lips and met her dancing eyes. Paul parted the curtains of the hotel room window to wistfully watch as Neil walked her safely to the airport taxi. Paul was afraid he would draw a crowd.

* * * * * * * *

Sandy's next visit came when the band was playing one-night stands across the U. K. Paul was relieved when her arrival was unremarkable. Neil had Mal meet her at he airport to avoid any mix-up in her getting to the right hotel. Between sound checks and performances in each town, the group sat around in the hotel resting, playing cards, or playing guitar. Sandy always had a suite or a private room to herself in each hotel for which Paul was relentlessly teased about his lack of sexual prowess.

The gig had gone well that afternoon. The crowd had been especially enthusiastic about "Long Tall Sally," Paul's favorite closing number. Paul was elated as usual after a rousing performance, and Paul and Sandy were finally alone, lounging in the living room of Sandy's suite Paul was completing a song he was writing. As he strummed and hummed, he noticed Sandy's despondency. I'm ignoring her, he thought. So to make her feel better, he abruptly leaned over and kissed her on the cheek. "I love you," Paul reminded her.

"I know, but I'm worried..." there was a pause in Sandy's voice, a hesitation. Paul was struck by the seriousness of her tone, the frailness of her childlike voice. She sounded so insecure that he looked up sharply from penning something in his notebook to stare at her. "Why are you worried, love?" The tone was solemn, pensive.

"Paul, I know you love me, but are you attracted to me?" she blurted. Her eyes were downcast. She continued to talk down to the floor, twisting her hands together. "I mean, I know I'm not as pretty as some of the other girls...you know, the girls that hang about downstairs waiting to see you..."

She didn't get to finish her sentence. Paul abruptly grabbed both delicate shoulders and stood up, pulling her off the couch. He stared incredulously down into her startled blue eyes. **"What do you mean, am I attracted to you?"** he demanded of her. The question caught him completely off-guard, and his control was gone, used up by trying to restrain his lusty feelings all afternoon. He must carefully guard his responses so he wouldn't become too physically aroused when she was around. She had been so close, her delicate scent wafting around his head all those hours. He had wanted to touch her and have her touch him. Now all his senses were stunned. As he towered over her, she looked as shocked by his reaction as he obviously felt by her question.

Paul's grip tightened on her as he lost all sense of control over himself. "I want to show you just how much I want you..." he whispered as his mouth roughly covered hers, kissing her thoroughly, hungrily His taut body pressed hers hard against the wall.

His breath became audible at this sudden emotional release. All he could think was how much he wanted her. He wanted her body so he could explore and enjoy it.

Sandy was totally surprised by his unexpected advances. Her small frame submitted as Paul's body pinned her against the wall and he continued to kiss her. She had never known Paul to act like this. The wild lack of control shocked her, but then his touch and the intense passion stirred something in her—a longing that she had never experienced. She wondered what to do. What should she do? What **could** she do?, she wondered. He was so much larger, heavier, and stronger, she realized she was, in effect, entrapped and at his bidding. She just had to trust him, as Cynthia had said. So she relaxed and analyzed the moment. She loved the feel of his strong arms around her as he clutched her. She noticed the rapid pounding of their two hearts. She was amazed at the growing bulge against her abdomen... evidence of his arousal for her.

And then it was over. As quickly as it had begun. Paul's senses were reeling at the electrifying touch and taste of her, and he fought to come back to reality. What am I doing?, he thought and released her. Angry with himself for losing control, Paul grabbed his guitar and strode out of the room, leaving Sandy gasping to catch her breath.

Well, thought Sandy, I wonder if that's what Cynthia meant when she said they should become intimate. The experience had been exciting, she had to admit, but she was very confused about how it suddenly ended.

Paul was beside himself, berating his rough treatment of Sandy. He was no better than that Colin Dodd bastard! He had wanted to handle her so gently when they could finally make love, but pent-up feelings made him treat her in this shameful way! She must hate him as much as he hated himself he anguished. Left alone just a few minutes with her and what had he done! He was not worthy of her uncle's trust.

To busy himself, he began strumming an intricate pattern. His fingers moved rapidly, head bent as he worked on the fancy riff. "Concentrate, he told himself, "block it out."[32]

Sandy knocked softly on the bedroom door. She had to talk to him, to discover the secret to his erratic behavior. Maybe that's the way it should be, but she didn't think so. She had to know. Now.

Paul continued to bang out chords as she timidly entered and sat down beside him on the bed. She listened for a few minutes, watching his long dark locks swing to the rhythm of his song. He was obviously struggling, head down, deep in thought on his project.

"Paul...Paul?" Finally she put her hand on his arm. Her touch was like fire to Paul. He couldn't shut her out any longer.

His handsome face turned toward her and she had his full attention. His hazel eyes looked very deep brown as he looked at her gravely. "Yes?" he said.

"Paul, I've got to know..." she started bravely.

"Yes?" he said a minute or so later as he continued to stare intently at her face.

The mood was tense. He knew he had some explaining to do. The time had finally come. All these months of waiting, holding back his emotions had to end. She deserved some answers. "Sandy, I'm sorry for what I did to you in there..." he nodded toward the living room of the suite. The afternoon sun streamed in the window making shadows on the rich maroon bedspread. "I just lost control, that's all."

They watched the shadows creep around them as the trees outside shivered in the wind, breaking through the sunbeam's light. Neither wanted to break the heavy silence. Sandy pushed her long flaxen hair behind her shoulders as she got up the courage to ask. "Why do you **need** control with me? Don't you love me? I thought people in love should be able to express that love together."

The questions were direct and simple. Paul stared at a picture of Sandy and her uncle on the dresser. He absent-mindedly strummed a few light chords as he prepared what he needed to say.

"I love you, Sandy. I want to marry you. But when I talked to your uncle about it, the only way he would agree to it was..."

He didn't have time to finish. She shrieked, "You discussed our lovemaking... or rather lack of it with him!" She was horrified and embarrassed beyond belief. "Paul!"

"I didn't bring it up, love. He did. Your uncle said that he didn't want you to get hurt. He said he wanted our physical union to come only after the marriage. I love you so I agreed. That's all there was to it."

"All?" She looked at him in disbelief. "All?" she repeated. "And I don't have any say in this? Am I a cow to be bartered? Am I a box of goods to be shipped that must arrive in pristine condition so as not to break the contract?" her voice rose.

"No, no, love, it wasn't like that..."

"Oh, I think it was. I am a person. I have some say-so, **the** say-so with my body, Neither you nor Uncle Roy have the right to control that!" Sandy insisted hotly.

Paul sat and stared at the picture of Sandy and her uncle again. His eyes closed and he realized that what he had done had shattered her. He had not treated her like a partner, but rather as an object. It hurt him that he had been so insensitive.

"I'm sorry. You're right. I didn't think." Paul said simply. He sighed and avoided her gaze. He wondered if she would turn away from him now. Was he still worthy of her love? She was right. She was right. He owed her respect as a person.

Sandy folded her hands in her lap and was very quiet. They could hear the swaying trees rustle outside the window. Birds that had gathered in the tree were surprised by the sudden motion and squawked as the shifting branches pitched against the side of the stone building.

"Do you love me enough to forgive me? To understand that I agreed to something I thought wouldn't hurt us..." Paul shifted his body around to face Sandy, suddenly needing to meet her eyes for reassurance. "I think, no, I **know** that our love is strong enough to withstand this challenge." he continued. He searched her face for understanding. She had to agree! He couldn't bear to lose her.

Sandy sighed and looked briefly away. "Oh, you're right. You agreed to please my uncle thinking it was the right thing to do..." she said in a voice full of flat resignation.

Paul interrupted as he leaned down to peer into her down-turned eyes. "Yes, I agreed because I love you so much. I was afraid that your uncle could keep us apart, and I couldn't let that happen. I would have agreed to cross the Thames on stilts if he had asked me to."

Sandy giggled. The thought of Paul on stilts anywhere was ludicrous! The stress of the situation had evaporated as she collapsed back to laugh out loud on the bed they were sitting on.

Paul relaxed a bit. He wasn't sure what her reaction meant, but at least she wasn't out the door yet. "Do you see?" he demanded.

"Yes, I see" she giggled still thinking of him on stilts.

She reached out to him, grasping his hands callused from years of guitar playing and pulled his face just above hers. She took his head in her hands and kissed him with urgency. Paul was surprised at this turn of events. She was so angry a few moments ago. "I love you, Paul. I want what's best for us together, not just you or just me."

"Yes?" he whispered.

"Do you want to wait until after our wedding to make love?" she said.

"No," Paul answered honestly.

"Nor, do I." Sandy said simply.

"How do you think you'd feel if I slept with you and then threw you away?"

"Are you going to do that, Paul?"

"No, I want you for life."

"Then there's no problem, is there?" She had him there. They both wanted physical intimacy. The wedding was only months away.

"What about my word..." he whispered as he kissed her slowly, "to your uncle?"

"He's not here...and I won't tell." Sandy whispered.

Paul let his favorite bass guitar slide off his lap to the floor with a resounding thud. His hands and arms had better places to be.

Paul's fingers, nimble from years of guitar playing, wove themselves through her silky wheat-colored hair and encompassed her head so he could kiss her thoroughly. He couldn't believe this was real. His heart raced. He could, at last, live out the fantasies haunting him since he met her. Pushing her down on the bed gently, but firmly, he continued to kiss her; but his hands left her hair to begin unbuttoning her silk blouse. Paul's breathing hastened and so did Sandy's. She was as anxious as he was for this, Paul thought. With her blouse open, he grew impatient. He wanted to feel her skin against his so he feverishly pulled his shirts over his head. When he looked down at his golden-haired angel,

Paul felt a pang of guilt. He realized that Sandy's hard breathing wasn't from excitement but from fear. She was clearly anxious. Her eyes closed, and she had instinctively crossed her arms over her open blouse. She looked scared out of her mind.

"Whoa, Sandy, you're shaking!" Paul coaxed. "I'm not going to hurt you, love." Paul was on all fours over her, bending to kiss her salty cheek. Sandy's eyes flew open.

She whispered, "What...why did you stop, Paul? Don't you want me?" She was still out of breath and shaking as he moved to sit beside her on the bed.

"Look, Sandy, ancient tribes might have sacrificed virgins, but I won't! Now I'm so frustrated I may go mad, but I won't take you by force. Don't tease me like that!" His words were spoken in haste and anger, and he immediately regretted them when he saw the tears flow faster down her face.

"Oh, Paul, I'm so sorry! Please forgive me. 'Tease' was what that Colin Dodd called me over and over. Do you think it was my fault he attacked me? Maybe I frustrated him, too." Her sobbing got worse, and she couldn't talk any more. She just covered her face with her hands.

"No, of course not," Paul comforted her by reaching down and pulling her head and shoulders into his lap and cuddling her. He kissed her forehead and stroked her hair, which hung off the edge of the bed and tickled his bare feet on the floor. " Making love has to be a mutual choice. Of course you didn't tease Colin Dodd. That swine assaulted you. Where we are concerned, I don't know quite what to think. I don't think I've been with a virgin before. I really don't know if I am just going too fast for you or if you've changed your mind and desire to wait like your uncle wishes. What do you think, Sandy?"

"Oh, I am so confused. I really love you, Paul, and I want us to have a normal relationship. If sex is what it takes..."

"What do you mean, 'if sex if what it takes...?' Our relationship is what we make it. Are you worried about losing me?" Paul asked incredulously. "Do you think that having sex is the way you'll keep me? Where did you get the idea that it's something we **need** to do to have a 'normal' relationship?"

"Well, Cynthia said..." Sandy began.

"Oh, I understand then! You've been talking to Cyn. Don't listen to her! She and John have a totally different relationship." Paul was clearly annoyed.

"Well, this is the first time I've ever faced this dilemma before. How do I know what is normal or what to do? I think Cynthia is kind to talk to me about such things. I've never had a friend share these sorts of things." Sandy pointed out.

"I guess you're right, love. It must be tough to be so new at all this." Paul sat thinking for a few minutes. He sighed loudly. "Do you think you'd be all right if we just went slowly with the physical bit? I want to touch you...I **need** to touch you, to let you know how I feel about you. I'll stop whenever you feel uncomfortable." Paul suggested.

"Well, to be honest, I've been looking forward to getting close physically, but I **do** think we need to take it slow. I get so scared sometimes." She gazed up into his huge hazel eyes and marveled at his amazing good looks.

"I don't mean to scare you, Sandy."

"I'll get used to you touching me, but would it be all right to wait until after the wedding for... well, you know? I think I'd be more comfortable with that because of my vows to the Church."

"Please trust me. I love you, and I promise you'll still be a virgin when we marry. It will be hard, though, because I want you so!" Sandy predictably blushed and looked down. "It's good to talk about it, love. I'm glad to know how you feel...emotion-wise, I mean," Paul laughed at his pun as he put his arms around her and bent to kiss her neck. Sandy laughed and wriggled like she was trying to get away, but this time there was no fear. Both of them felt better. They had finally clarified their relationship. Sandy trusted Paul completely to honor his promise, and Paul was relieved knowing he could show his love to her physically even if there were limits. He realized there would still be lots of cold baths in the next few months, but at least they

could explore each other a little more and relieve some of
the tensions.

LONDON

Laughter floated on the breeze down Gower Street.
Gas streetlights shone on two shadowy figures as they staggered down the steps of the Saddle Club, a public house
where the local musicians liked to drink. "Bloody hell"
swore George as he tripped over his own boots and hung
onto the wrought iron railing. Ringo, who was behind
George, clung to the railing laughing and waiting for his
friend to catch his balance. Then with arms around each
other's shoulders, they swayed down the sidewalk.
    "Taxi?" George suggested.
    "Nah. Let's go first class...let's take the carriage." Pass-
ing by the many autos waiting to serve them, the two men
stopped in front of a driver dressed in knee boots and a
fancy gold livery. His huge bay gelding snorted and pawed
the pavement, anxious to pull the shiny carriage.
    "Take us to #4 Green Street on Park Lane,[33] man."
Ringo said grandly, gesturing with his arms outstretched.
Then both of them ran and crawled into the carriage laughing riotously. They clearly had a few too many pints. The
driver clicked to his horse and shook his head as his two pa-
trons howled the naughty lyrics of a limerick to the rhythm
of his horse's hooves.

* * * * * * * *

The next morning after complaining bitterly about
their aching heads and swearing they would never drink
that much again, George and Ringo settled down together
in the living room of their shared flat with steaming cups of
strong tea. Sipping silently, they regarded each other, both
avoiding a topic that each knew must be discussed. After a
while, George shifted his eyes toward Ringo and said pen-
sively, "Well, maybe she was in her cups last night. Paul has
said she rarely drinks alcohol."

"Don't fool yourself. You've always been stuck on her, George. She's a slut and Paul needs to know. You saw how she behaved last night...like..."

"Just like every other bird in the club," George finished his sentence.

"Yeah, but you've got to admit that if you were going to marry her, you'd like to know her other side. I'd rather it come from me mates than to read it in the paper or hear it on the telly." Ringo insisted.

"Yeah, well, it's going to cheese Paul off to hear it from us." George lamented.

The two dark-haired men sipped their steaming breakfast tea in silence once more. Finally George nodded, "Let's go to the practice early so we can talk to him. It's got to be done."

* * * * * * * *

Paul's head was bent over his bass guitar, intensely concentrating on the chords he was playing. As he strummed, he eyed the words they would be singing with it today in their rehearsal.

Still nursing hangovers, Ringo and George entered the studio door very quietly, easing into chairs facing Paul.

"Hiya, Macca" George began.

Paul paused in his playing to jot down notes on paper next to him. "Hiya" he answered.

"Is Sandy coming to see you this weekend?" Ringo asked.

Paul shook his head, "No, she's getting some fittings done in Paris, I think." His eyes looked so dreamy when he spoke of his fiancée. George crossed his arms, stared at the floor, and looked very uncomfortable. Paul was the one who had invited him into the group, and they had been close for a long time even riding the bus to school together as young children.[34]

Ringo snorted, "Fittings, eh?...Paul, she's here, not in Paris. Here in London."

Paul stared open mouthed at Ringo, eyes wide. "What do you mean, don't rib me."

George shifted uncomfortably as Ringo continued his accusations. "Paul, I'm telling you we saw her last night at the Saddle Club. And she wasn't alone. She was hanging onto this teddy boy type.[35]

Paul stared incredulously at his friend. "What? Ringo, stop, you may resent her, but don't try to give her a bad name. She's going to be my wife!" Paul was getting upset and rose from his chair. Ringo rose too and Paul's fist shook as he tried to keep from punching his friend. The shorter man stood his ground.

"Paul, I'm trying to help you. George was there. George, tell him!

Paul and Ringo then looked to George, but George sat quietly still staring at the floor. Finally he looked up and he had a pained expression on his face. He let out a long breath, expelling smoke from his cigarette. "Paul, he's right. Sandy was at the Saddle Club last night. We saw her. She was not acting at all like herself. She was really partying pretty heavy."

The door opened and John stepped in carrying a guitar case and a duffel bag. "Hiya, mates!" The relaxed anticipation on his face shifted abruptly to apprehension and shock as he sensed a disagreement among his other band members. He froze there a moment, looking from friend to friend, trying to assess the situation.

"Partying?" Paul exclaimed. As Paul's temper exploded and he reached out to strike Ringo, John managed to push between the two angry men, blocking the blow.

"Take it easy, mates!" John warned. "What's happening here?"

Paul turned his back on his three friends and tried to digest what George and Ringo had said. How could it be true? Sandy, his sweet innocent Sandy, was in Paris gathering her trousseau for their marriage. They must have seen someone who favored her. That was it! She would never be in a club with another man.

"Are we going to play or not?" John demanded looking from one man to another. And all four friends began to busy themselves getting their music their instruments ready and tuned, becoming members of the band, and putting their private lives aside once again.

"Poppermost"[36] rang out four times as each member verbally committed in their accustomed manner to shut out the troublesome world for this session. This was their way of preserving their musical creativity in spite of what was going on outside these studio walls.

* * * * * * * *

Following their practice session, Paul packed his guitar and gear and left quickly and silently, avoiding his friends' eyes. The other three sat and looked at each other silently.

"What are we going to do?" Ringo asked after Paul's exit. "He clearly won't believe us."

"Tell the tale, Ring" John growled.

"Well, this girl Sandy that has Paul droolin' is steppin' around." Ringo said somberly. His dark earnest eyes peeking under a brown fringe of hair.

"And how do you get that? She stays right with us when she's in town. I haven't seen anything unusual from her." John said. "She's almost as meek as Cynthia."

George spoke up then. "We saw her last night at the Saddle Club, and she was hanging all over some teddy boy type like a tramp. I've never seen her act like that with Paul even, and he's getting ready to marry her."

"And you're sure it was her..." John paused as Ringo cut him off.

"Bloody hell, yes! She's hardly one to be confused with a lot of other birds. That long blonde hair and that angelic face!" Ringo argued, "It was her all right. I'd stake me life on it."

George added, " I've never seen the like of the show she put on last night. She could have passed as Maggie Mae, that one."[37]

"Hmmm," John pondered, fingers drumming on the table beside him. "I wonder if that's because we've never seen her have too much drink. A little too much rum and she might become a different person for Paul to see."

"Yeah, we've got to get Paul to see her for the person we saw last night." Ringo said, "Maybe if we get her drunk the next time she comes to visit..."

"I think it would be a shame for Paul to be wed to someone so deceitful. He'll never be able to trust her with other men as long as a bottle is around." George agreed.

"Okay, lads," John suggested, "We'll help her have too much to drink next time she comes to see Paul for the weekend. We'll get the truth out of her."

George and Ringo nodded their agreement.

BLACKPOOL, ENGLAND

Paul and Sandy had settled into a schedule of talking on the phone every day and seeing each other every other weekend. This wasn't nearly enough time for Paul, but he had to agree that she needed to make wedding preparations. So he cherished the time they had together. She'd fly in from Germany to meet him anywhere. Brian would arrange security men and a car to get her safely into the hotel. There were lots of young girls who would hang about hoping to get to talk to the band. They had become quite popular in northern England.[38] Sandy remembered her original experience trying to get to Paul and was frightened of repeating it, but she trusted Paul and his friends to protect her.

Sandy was coming this weekend and Paul was overjoyed. The other three band members were equally excited as they anticipated putting their plan into action to expose Sandy's divisiveness. An added bonus this weekend was that their concert had been canceled, so they could party without having to worry about being fit to work.

"Oh!" John sighed explosively as he sank into a padded chair in the shared suite. An afternoon show, the only one of the day, was over. Joy of joys, he thought, maybe we can get a little rest tonight. He loosened his tie and sank back into the cushions. "Come here, love" he patted his lap for

Cynthia who moved over to join him. Paul and George stood near a bar area, mixing drinks as Ringo strode in briskly, his tie and coat already off and his collar open.

"Fix one for me," he called to his friends at the bar, "very strong."

"Us too!" John chimed in as he nuzzled Cyn's neck.

"Hey, what you think we are, room service?" George muttered as he kept filling more glasses with ice. He tossed an ice cube towards John, but John was involved in a deep kiss with Cyn at that moment so he didn't notice.

"Eh, Macca, Sandy coming in tonight?" The question came from John as he continued to stare into Cyn's eyes, but the other two men glanced at Paul and listened for his reply.

"Yeah, right you are!" Paul replied. And as if on cue, there was a knock on the door to the suite and the dazzling blonde entered bags in hand. John immediately dismissed the prospect of a quiet evening with Cyn. This meant their plan was on.

"Hello, love" Paul sang out and went over to meet Sandy. His light kiss and the warm embrace didn't go unnoticed by the others in the room. Eyes met and faces expressed grim determination to carry out this evening's plan as Paul and Sandy wrapped themselves in each other's arms and whispered together.

"Come on, love. Let's get you settled in," Paul offered as he picked up her blue tapestry bags, and they left to go to the suite next door.

"Everyone still in?" Ringo asked as he eyed his friends. Around the room, affirmative remarks were heard. "Let's go over it again then, mates" Ringo urged as they all gathered around John's chair to review their strategy.

* * * * * * * *

The party was still young as each of the other three band members took turns spiking Sandy's drinks. About twenty people lounged, stood, and danced in the living room area of their suite. Beat music blared, but went unnoticed by the hotel's other guests as the Beatles' road manager had reserved the whole floor and the suite directly below, since they had the evening off to party. Neil stood at the door to the suite helping the two security guards check IDs as people came and went. One of the guards said in passing to the other, "Looks like a fun crowd," The other shook his head at the antics of several guests inside and made a comment on how it was going to be a wild one. Neil, hearing their conversation explained that sometimes the band needed this to relax.[39] Doing one or more concerts every day was bound to cause burnout. Neil thought it was okay for the lads to have their fun as long as they were ready for tomorrow night's show.

When they first planned this party, the concert had been cancelled due to problems with the lights in the hall, but now with the concert back on, they'd better have their wits about them to play Blackpool Hall live. Neil frowned as he spotted John pulling Paul's girl out to dance. From the look of her, she'd had quite a bit to drink. Neil hoped fervently that John would have the good sense not to make Paul mad or jealous. He'd had to pull those two apart a couple of times in the last few weeks. Come to think of it, Paul seemed to have a chip on his shoulder lately. The others seemed after him about something. Wonder what it could be. Touring was good for their career but only as long as they could stay rational. Well, Neil thought, that's the way of good friends. And being artists, it was to be expected that all four of them would be temperamental. Sometimes Neil felt more like a parent or baby-sitter than a road manager. He sighed aloud. It's all part of the job, he thought as he leaned against the gray wall beside the door.

* * * * * * * *

John swung Sandy around roughly as they danced. He noticed smugly how pliable she felt as he put his arm around her waist and pulled her close to him. She was clearly enjoying dancing and threw her head back, laughing as John clutched her even tighter.

"Hey, baby," John whispered close to her ear, "you're beautiful. I'm glad you're having a good time." He squeezed her with both arms as he pulled her up against his body.

"Please not so close" Sandy whispered and then burst out giggling as John whirled her around. "No, John, please don't..." she urged as he licked her ear.

George and Ringo were watching closely as they had one hand holding a drink and the other wrapped around shoulders of pretty local girls Neil had procured.

As soon as John let go of her, Sandy thanked him for the dance and tottered around to look for Paul. She looked lost and very unsteady as Ringo led her into one of the adjoining bedrooms. She never saw Paul because Cynthia had him busy showing his bass guitar to several guests. Sandy was at the mercy of Paul's three friends, but she didn't suspect that anything odd was going on. She giggled innocently as she staggered over to sit on the side of the bed. Her waist-length ash blonde hair flowed about her shoulders as she swayed to the roaring music from the other room. "You made me cry...when you said 'good-bye'...ain't that a shame..." she sang with the Fats Domino record that was blaring throughout the suite.

"What now?" asked George as he peered at Paul's girlfriend.

"She sure doesn't act like she did the other night at the club," observed Ringo.

"She's just silly; she's not acting seductive at all. She didn't even want me to hold her tight when we danced. And she's definitely had a pint too many. She's liable to pass out!" John exclaimed softly to the other two.

"Yeah, she's thoroughly pissed[40] all right," observed George.

John frowned at his two mates. "Are you sure of who you saw at the bloody club? Maybe you two were as pissed as the girl you were watching."

"No, it was her all right. I'll bet she won't act the slut because we're all Paul's mates." Ringo said. "I'll get Mick to approach her. He always has good luck with birds."

Meanwhile, Sandy sat happily on the bed swaying to the music, ignoring Paul's friends having their private conversation near the door. Ringo returned with his friend, Mick,[41] and they all stepped behind a dressing screen close to the door.

"Mick, we want you to entice Sandy here to make out with you a little bit. No rough stuff, just a little friendly persuasion. We suspect she may be two-timing a friend of ours, and we want to see if she's that kind."

Mick obligingly slipped around the screen and went down on his knees in front of the beautiful girl sitting on the bed. She was obviously tipsy. He took her hands and whispered to her for a while. John, George, and Ringo saw her giggle and shake her head. "No, I like you but I can't." More whispering occurred and Mick tried to kiss her. Sandy pushed at his chest. "No, please!" and turned her face away. Mick glanced at the other three men standing behind the screen and raised his eyebrows as if to say, 'Do I go on?' Ringo waved his hand as if to say, 'Come on, do it!'

Mick then pulled Sandy up off the bed and pulled her body close to his. He whispered to her for a minute or so. Sandy pushed at his shoulders. "No, please! I want Paul! Help!" She had had so much to drink she barely spoke above a whisper, but her intent was clear. There was rising panic in her tone as he attempted to plant kisses on the squirming girl.

"Enough!" John commanded, stepping away from the others as though he would help her if needed. Ringo and George both nodded their agreement.

"We'll help you find Paul," George offered and reached for the girl's hand. After Sandy, Mick, and George had left the room, John and Ringo stared fixedly at each other, arms crossed. After a long silence, John said, "You know what we just did was despicable. That girl's as innocent as Paul says she is."

"No," Ringo insisted. "We saw what we saw. She didn't fall for this tonight because Paul was right in the next room, but I'm going to carry my camera with me every time I go clubbing from now on. We're bound to catch her at it! Paul doesn't deserve the heartache that one will bring to him."

"Son, you better be right or Paul McCartney will have your head." John admonished. And Ringo knew he was right.

* * * * * * * *

Meanwhile, George and Mick guided Sandy back down the hall to the party in the living room. They were supporting her with their arms around her waist. The group literally ran into Paul coming around a corner.

"There you are!" Paul announced as he grabbed Sandy by the shoulders. "Where have you been?" George and Mick said nothing. They just thrust Sandy gently at Paul who put his arm around her. Paul supported her as she wrapped her arms around him and snuggled into his shoulder.

"Hey, love, where have you been? I've looked everywhere for you." Paul persisted. Mick had already disappeared, but George still stood nearby, so Paul looked at him as he struggled to support his limp fiancée. "George, she has really had too much to drink! I've never seen her do this!" he whispered to his friend. As George just shrugged and shook his head, Sandy reached up on tiptoe to whisper in Paul's ear, "I want to be alone with you."

Grinning broadly, Paul told George, "If anyone wants to find me, we'll be next door in Sandy's suite." He gave George a sly wink.

"Right!" George nodded as he turned to join the noisy throng in the living room. He was relieved that Sandy hadn't told Paul about their efforts to reveal her infidelity.

As Sandy and Paul left the group's suite, he also whispered their destination to Neil who continued to guard the door. Neil checked the hallway to make sure there were no fans there, and then gave Paul the 'thumb's up' sign.

The Beatles had so little privacy with the ever-present hordes of fans and reporters that they had developed hand signals to communicate.[42] "Have fun!" Neil laughed as he grinned at the noticeably drunk blonde clinging to Paul. The next hand signal that Neil gave Paul wasn't universally known. In the group's sign language, it wished Paul hot sex. Paul gave him a warning frown, but decided to ignore his rude implication. "Call before you come back so we can look out for ya!" Neil urged, "that is if you come back tonight, you lucky bloke!"

When they were alone in Sandy's suite, Paul decided to embarrass her a little. He loved to see her blush. But when he put his hands on his hips and asked why she wanted to be alone with him, he was the one thrown off-balance. The angelic creature grasped his face and pulled it closer to hers. Standing on tiptoe, she ran her tongue around his lips and then kissed him gently on the mouth. Her kiss held a promise, an invitation for more intimacy.

After recovering from the shock, Paul couldn't resist wrapping his arms around her tightly and deepening the kiss. His hands explored her back first, and then as he became more passionate, his hands roamed to other curves of her body. Realizing how excited he had become, he broke off the kiss. Still hugging her close to him, he hid his face in the thick mass of blonde hair smothering her shoulders. She smelled like lavender, a scent that always meant home to him.[43] It excited him even more! Breathing hard, he heard her say softly, "What's wrong? Didn't I do it right?"

"No, no, love," Paul laughed slightly as he looked down into her crystal blue eyes. He was still breathing hard. "Love, we shouldn't be alone like this. You know you want to wait..."

"Yes, but can't we show how we feel about each other?" Sandy cuddled against him and giggled. Paul shook his head in amazement at how relaxed the liquor had made her. He realized that Sandy was just saying what she honestly thought. She was so naive and vulnerable. He hoped that he had the strength to protect her.

"God, Sandy, you don't know what you do to me," he groaned as he ran his hands through her long golden hair. "I'm afraid I'll ravish you if we get started, love."

Sandy smiled slightly and then frowned as she touched his face. "You're always a gentleman, Paul, but I'll stop you if you try to go too far."

Paul thought she just looked adorable as she blushed.

"Oh, you will?" Paul growled as he suddenly swung her up into his arms. It was a short three steps to the couch. Paul smothered her surprised yelp with a kiss as he put her down on the burgundy upholstery. He sank smoothly to his knees beside the couch and leaned over her as he stroked her hair. Sandy gazed up at his wide eyes that usually looked so dreamy. They had a wild look that along with his flared nostrils gave her the first sense of the power a woman has over a man.

"I love you, Paul," Sandy whispered, suddenly feeling shy after Paul's show of bravado. Paul laughed as he bent to hug her. As he held her tightly, he told himself that he had the rest of his life to make love to this gorgeous girl. He knew that the lack of inhibitions tonight was due to the liquor in her system, not a sudden change in her decision to wait on having sex.. He could hear his heart throbbing, demanding the satisfaction his body needed but couldn't yet have.

"I love you, Sandy," he gasped into her sweet smelling hair. "You're what I need." After a few minutes of holding her close, Paul felt her go limp. "Sandy?" he whispered and drew back cautiously to look at her face. She had passed out from too much liquor. Paul left her on her side sleeping peacefully on the couch while he went into the bathroom to take the longest cold bath of his life.

God, he wanted her so badly! He could hardly stand it! To have her so willing and so close was difficult. He mused whether he should further tempt himself by staying the night with her here in her suite. No, he decided he had made a promise to her about waiting until after their wedding for sex, so he'd better go back to his group's suite to sleep. He had resisted the urge tonight, but he might give in if he stayed any longer.

After tucking her in her bed, he called over for the security men to check the hall for him. A groggy Neil mumbled, "What in hell? Paul, it's 5:00! The security blokes have left. I'll check the hall myself. Just a minute...all right, come 'head."

Surprised at the time, Paul glanced at his watch and asked, "When did the party break up?"

96

"About an hour ago. I had just gotten to sleep! Get over here now!" Neil grumbled.

* * * * * * * *

The next morning, everyone in the Beatles' suite was slow to move around. Over tea and coffee, though, they slumped in overstuffed furniture around the coffee table and stretched out their long legs to compare notes about the success of their conquests last night.

"I had me four of 'em!" John bragged. "The last one was the best. I shagged her in the bathroom!" he laughed. "It was just fantastic."[44]

"Oh, the strawberry blonde?" George questioned.

"Yeah, she made a lot of noise. She was built though!" They all laughed.

"How about you, Rings?" John asked.

"Just one, but, man, she was fab! I'll bet Paul's the one though who has something big to report. Neil said you were in Sandy's suite until 5:00 o'clock." Ringo said.

"Oh!" Paul's friends chorused as they nudged him and laughed. "Tell us, Paul!" They snickered like schoolboys. George reached over and slapped him on the back.

"Did you finally remember what your John Thomas is for?" John teased as he put his tongue in front of his top teeth and made a face as he leaned close to Paul.

Paul rolled his eyes and blew cigarette smoke at John. "It is none of your business, but...we didn't do it."

"Ahhhh!" the others chorused in a disappointed tone.

"What's your problem, won't the soldier salute?" George called out.

John added, "you need instruction, son? He's been deprived too long!" He leaned forward into Paul's face. "You can watch me next time." Paul swatted at him, which prompted John to giggle delightedly.

Ringo just laughed, "Come on, Paul! Don't tell us you've forgotten how!"

Paul shook his head. "Oh, sod off! Sandy and I have decided to wait until after the ceremony. Now shut your bloody mouths!"

Ringo, George, and John exchanged secretive glances as Paul bent to sip his steaming tea. They all hoped that Sandy was not playing their friend for a fool. If so, he would be devastated because he seemed so much in love with her.

LONDON

George, Ringo, and John, dressed in turtlenecks and sport coats, descended the stone steps to the Saddle Club on a mission each hoped would be unsuccessful. Laughter and live rock music greeted them as they scanned the huge underground room. The place smelled of stale beer and sweat, common for clubs frequented by the youth of London. It reminded them of the Cavern where they had often played in their hometown, Liverpool.

After Ringo, George and John grabbed a table and drank a few pints, the crowd began to change over from the teens to the young twenties crowd, who could stay out later and party wilder. The Beatles were well known at the time, but not yet famous. Their presence drew the attention of the crowd. Local band members stopped by their table to chat about music and introduce friends. Late into the evening a long-legged beauty with waist-length flaxen hair appeared in the crowd near the bar.

"Hey, look at the yellow bird..." George drawled setting his beer down on the table with a thump. John glanced his way and saw the interested look on his face. Then he followed George's gaze to a luscious-looking girl in a tight black mini-dress. Rory Storm,[45] a former band member who'd come to visit with Ringo, took note of the blonde as well.

"O-o-h, yeah, th-th-that's a hot p-piece o' p-pie," he said, nodding his head at her as he flicked ashes on the floor. " Sh-sh-she s-seems to c-c-come and g-go...don't s-s-see her m-much, but whe-whe-when she's ar-round, sh-sh-she's a w-w-w-wild one!" Rory observed.

"Uh-huh" John said, "I'm going to see if she likes to dance, among other things. Got your camera, Ringo? Follow us when we go off alone." The swirl of smoke and the throbbing beat of the music went on as John approached the bar to make his conquest.

* * * * * * * *

The next day, John, George, and Ringo could hardly wait to get Sandy alone to confront her about her despicable behavior of the night before. They arranged for Neil to get Paul out of the suite, and began accusing her. Of course, she denied everything.

"No, I wasn't at this Saddle Club last night!" Sandy said indignantly. "I just flew into London this morning. Neil picked me up at the airport."

"Yeah, you made it look that way, but you definitely cheated on Paul last night with another man. Just admit it, you slut!" John's voice rose in volume as he spoke so that the last two words were fairly shouted. Sandy gasped but stood her ground with her hands on her hips.

The argument went on, and John began to get more and more worked up at the thought of his best friend being humiliated. George and Ringo noticed and began to get nervous fearing John's actions would become violent. "He may lose it," George said in an aside to Ringo. Then George suggested, "John, let's wait a bit to discuss this until Paul gets back. Perhaps it will help..." He didn't get to finish his effort to calm John.

Sandy now frightened of John's anger, made an effort to get past them to the door. "I need to go..." she murmured as she tried to move out of the corner Paul's three friends had her in. This effort to escape was the crack that was needed to burst John's fragile rein on his pent-up anger. John's control snapped, and he grasped the petite blonde by the hair and neck. "You will listen..." he began in a low threatening voice, his face very close to hers.

99

Sandy's face was very pale, and she was intimidated, but she whispered forcefully, "I love Paul, and I would never cheat on him!" which incensed John more than ever.

The sight that greeted Paul when he opened his bedroom door at that moment was one he could not have possibly conjured in his wildest nightmares. His best mate John was clutching the girl he loved by the neck. He had his hand poised to slap her.[46]

Paul was so shocked by the scene that he was unable to act until he heard Sandy gasp, "Please let me go! I can't breathe."

"Let her go, John!" he ordered coldly. John and the other two men turned to look at their friend, now aware of his presence. John then looked down at his right hand which was drawn back ready to strike as if seeing it for the first time. He immediately released Sandy.

"Paul, they're accusing me of horrible things that I would never do!" Sandy called frantically across the room. She instinctively reached out toward Paul as she begged his help.

"Shut up, you bitch!" John snarled and pushed Sandy backwards. By accident, she hit the nearby chest of drawers pretty hard. She stayed frozen against the piece of furniture as though afraid to move. Then she collapsed on the floor at John's feet.

"Now you've done it, John!" growled Ringo.

"John, you bugger..." George began.

"Well, you know what she is as well as I." protested John hotly.

Paul was enraged. There was his beautiful fragile fiancée crumpled on the floor with his three best friends standing over her with clutched fists. Their scowls told him John wasn't the only one who had participated in Sandy's persecution.

"You bloody bastards! What have you done to Sandy?" he railed as he angrily pushed them aside to get to her. Paul stroked her hair and bent to her face to hear her breathing. "I think she fainted again." He gently tapped her cheeks as he urged, "Come on, love, wake up."

John folded his arms and looked up disgusted at the ceiling. "Will you quit it, Paul? She's okay. She deserves what she gets, that one."

"That's enough!" Paul glared up at John. "What's wrong with you?" Glad she was alive, he forgot her for a moment in his anger toward John. He leaped up, grabbed John by the lapels of his black coat. Paul shook him and howled, "What did you mean by that?"

"Now calm down, Paul," Ringo said. "John didn't mean to hurt Sandy. But you've **got** to listen to us. She's no good, that one." He shook his head sadly.

"What?" Paul looked incredulously at the shorter man and brought his face close to him while still holding John. Ringo didn't seem to be intimidated by Paul's action.

George stepped between Paul and John, prying Paul's frozen hands from John "Now Paul, I know you've had trouble believing Ringo and me about seein' Sandy steppin' around, but we've got proof now. She made it with John...and we've got the bloody pictures to prove it."

"What? If you've got pictures then John forced himself on her, that's what!" Paul shouted losing all control as he lunged at George.

"Easy, mate," John chided as he and Ringo grabbed Paul and hauled him over to the bed.

"No!" Paul yelled, "let me go!" as John and George sat astride him to hold him down.

"Macca, you'll listen to us and you'll listen to us now!" John said emphatically.

The only sound in the room besides the ticking of the bedside clock was the heavy breathing of the four intense young men. The stillness was interrupted by a feminine moan coming from the floor. "Paul..."

"You've got to let me up." Paul urged frantically. I've got to get to her. You can't just let her wake up and think no one cares." Paul's eyes flashed at all three of his friends. "I warn you. You let me get to her or I'll murder you." Paul growled.

"Okay, but you'll give us a listen when you get her taken care of," John growled reluctantly as he got off Paul's chest. George had already stood up.

"Bastards!" Paul hissed at them in a low tone so Sandy wouldn't hear as he rolled off the bed quickly to cradle Sandy in his arms.

"Are you all right, love?" He stared into those gorgeous wide blue eyes and kissed her lightly on the cheek.

Sandy looked dazed and blinked up at him obviously dizzy. "John..." she said as her eyes focused and she drew in her breath quickly. "Why did you hurt me?" she said quickly as she sat bolt upright and stared at the three scowling men who stood with hands on their hips.

" I did nothing to you!" she gasped.

"The hell you didn't!" John leaned over her accusingly. "You gave me these red marks on my neck" he said as he jerked his shirt collar open, "and you offered to fuck me, you scrubber!"

Sandy's mouth fell open as she stared at John. Her face turned a bright shade of red, and she clutched Paul's arms around her as she began to tremble.

Paul immediately stiffened. "John, you bastard, you didn't...tell me you didn't...."

"I wouldn't do it, Paul. You're my mate, and I knew it would hurt you!" the irate John insisted, "but the little harlot offered for me to take her and seemed bloody disappointed when I wouldn't! She had a hot cunt, that one!".

"I want to go back to my room, Paul. Will you take me there?" she made a choking sound and tears streamed from her eyes. Sandy stared at the floor overcome with embarrassment. This whole situation was incomprehensible to her. She felt she had to escape.

"Can't deny the truth, can you?" accused George, bending down to look her in the face. "We've even got photographs of you rubbin' yerself all over John."

Sandy shook her head wildly. "I swear it's not true. I could never do what you said.

Paul, you believe me, don't you?" She looked from one Beatle to another as the clock's steady ticking once again filled the silence.

"Yes, love, I believe you. Let me get you to your room safely." Paul said gently, "come on then," as he helped her stand. Then he swung her up into his arms, cradling her gently and kissing her cheek. Much to the others' disgust, Sandy promptly snuggled her cheek against his shoulder hiding her eyes against his neck. "I'll talk to **you** when I get back," he frowned ominously at his three friends, still immobile but angry-looking.

* * * * * * * *

In the living room of Sandy's hotel suite, Paul and Sandy sat on the couch together to try and calm down from the madness they had just experienced next door in the group's suite. "Paul, why would John and George and Ringo say these awful things about me? I have never done anything to them." Sandy wondered.

"I don't know, love, but I'm going to find out. They will apologize, I'm quite confident." Paul assured her. A few tender kisses later; Paul whispered good-bye and reminded her to bolt the hotel door. She settled down to ponder the evening's strange events. Paul's friends were a little strange, but she couldn't understand how they could treat her so horribly.

When Paul returned to the suite, Ringo was shaking his Pentax camera in Neil's face. The road manager looked confused and a little defensive. "I got it for you as fast as I could" he insisted. "I had to have it specially done, you know. You expect miracles, you do!"

Paul shook his head as he poured himself a stiff rum and Coke. They'd all gone potty. The touring had made the lot of them daft. What would he do for a job now, he wondered. He'd left art school for this. He'd probably have to get a real job like his Dad[47] now, selling stuff. The band had been fun while it lasted he mused.

An envelope slammed down on the bar in front of him interrupted Paul's thoughts. Paul's eyes swung up to George's stony face as all of the other three gathered around him. "We're having a meeting" declared John, eyes locked fiercely on Paul, but nodding his head at the door. His tone warned the other five people in the room that it was time they left. Neil closed the door behind the last of the visitors, said he'd be in the coffee shop downstairs for a while if they needed him, and then disappeared out the door, locking it behind him.

The four were alone at last for the meeting of the minds that was long overdue.

"Where in hell do you get off attacking the girl I'm going to marry?" Paul began. His hostile gaze swung to include all three of them.

"I didn't believe it, Paul, to start with when the other lads said Sandy was acting like a slut." John nodded toward George and Ringo. " I had to see for myself. And I finally did. We went to that club last night where she hangs about. She came onto me, Paul."

"No!" Paul said emphatically.

"Here are the pictures." George held the envelope in front of Paul.

'Look at them!" ordered Ringo.

"We're your mates, Macca. We love you like our brother. Look at the bloody pictures!" John said. While John was staring Paul down at close range, he took the envelope from George and pressed it to Paul's chest. Paul grasped it finally, shaking his head.

Minutes later, Paul sat awestruck as he looked through the pictures. The other three men sat smoking, long legs stretched out on the coffee table. They watched Paul warily.

"There must be some mistake," Paul protested.

"It's her." John said emphatically.

"No!"

"I ought to know. From what you've said, I got farther with her than you, and you're engaged to her! I could have gone all the way, but I didn't because you're so hung up on her. Look at the bloody pictures. They tell the tale." John said, not backing down at all.

"Paul, some birds just need to play the virgin," George suggested. "They think it turns a bloke on."

"A lot you know," huffed Paul.

"Hey, I was in Hamburg. I pulled birds there just like you. We all grew up there[48] Paul. You know it's true." George said quietly staring at his friend. George obviously was tired of being treated like an inexperienced juvenile.

"You tore Sandy apart with your ugly talk, John. She couldn't have willingly done what you said. You saw how it affected her." Paul insisted, trying to change the subject.

"So she's a good actress," John shrugged.

"I'll talk to her...see if we can make some sense out of this. There must be an explanation." Paul said as he leaned back, his hands behind his head.

"Drop her, Paul, she's bad news," warned Ringo.

"Yeah, do yourself a favor," added George.

"Do us ALL a favor," John said emphatically.

* * * * * * * *

Sandy and Paul sat alone in her suite on the couch. "I don't know what to say, Sandy, it's as though someone has gone to an awful lot of trouble to set you up." Paul began.

"What do you mean?" Sandy sounded apprehensive.

"Well, the lads have these photographs, you see." He held up the envelope.

"Let me see!"

"Uh, no..." Paul looked uncomfortable. He put the envelope in his suit pocket.

"Why?"

"They really are obscene. I don't want you to be embarrassed."

"John said I was in these pictures, so I won't be embarrassed, Paul."

"The only thing I can think is someone must have drugged you or slipped you something in a drink to get these photographs. You couldn't have done it willingly." Paul surmised.

Paul put the photos on the coffee table in front of them. When Sandy looked at the first one of John kissing her with his hands on her rear, she gasped and covered her mouth.

"See, I told you, now let's put them away." Paul said as he once again put them in his pocket. He reached to hold Sandy's hands in his, but she pulled away.

"No. I need to see, Paul." Sandy's face was serious. Paul sighed as he withdrew the envelope from his jacket and handed it to her. Sandy shuffled through the eight photos, blushing redder by the minute, and when she got to the one with John removing her blouse, it was too much. She fainted, scattering the vulgar photographs around her as she dropped to the floor. She awoke on the couch with Paul kneeling beside her.

"I told you not to look at them. I was afraid it would upset you too much." Paul fussed as he held a cold cloth to her forehead. "I told the lads you were too sensitive for such rubbish. Those bloody pictures belong in the dust bin!"

When she could finally talk, she whispered "I'm sorry, Paul." Tears were running down her face, and she looked so miserable. She covered her face with her hands. "I'm so sorry, Paul."

"What do you mean, Sandy? Why are you apologizing? They're the ones who had better apologize! They **drugged** you, didn't they? You wouldn't do those things **willingly!**" Paul looked alarmed. From his kneeling position, he hugged her as she lay on the couch.

"No, no, Paul, I don't think your friends did anything to me. It's not me in those photos," she assured him hastily. "Let me see them again." she said as she pushed Paul away and reached down to the floor with one hand to gather them together.

"No! You've already gotten too upset. I don't want you to faint again." Paul answered.

"I just need to see one more time..."

"Sandy, no! Now that's enough!" Paul looked determined.

"Paul, I think I know who it is in those photos, and if you'll let me show you something in one of them, we can prove it to the others." Sandy smiled slightly; "Please...I won't faint. I'm over my shock."

Paul hesitated. "Do you really think you can clear this up?" When Sandy nodded, he scooped up the pictures by his feet and handed them to her. She tried to sit up, but he put his hands on her shoulders. "Uh-uh," he said. "You lie back on this couch. That way if you do faint, I won't have to worry about you hitting your head."

Sandy smiled and began to look through the pictures. "There! See, it's not me," she declared triumphantly, pointing at the picture of her look-alike undressed from the waist up.

"Sandy, you forget, love, I've never seen you naked. How would I know?" Paul reminded her.

Sandy blushed. "Look at her side. See the large birthmark here. I have none!" And with that statement, she stood up and began unbuttoning her blouse. Paul stared at her in surprise.

"No, love, no, you don't have to prove it. I believe you!" Paul said hastily.

Sandy blushed but continued removing her blouse. "I want you to see..." She seemed determined so Paul sighed and turned his back while she disrobed to the waist. Holding her blouse around the front of her body, she said, "Okay, look!" Paul turned to look at the bare side of her torso. No mark was evident, as it had been in the photo.

"Your friends HAVE to believe me now," she stated happily.

"I don't know if I want you to prove it, not this way anyhow." And he laughed mischievously as he grabbed her shoulders and kissed her.

A quick knock came on the door and Neil[49] popped in, striding toward them confident that it was all right for him to enter. There was never anything between Paul and Sandy that they required privacy for, or rather there hadn't been. He suddenly took in the situation...Sandy bare from the waist up except for a piece of cloth held over her breasts and Paul holding her shoulders with the surprised look that he had been interrupted. Neil, quite naturally, froze in his tracks.

"Oh, sorry, so sorry..." he began apologizing as he backed toward the door. "Ummm, Paul, Brian needs to see you next door about schedules." Neil, usually so unaffected by anything that happened, turned beet red as they continued to stare silently at him. As he stumbled backward, he ran into the open door, and tripped through the opening. He then slammed the door shut behind him.

Paul and Sandy still stood as they had, her arms clutching the blouse over her chest and his arms holding her.

Then their eyes met and they burst into riotous laughter, both from the relief of absolving any doubt of Sandy's guilt and from the absurdity of getting caught in a provocative but innocent situation.

"I'll step in here to get dressed," Sandy gestured to one of the bedrooms off the living area."

"Okay, love. I'll fix us a drink. I think we need to celebrate..." Paul replied as he stepped over to the bar area.

"Paul" Sandy said as she came back fully dressed. "I know how to prove to your friends that I'm being honest," she said as she accepted her drink.

"Yes, you said you knew the woman in the photos. Can you produce this person?"

Sandy smiled brightly. "Yes! Let's sit down and plan a little surprise for your friends." And with that, she sat on the couch and patted the space beside her.

After their strategy session, Paul rose to go. "Let me know as soon as it's arranged, " Paul urged.

"I will," Sandy promised.

Paul pulled her close and kissed her thoroughly in a long slow kiss full of the promise of sharing their lives together. He left to go back to the group's hotel rooms feeling exuberant. He fairly danced all the way back.

* * * * * * * *

The next night at Paul's suggestion, Neil, Mal, and the four band members descended into the noisy smoky Saddle Club for an evening of socializing. Rory Storm and the Hurricanes paused after belting out the song, "Lucille" to note the presence of the Beatles and another local band in the audience. As Paul waved to the clapping crowd with the rest of the band, he was scanning the room looking for Sandy. It was difficult to keep watch because so many people were crowding around the group talking and seeking autographs.

A beautiful flaxen-haired girl soon began to weave her way through the packed crowd toward the table. Neil punched Paul; "There's your bird, Paul." Everyone at the table including Paul showed surprise when she passed by him and slid unexpectedly onto John's lap. John, his eyes huge, for once was without words. He gestured to Paul with his hands in the air meaning that this was none of his doing.

When Paul laughed and held his ale up to toast John, the rest of the party at the table looked at him in astonishment. George nudged Ringo and whispered, "He's as potty as she is!"

A few minutes later another flaxen-haired girl wearing an identical black jumpsuit threaded her way through the crowd to slide onto Paul's lap.

"Blimey!" exclaimed Mal.

"They're identical!" shouted Neil over the roaring rock music.

"Hello, love," Paul looked into the blue eyes so close to his. "Are you Sandy?"

"You don't know, do you?" she teased.

"No, I don't, so please be kind and tell me." Paul's hazel eyes were serious. He bit his lower lip slightly as was his habit when perplexed, and his large eyes looked huge.

The blonde laughed delightedly and wrapped her arms around Paul's neck. "Yes, I'm Sandy. Give me a kiss."

"Not so fast! What's my favorite fable?" Paul asked as he thought back to the day they met.

Sandy giggled. "Brer Rabbit. Do you believe me now or do I need to take my jumpsuit off to prove it?"

"Well, not right here and now. Give me a kiss!" He wrapped his arms tightly around her and kissed her deeply.

When John saw Paul kissing the girl identical to the one sitting on his lap, he held her away from him a little to get a better look and questioned, "Who are you? You look just like Sandy."

The girl tossed her long hair and giggled. " She looks just like me. I'm Candy..."

"You certainly are! And I'll bet you taste sweet." John interrupted, smiling admiringly.

"I'm five minutes older than she is. And you already know me, at least a little bit." she said coyly. "We met here last night. Don't you remember?"

"Oh, I remember. I sure do!" John grinned. Turning to the others at the table, he gestured to the two blondes and exclaimed, "Twins!" over the din of the club. "This is Candy, Sandy's sister!" Each man nodded in turn at her as he was introduced.

Candy then whispered in John's ear, "I hear you've been giving my little sister a hard time for some things I've done."

"Yes, I'm sorry. We did jump to some conclusions. Who could imagine this?" John replied overwhelmed at how they looked the same in every way. "You two are bloody identical!"

"Not really," Candy corrected him. "You see what is on the outside. We both chose not to take the vows as nuns, but I am, shall we say, more social than she. Sandy has been secluded at our place in Germany while I jumped right into a career of modeling here in London. She hasn't had the same experiences as I."

"I understand." John said simply. He looked at her as if wished he had shared some experiences with her. He stroked her shoulder gently as he gazed into her eyes.

The rest of the evening they celebrated that tensions among them were cleared up. When it got a little quieter, between sets, George, Ringo, and John all apologized to Sandy and Paul for misunderstanding the situation and mistrusting Sandy. "Look, Sandy, we had no way of knowing. We thought you were steppin' round on Paul," Ringo, always so kind, told Sandy.

George nodded and added, "It's like we're brothers, the four of us," he pointed around the group as he spoke. "Forgive us, please, for doubting you."

John stared down at his feet during the apologies, Paul noted. Finally he looked around at the partying crowd in the club and only glanced briefly at Sandy as he said, "Sorry, it's pretty easy to mistrust when we live like we do." Paul reached out and punched John's shoulder as John shared an embarrassed grin with him.

Sandy realized how hard it was for John to apologize. Paul had shared with her how John rarely showed his true emotions. Since she had also lost her parents early in life, she could understand that John protected himself by putting up a brave front. She was very gracious to all of them. "I know that you were just trying to protect Paul. He is lucky to have such good friends." She gave each one a hug, and the discord, which had wrenched the entire group for the last few months, disappeared as they socialized the rest of the evening.

Hours later, when Paul kissed Sandy good night at the door of her suite, he whispered, "I love you, and I never doubted you."

"I know," she whispered back, "and that's one of the reasons I love you. I need your love"

"You have my love forever, whatever happens," was Paul's whispered response.

* * * * * * * *

Brian had been sitting so long he was getting drowsy. The Whitehall music offices were quite cluttered, he thought idly. The heavily laden desk that faced him reminded him of how much was stacked on his desk at his office at NEMS, his record store headquarters. Here he sat, wasting time waiting for someone to come and talk to him about this gig they had booked for The Beatles. It wasn't that he didn't manage the number one rock group in Britain and Scotland. It was true that the group hadn't been able to get on the charts in the U. S. yet, but that didn't matter. Well, he decided, they could bloody well get to him in the next ten minutes or he would leave, he decided. A tall muscular dark-haired man filled the doorway, and Brian let out a sigh of relief. At last, he was going to get some attention. "Good morning, Mr. Epstein," purred the stranger. "I'm Vladimir Kreiskop," as they shook hands.

"Pleased to meet you, but I was told I would be meeting with Sir Harold Whitehall today. He usually handles the bookings requested by this company."

"I'm now handling your bookings. I hope that doesn't displease you, Mr. Epstein."

The massive man moved in one fluid motion to his chair behind the desk. The man moves like a big cat, thought Brian, what an unsettling idea.

"I suppose that's acceptable. Is Sir Harold ill?" Brian inquired. Kreiskopt met the music manager's thinly veiled challenge with a full minute of stony silence. He enjoyed watching as the neatly dressed businessman squirmed waiting for his reply.

"No, Mr. Epstein, he is fine. Now shall we get to the business you're here for?" the Russian finally droned.

"I'd like to talk to you about this booking that your firm has arranged on the southern tip of England. The papers say that my boys will be performing on a stage that will not be available for sound checks until the actual day of the opening performance. I'm concerned about safety. Something could happen to my boys. I need to have access to this stage before hand. I am firm on that."

Kreiskopt shook his head. "I'm sorry, that is not possible." Brian followed his eyes to a large tan envelope marked 'Plans For Crown Estate' lying on the desk.

"Well, at least I could review the plans to be sure that stage will be sturdy enough."

Again Kreiskopt shook his head. "No, we'll handle everything, Mr. Epstein. You just make sure your band is in tip-top shape. This client, Mr. Crown, has asked quite specifically for your group. We don't want to disappoint his nieces who will be in the audience. This will be a special occasion in many ways."

Brian stood and angrily stabbed the air with his finger. "I will not be treated this way. The Beatles are going to be bigger than Elvis! I demand that I be shown the plans! I know you have them! I've been staring at this envelope all morning!" he pointed to the large tan envelope that Kreiskopt had fingered throughout their conversation. "I've stared at this envelope the whole time I've waited for you. I intend to see the bloody thing!" When Brian reached out and grabbed the envelope that was marked 'Plans For Crown Estate,' Kreiskopt didn't react. He remained seated as Brian stepped quickly behind his own leather chair. Kreiskopt calmly warned, "Mr. Epstein, you really don't want to see that." as Brian frantically ripped out the contents of the envelope.

"Ah, ha!" Brian immediately exclaimed, his pale face flushing with satisfaction. "There can be nothing too secretive about building plans for a stage!" But moments later he exclaimed, "Oh, my God!" As the blood drained from his face and he stared first at the documents and then at Kreiskopt's frown. Epstein's stunned, thought the Russian. Well, he asked for it, he thought smugly.

"What...? How...?" Epstein began.

"Yes, yes, sit down, Mr. Epstein." he said condescendingly. When he perceived Brian's quick glance at the closed door, he added, "I assure you, the door is locked and guarded. You can't get out right now."

Brian stiffly sat back down on the chair, once again staring at the blueprints on his lap.

"You see, Mr. Epstein, you weren't supposed to see that. Don't you wish you had listened to me before? Now you're part of the plan. It was to be avoided, but now it's unavoidable." "No..." Brian exhaled looking frightened.

"You have no choice, Mr. Epstein."

As though suddenly waking from a stupor, he leaped from the chair and frantically tried the door handle. "No, I won't...this is too monstrous."

"But you will. Come and sit down." Kreiskopt chided.

"No, you can't force me to be a part of this scheme." Brian insisted.

"Oh, we can't? Well, Mr. Epstein, have a seat and take a look at our intriguing photo album we have here. Your photographs really don't do you justice."

Stricken, Brian turned and gazed with glassy eyes at the bound album Kreiskopt laid close to the edge of the desk near Brian's chair. "Memories are so sweet, aren't they, Mr. Epstein?"

Brian slowly perused the photos of his last holiday and covered his mouth to restrain his response. He had the look of a man who was living his most fearsome nightmare.

"You're a fine man, Mr. Epstein. Christoph said you were tender and loving, quite like a father. What a shame those narrow-minded parents of your teenaged audience might not understand how loving you are.[50] You know that a man in your station of life should always maintain a sterling reputation." Kreiskopt shook his finger condescendingly at the obviously disturbed man in front of him. "I understand homosexuality is even against the law in your country, isn't it?"

"You bloody bastard!" Brian fumed at him and crashed his fist to the desk.

"We wouldn't want to ruin your boys' career, after you've put in all this work. Just when the Beatles were moving up from a regional band. They were just getting started."

Brian sat quietly, anger building up inside. "Now just calm yourself. We will take care of everything. I guarantee your boys won't be hurt by our plans. Just go on as though you knew nothing of this, and your little secrets in this photo album won't get leaked to the press."

"But, but..." Brian stammered, "Th—those plans say 'missiles'. You expect my boys to play on top of a stage covering bombs? How can you guarantee their safety? Who are you going to blow up? "

Kriskopt sighed. "Mr. Epstein, I assure you the stage that is being installed is just a storage area. Nothing more, nothing less. The missiles will not be launched there. They are just on hold here, and this is a convenient way of —shall we say—omitting the truth so as to avoid misunderstandings? Exactly as it is with **not** publishing your vacation photos in <u>Life</u>," Kreiskopt sat back in the leather chair, hands poised in front of his face, fingers together. "There's a thought," he pondered aloud.

"So do you agree that if the stage is the right size for your singing group and the hall is adequate for Mr. Crown's guests, the show will go on? We don't want to deprive The Beatles' fans in any way. We just want to share the use of the stage, or should I say, the space under the stage."

Brian nodded silently.

"Well, we're agreed then. Now are there any other questions about the arrangements on this performance?"

"No, no, that's it." Brian said with resignation. "Do you swear no harm will come to them?"

The Russian smiled cruelly. "I believe, Mr. Epstein that you're not in a position to ask for concessions." He pursed his lips and stared at his fingertips as he paused. Then he shrugged and threw his fingers upward in a gesture of resignation. His smile this time was conciliatory. "I promise. It would not be in our best interest to have an incident at this concert, I assure you. We are trying to keep a low profile."

Brian suddenly realized he hadn't been breathing and took a deep gulp of air before he rose and moved to the door. Kreiskopt was beside him in an instant putting out his hand. Brian reluctantly shook it and then stepped warily out into the hall after the door was unlocked. "Good day!" Brian said to Kreiskopt. Glancing left and right, he noticed security men positioned casually. Their eyes pierced him as he hastily walked down the hall to the exit. Have I made a pact with the devil, the frightened man thought as his heart pounded rapidly.

Once outside, Brian paused to lean against the burgundy brick building. He needed a moment to compose himself. Even though the sun beat down uncharacteristically warm, he shivered under his wool overcoat. With his eyes closed, he mentally replayed the meeting with Kreiskopt. He had to go along with this terrible plan. How did that bastard get those condemning pictures? How would his parents react if they saw them? How would the fans react to The Beatles if they knew his dreadful secret? Brian shuddered. He knew. No matter what he had to do, he must keep those pictures from surfacing.

Walking to his car, Brian began to think again about his young lover, Christoph. Beautiful boy. Slender, eighteen-year-old Christoph had flashed his black eyes at Brian during a holiday to Greece. Brian met him in the lobby when Christoph needed money to pay his hotel room bill. Brian was more than happy to oblige. Christoph watched in surprise when Brian soothed the hotel clerk with a wad of money. Over drinks in the lounge, Brian asked him if he had a girlfriend.

Christoph shook his black curly locks and laughed. "No, women don't interest me." He plucked the olive off his hors d'oeuvre pick with his tongue in a most sensuous manner, causing Brian to involuntarily gasp. Brian's eyes were locked on the handsome charismatic boy. He was mesmerized as the young Greek delicately crunched the olive with his white teeth. "Perhaps you feel the same way?" He leaned forward and confided, "From the look in your eyes, I think so."

"Check please!" Brian called briskly. Christoph blushed and put his hand shyly on Brian's.

"Thank you, Mr. Epstein," Christoph said sincerely. "I don't know what I'd do without you. I have no money because of the robbers and now I have you, my friend. Brian remembered the look of awe on Christoph's face as they entered the grand suite. "It's a beautiful place. You stay here alone, Mr. Epstein?"

"Please call me Brian," he said as he took off his suit coat. "And yes, I do. Would you like to get comfortable, Christoph?" Brian put another vodka in the boy's hand.

"Mmmm" Christoph murmured as he sipped the whiskey. His eyes intent on watching Brian loosen his striped tie.

"Let's go in the bedroom," Brian suggested as he walked to the open door. "We'll be more comfortable there."

* * * * * * *

The weeklong affair had ended with mutual satisfaction. Brian could still see the fond look on Christoph's face as he saw him off at the airport.

Brian's thoughts of Christoph and his Greek holiday ended as a passing taxi blared his horn. Brian leaned against his sleek black car scolding himself for being so preoccupied. "Oh!" Brian murmured in disgust as he climbed in the driver's seat.

Brian fantasized about his homosexual conquests when he was under pressure. Lately, he needed more than fantasy to relieve his stress. Maybe I'll find a lad this afternoon instead of going back to the office, he considered. The expensive car headed for the East End of London where young men were always in need of a few quid.

* * * * * * * *

October brought interviews with music journalists and more touring in northern England for the Beatles. Practice at Abbey Road Studios intensified as the Beatles prepared in earnest for live radio and TV show dates Brian had arranged for the Fall. Pressure was on in other ways too. Their popularity had grown from playing so many clubs around the U. K. Radio and newspaper attention increased to the point that the four were recognized and crowds gathered wherever they went. This sometimes made life difficult. They felt lucky to still move around individually when they were discreet.[51]

The four had been living together twenty-four hours a day for so long, they had become brothers. They shared everything. The four of them could fight among themselves, but they were fiercely protective if any one of them was threatened.[52] The hours were long and as best friends will, Paul and John got into a row or two from time to time over how their songs should be presented. They composed collaboratively and individually in competition with each other. They often came together after near completion of a song, helping each other to finish it. Both strong-willed individuals, an occasional difference in opinion over the arrangement of a song was inevitable. They didn't know their last argument would have such a tragic and final ending.

* * * * * * * *

The clock said 5:15 A.M. Wellington had just settled in with his first cup of coffee, hoping to get some paper work done. The gray mists of London swirled about outside his vantage point obscuring all but the tower of London. Roy leaned back in his plush office chair and reflected on his career with Interpol. Forty years of living in the spy network

117

had provided brilliant travel opportunities and more than enough excitement. Being a field agent had given him the thrill of living on the edge that he had needed throughout his life. The trim gray-haired man had liked life in the fast lane, but now he felt something was missing as he faced his eminent return to retirement after this interim duty. He found himself longing for the companion he had never had all these years. The prospect of puttering around a little flat alone made him wish fervently that he had someone to share the joys of retirement.

The secretive nature of his work as a field agent never allowed him to offer the security and safety that he felt a wife needed. And he didn't think it would be fair to either of them to live a double life. Secrets spawned pain. No, it was much better to be independent of anyone. That way if a mission went badly, there was no one at home waiting and worrying or needing censored explanations. Roy rubbed his eyes and remembered how he had had a double life thrust upon him unexpectedly despite his wishes.

It was 1942, and Roy was working undercover for the Allies tracking the German troop movements in occupied France. "Hey, you, farmer, give us some fruit!" a massive blonde German demanded as Roy wheeled his decrepit cart across the road to the shade of a huge oak tree. The leafy canopy overhead swayed in the breeze as Roy was surrounded by excited German soldiers picking at the apples and pears on his cart.

"Take, eat!" he encouraged them as he removed his flat peddler's cap to wipe his sweaty brow. The men needed little encouragement. The malnourished soldiers devoured the fruit hungrily as they chatted casually about the day's plans. Roy made note of each tidbit of information as he slyly feigned a nap leaning against the ancient tree. Headquarters would be thrilled to share this knowledge of troop movements in a few minutes Roy mused.

But when he cranked up the battle-scarred portable radio set to call in this latest intelligence information, he was given horrible news. His only living relative, his sister Jane, had been killed along with her husband in an air raid on

Berlin, leaving their two babies without a home. "Get me into Germany," he demanded. "I've got to get to my nieces!"

It wasn't too difficult to slip from occupied France into Germany in the disguise of a priest, but tracking the girls to a convent proved to be a challenge. Guilt overcame him as he finally gazed at the golden haired babies sleeping in their cribs. Sister Margaret patted his shoulder as he broke down and cried over the futility of the situation. "Don't worry yourself, Father, the little girls are happy and we can keep them right here as long as you need to pursue your vocation. We will care for them as our own." Although Roy was ambivalent about what to do, he reasoned that in the dangerous war conditions, the babies were safer here. He continued his undercover work, but he was fortunate enough to obtain a transfer to work within Germany so he could be close to the girls. He looked forward to his weekly visits even though it was difficult to live a double life.

The red phone on Wellington's desk rang, and it brought him immediately back to reality. "Damn it, what could someone want at this hour?" he grumbled as he reached for the phone that scrambled the caller's message for security reasons.

A brisk British accent met his ear. It was the head of the surveillance team for the singing group that would be playing at Crown's estate. "Sir, its Hopkins. We've got a problem down on Abbey Road. A member of the Beatles has wrapped his little red roadster around a tree. It's a bloody mess."

"Good Lord! Have you put it all under wraps?"

"Yes, sir. We've moved it in a nearby indoor parking garage. I wanted you to be aware of it, though. We need to act fast. Please advise me how to proceed as soon as possible."

"Is he dead or just badly injured?"

"He's dead, sir. Obviously killed instantly.[53]

"Right. I'll get back to you." Wellington responded.

After hanging up the phone, Wellington leaned back and wondered what to do. The movement of these missiles had been planned for months as had the maneuvering to get a team in there to disarm them before they were shipped to Cuba. A cancellation by this popular singing group or any sudden splash of publicity about the event would jeopardize the entire operation. The Russians would back off and plan another shipping route if there were any irregularity at all. Wellington sat and thought about the alternatives. No, the plan had to go on in spite of this unfortunate event. Maybe he could find a double for this singer to go with the group just long enough to complete the mission.

Wellington picked the phone and called one of his assistants. "Harry, could you help me out? We need a double for a chap that Agent Hopkins is holding at a parking garage on Abbey Road. He can supply details on the man. Do whatever you need to...plastic surgery, implants, contact lenses, whatever the cost...it's a code red. See to it immediately, will you?

"Yes, sir. I'll get over there straightaway." the younger man briskly responded.

* * * * * * * *

That morning Brian was just getting ready to leave his posh Belgravia townhouse on Chapel Street where he lived alone.[54] When he answered the ringing doorbell, he was surprised to see two unfamiliar gentlemen in expensive suits and topcoats. Showing police badges, one of them said, "May we come in, Mr. Epstein? We have matters of extreme importance to discuss with you,"

"Of course," Brian said ushering them in. The next hour was perhaps the worst in his life. Breaking this news to the boys would be even worse, he thought. The hardships and successes they had experienced together had made them a self-contained family. They would figure out quickly about this double among them. But as the men explained, it was to be pointed out to them how this would keep their career going. Brian agreed the matter of national security was to be kept secret. He was comforted by their assurance that there would be no danger to the others in this whole mess. The boys should never have to be aware of anything other than putting on a good performance at Crown's estate.

120

As John, George, and Ringo meandered into the studio at 10:00 that morning, red-eyed and hungover, to do some overdubs on the newest recording, they were surprised to find Brian chain-smoking in a chair near the drum set. Usually, only George Martin, their producer, and Neil and Mal, their roadies were with them in the studio.[55]

"Boys, Paul won't be here for a week or so. He's had a death in the family." Brian's hand shook as he tapped his cigarette into an ashtray.

"Not his brother, Mike?" George said sounding panicked. George and Mike were close in age and had been schoolmates.[56]

"No, a distant relative, but he has to be gone awhile so just work without him."

"Brian looked upset," observed Ringo after he had left.

"Too much partying with his little boys," grumbled John.

"Poor Paul, hope he's okay" said George.

"All right, let's go. Tape's rolling. Red light's on!" George Martin's refined tones came over the speaker into the studio. "Let's go!"

* * * * * * * *

Paul had been gone ten days when John arrived in Abbey Road studio to see him practicing chords on his bass guitar.

"Hiya!" John offered their usual greeting.

George and Ringo came in and the other three all said "hiya!" simultaneously, which made them all laugh.

"Who died?" George asked as they all huddled around Paul.

"Me Aunt Bet" Paul answered, "I had to stay a while to help out."

The other three who were beginning to get their instruments ready mumbled "Sorry". John said, "We've been working on our sets for the radio shows since you've been gone. Neil can get you a song list and we'll run through it together if that's okay."

121

"Fine," nodded Paul.

They spent the next five hours practicing with only thirty minutes to eat sandwiches. Then it was time for a gig at a club five hours away. By the time 1:00 A. M. rolled around and the van was heading back toward London, they were exhausted. As they piled out of the van, dawn was just beginning. After hauling all the cases and amplifiers back into the studio, and Neil and Mal had left,[57] John, George, and Ringo faced Paul, arms crossed and faces sullen.

"Who are you?" John said accusingly.

Paul stared back at them equally serious. "I'm Paul."

"You're not! That's a load of rubbish!" John flung back.

"I am Paul, but not as you know him," he answered.

"Quit speaking in bloody code. Tell us who you are and what you did with our mate Paul!" John insisted.

George looked especially disturbed and took a step forward. Ringo promptly put his arm across his chest, blocking him.

"Maybe we ought to sit down," Paul suggested.

"Maybe you better bloody tell us the bloody truth before we bloody murder you!" John warned angrily, his fists clenched at his sides.

"Paul is dead," Paul's look-alike said.

"What?" George exclaimed. There was a stunned silence as they tried to absorb the tragic news. George, John, and Ringo stood motionless with their eyes fixed on the man they knew as Paul McCartney.

The man who looked like Paul nodded and continued his strange tale, "Yes, September 13th, James Paul McCartney left these studios in his little red sports car at 4:45 A.M. and never made it home." The stunned silence continued as the three stared in shock at each other.

"It isn't possible..." George's voice cracked.

"He hit a tree just off Abbey Road. Head injury. He was killed immediately. I'm very sorry."

John began to laugh hysterically. He couldn't stop. It was clear that he was terribly upset about this tragic news.[58] He fell onto his knees on the floor. Tears ran down George's face. Ringo got up and walked to the window, biting his bottom lip. He looked ready to cry.

After about ten minutes, Paul spoke again. "Brian, your manager, arranged to have me join you to see if I could try to fill Paul's shoes. No one can, but if you'll let me have a go, maybe we can at least fulfill your bookings this month. I really think I look enough like him to get away with it."

John's head raised slowly and he had a hostile look on his face.

"Brian..." he whispered hoarsely, "that bloody bastard...all he cared about was the business, keeping the bloody money coming." John's voice was progressively louder, and he was fairly shouting when he finished his accusation. His eyes flashed at Paul. "He could have told us!"

They all sat in silence. It was difficult to think clearly. The uncomfortable trip in the van had added to their lack of energy.

George sighed, "Yeah, Brian handled it wrong. He's a bastard. I can't imagine life without Paul. We can't go on without him. No." He shook his head emphatically.

Ringo nodded, "But there's nothing we can do for him, but keep good thoughts."

John sat stoically.

"You blokes decide," Paul said. "I know your songs and routines, but if you don't want me in your band..."

John turned to look at Paul. "It's not **that**, man. You did a fab job last night. Just bloody amazing. It's just that this is such a shock! Paul was our mate! This is so sudden. Can you understand? "

"I can," Paul said simply and left. "I'm very sorry about your friend," he said softly before he closed the studio door.

The other three huddled on the floor together and talked and laughed and cried and hugged and reminisced until the others began to come in at 10:00 A.M.

* * * * * * * *

"I didn't think you lads would be up this early after the road trip last night," Brian greeted them as he strolled in, dapper in a pinstripe suit and an ascot.

"Oh, really?" John rose. His voice had an edge to it as he rose from his chair. George and Ringo cut their eyes at each other as they blew out their cigarette smoke.

"Well, Brian, what did you think we'd be doing, visiting the graveyard?" John quipped emphatically as he shoved Brian back against the wall. Brian was aghast. He wasn't a frail man, although slightly effeminate, and he certainly wasn't used to being treated in such an ungentlemanly manner.[59] John shoved him again. "Well, Brian?" he said sarcastically.

Brian glanced up at the glass-walled control booth. George Martin, Neil, and Mal sat transfixed by what was going on below them. They had seen this side of John many times but not toward the upper middle-class agent of the group.

"John, uh..." Brian seemed at a loss for words.

"Why didn't you just TELL us about Paul?" George said, rising to stand nearby.

Ringo got up too. "It wasn't right the way you handled this."

"No, all you bloody cared about was making money off us." John said once again pressing his fists against Brian's shoulders.

"No, no" Brian shook his head as tears streamed down his face. He reached for his handkerchief, and John let him go. Brian mopped the tears and then began straightening his shirt and tie while John glared at him. "This is so hard," Brian continued. "Is the intercom on?" The three long-haired musicians glanced toward the glass wall of the control room to see the other three men nodding. "You chaps need to turn everything off up there and come in. We need to talk."

When George, Ringo, John, Brian, Neil and Mal, and George Martin, the seven people who comprised The Beatles' production team, were seated on stools, chairs, and amplifiers in a semi-circle, Brian tried to compose himself. It took several attempts before Brian could speak. Brian's hands shook as he lit a cigarette and stared at the floor.

"Paul is dead." Brian blurted out finally. George Martin's, Neil's, and Mal's shock was obvious and everyone in the group had tears, even John. "He died in a car crash."

"No!" George Martin and Neil spoke at the same time as they lurched forward in their seats. George Martin clutched his temples in shock.

"It can't be true!" Mal groaned. The ex-bouncer with the big frame and an equally big heart cradled his head in his hands and began to rock forward and backwards. "It can't be...no, it can't be." Mal was a gentle soul although he looked like a brute. Although he had recently joined the group as a roadie driving the van and loading their gear, he was very close to all of the band members. They accepted him as they did Neil in their pub-hopping and womanizing.

Silence followed.

"Where is he buried, Brian?" George wanted to know.

Brian looked very uncomfortable. "He was cremated and his ashes were scattered in Strawberry Fields."

John began laughing again hysterically. "That's irony!"

George spoke over him to the non-Beatles there, "That's a charity-type home near John's Aunt Mimi's house.[60] It had lots of green fields that were good for playing ball. John and Paul used to go there together. Paul liked that place."

"Yeah, but he bloody well wasn't as good as I was at climbing the stone wall!" John giggled and then he stopped laughing to whisper bitterly, "Now he can't ever climb the wall again, the bugger." John stared at the floor, as everyone was silent.

After a while, Brian spoke again. "I found a musician who looks a lot like Paul and asked him to try joining the group to see if we could at least keep the band together for the rest of our bookings this month. How do you think he did last night?"

Neil and Mal stared in confusion at Brian. "You mean that bloke who played with the band last night was...why, we didn't even know!" Neil said.

Mal added, "Bloody hell! He even acted like Paul in the van last night."

"When did Paul have his accident, Brian?" George Martin asked.

"It was after the last recording session. His little roadster hit a tree. The imposter told us." George stated coldly. The way he said the word 'imposter' gave Brian a cold chill.

Brian said, " I helped him learn our Paul's mannerisms and the songs from the tapes we've been making. I'm sorry. I handled it all wrong. I knew you'd see through the deception." He looked directly at John, George, and Ringo. "But I hoped that way you'd at least have a chance to see him and give him a go." Brian shuddered at the memory of the impassive government agents at his door and at the vile Russian who had threatened him with blackmail photos. He had to convince his boys to accept this replacement. He wondered frantically what these agent people would do to all of them if they didn't cooperate and perform at the Crown Estate.

John puffed on his cigarette and shook his head, looking down at the floor. George gazed steadily at Brian. "We're not The Beatles without Paul."[61] Brian had the momentary thought that George resembled a bulldog: loyal and tenacious. George had a direct manner that could be quite intimidating.

"Look, you have a choice here, lads. You've won the Mersey Beat poll, you've recorded for BBC and you've got a record just released that's climbing the charts."[62] Brian spoke hastily, his words tumbling over each other.

John continued to shake his head and stare at the floor. "We've fuckin' had it now."

"Oh, no!" Brian looked pleadingly from Ringo to George and back again. "Let this new bloke take Paul's place. You've got fans that know and love Paul. If they find out, it's over. Do you want to throw all that away?"

Brian had more than one reason for wanting this young singing group to succeed. He had been unsuccessful in each venture he tried from furniture sales to drama to record sales. His wealthy family had already pronounced his managership of this band a worthless project. He needed to prove to his parents and his younger brother, Clive, that he could be successful at this!

"TAKE HIS PLACE??!!" John shouted as he impulsively leaped to his feet and kicked the bass drum sitting nearby. Ordinarily, Ringo would have protested vehemently, but he was so shocked about the reality of Paul's death, he didn't move a muscle. He sat stonily watching John's violent destruction. John managed to smash Paul's Hoffner bass over a chair before Neil and Mal subdued him. Slivers of the mahogany-colored wood peppered everyone in the room. No one reached up to deflect or wipe away the remnants of Paul's beloved instrument as they landed on shoulders or trousers. "He's gone! My old friend is gone!" John wailed as he slipped out of Mal and Neil's grasp to his knees on the floor. Tears were streaming down his face as he lamented, "And you want someone to take his place? Well, fuck you, Brian Epstein! You bloody bastard!" Ringo put his face in his hands when John fell to the floor and George sat stoically staring at the microphone, which was used by Paul the last time they played together. George Martin gaped openly at John's outburst, but the hurt look in his eyes conveyed empathy for John's agonizing pain. He had a deep respect for the bond these boys from Liverpool had for each other.

Brian shifted uncomfortably, but he was desperate to have the boys accept this substitute. They didn't know nor could they know what was at stake here! The agents had made it clear that no one else could know about the stage and its dangerous cargo. Missing the gig at the Crown Estate could endanger all of them, Brian felt quite sure. Despite John's hysteria, Brian tried again to make his point. He spoke calmly but his voice quavered at the end of his speech. "Do you think Paul would want you to ruin your success because he can't share it with you? We can't bring him back! And we'll never get this chance again to secure the careers you've always wanted." Brian implored.

They all sat in silence again as everyone considered the situation. Finally Ringo stood up. "I need a pint. Let's go mates," Ringo said as he helped John up off the floor. He gestured to George who rose to follow.

"Come 'head, then," Neil said as he gestured for them to follow him to the door. "Let's go to the Grapes,[63] shall we?" George, John, Ringo, and Mal headed for the door leaving Brian and George Martin to stare at their retreating backs.

"Well, such disturbing news. He was such a good chap. Very talented. Yes, he'll be missed," George Martin mused. "Brian, I'll see you tomorrow. I'm going to go home a while. I think the lads are right. We all need time to take this awful news in." He rose to go and extended his hand to Brian, but Brian was too self-absorbed to notice. "Cheerio, then!" he nodded as he withdrew his hand. Brian sat alone mumbling after the producer had left.

"My sweet Lord," Brian whispered, "they've got to give it a go or we'll all be killed!" Numb legs carried him outside to his Aston Martin for the ride to his flat. Maybe I'll just take a tour by the docks on the way home, he thought, as he eyed some rough-looking boys clad in leather along the street. Yes, he decided, finding a young lad for the evening would get his mind off this terrible tragedy.

* * * * * * * *

The next day, Brian poked his head cautiously into the silent studio to see if George, John, and Ringo were practicing. "Come 'head!" a gruff voice roared near his ear.

"OH!" Brian shook as he exclaimed and glanced behind the door to see John. A quick glance around the room confirmed that Ringo and George were also there, sitting silently. "You startled me, John."

"Mal! George! Neil!" George Harrison called to the three figures in the control booth. "Come on down! We need to talk!"

As Brian sat on a nearby stool and waited anxiously for everyone to be assembled, Brian's thoughts raced. His determination outweighed his fear of their reaction so he began his argument. "Now, boys, we've got to go ahead with our commitments. Even if you just let his chap help out until we fulfill our current bookings..." Brian's shaking voice trailed off as he looked at the solemn faces around the circle. A full five minutes passed while all seven of the men lit their cigarettes and smoked in silence.

128

Finally John spoke. "Paul is gone. We can't do anything but remember him." His voice sounded flat and without emotion. His face was bland, but a tiny tear glistened at the edge of his left eye. He stared across the room with a poker face.

"Yes," Ringo agreed and the others nodded. Brian's heart raced wildly as he realized that they might have accepted Paul's demise.

John's next words brought a sigh of relief from Brian. "Let's give this new chap a go," John suggested.

"Okay," George said and Ringo nodded his approval.

Always thinking, Neil said, "What about his family? Won't they know?"

"There's no one he sees daily there. He's not really close to anyone but his brother, Mike, and they only see each other briefly maybe twice a year." George informed them. "The problem's going to be his bird."

"Yeah, Sandy," Ringo added, "she'll definitely know it's not him. Birds know these things, even though they've never shagged."

"That's a problem," Mal agreed, "She's a nice girl, but he could eventually break up with her." Everyone looked around at each other trying to assess agreement.

"No one but us must ever know," stated Brian earnestly. "It is imperative, boys." The group continued to sit and chat and chain-smoke for awhile. "I'll call Paul and tell him he's 'in' this afternoon. Then we've got a lot of work to do," Brian said as he stood to leave.

* * * * * * * *

The rest of October was busier than ever with more interviews with music journalists, a recording for Radio Luxembourg, local TV appearances, and nearly daily performances all over the north of England.[64] The Beatles were getting tired of sleeping in the van after gigs, but it was all worthwhile when they saw their records climb the charts. Spending so much time together also had the effect of bonding the four of them and Neil and Mal as a family.[65]

Two days before their scheduled gig at Crown's estate, Paul arrived on time to practice to find the other three band members there uncharacteristically early. He sensed they had been talking about him. "Hiya!" he said as he put his guitar case down.

"Hiya!" answered the other three automatically.

When Paul had seated himself with them, John said, "We need to talk."

"Okay," Paul steadily returned his gaze. He knew some things had to come out.

"Paul, we want to know some things about you," he said.

"Like what?" Paul asked.

"Like your real name, and where you're from...and you've obviously been in a band, so which one?" George answered him.

"Well, " Paul began, "my real name is William Worthington, but my mates call me Billy.[66] I'm from Manchester, the son of a fisherman. And I've played guitar since I was ten. I've been in three bands, all of which folded after a bit."

"How can you just leave your life?" Ringo wanted to know.

"My Mum died when I was born. My Dad died last year, and I have no sisters or brothers. I was waiting on tables all day and playing guitar at night in a club when Brian found me. This looked like a great opportunity to join a band that had some potential."

John, George, and Ringo exchanged glances. Paul, he had satisfied their curiosity. He had been prepared for this exchange. Agent Hopkins had said it was to be expected.

"We still miss the old Paul fiercely, but we're glad you're with us," George assured Paul.

"I think we should pay tribute to Paul somehow, " John suggested.

"Yeah, I feel like I missed saying good-bye to him," said George. George had always felt like Paul's little brother because Paul and he used to ride the school bus together and had shared many good times before either had joined the group. Paul had encouraged John to accept him into the group.[67]

"I hate funerals and that, but everything does seem unfinished with him somehow." Ringo commented sadly. "He was a good lad."

"I feel so guilty about the right slagging[68] time we had just before he left in that bloody car," John said with conviction. He sat with his head in his hands. Both George and Ringo reached instinctively to pat him on the back.

"Paul knew you cared for him, John," Ringo said.

"Somehow we need to share the news of his death, but we can't TELL anyone," George sounded frustrated. He tossed his head back shaking his long dark glossy locks.

"Let's do things symbolically when we can in his memory. We don't need to explain it to anyone else. But we'll know," John suggested excitedly. His eyes lit up with the thrill of the secret.

"Yeah, secret signals, like a code," agreed George, nodding.

"Yeah, " Ringo said, "Paul would have been chuffed about that! He'll get a laugh in heaven." He gave a hearty chuckle pointing with his cigarette toward the ceiling.

"Well, to begin with," Paul announced, "I'm going to write a tiny P with a halo around it on my wrist to remind me today of the Paul you loved," Paul said and did so with black ink. The other three in turn did the same.

And so they began a secret tradition of finding ways to pay tribute to Paul through symbols. References to him and his death were planted over the years on album covers, in photos, in song lyrics, and in reverse tracks of records by his three friends who loved and missed him and by the one man who succeeded in replacing him.[6960]

Having ended their meeting, as the four stood, they in turn shouted "Poppermost!" to show they were blocking the world and their problems out. Practice that day was most productive as each member threw himself into preparation to entertain at the Crown Estate. Brian kept reminding them that this was a really important gig, but they couldn't yet figure why. They just knew Brian said they'd better be in best form.

* * * * * * * *

"Brian hired two bodyguards to go with us to this gig today," George informed the others as they arrived at the Abbey Road Studio. He nodded toward two heavily muscled men dressed in coat and tie like them. "Look at the muscle."

"Wonder what's shakin'?" Ringo mused.

"Don't know. But this gig must be important like Brian said. He seems more flighty than ever right now." Neil remarked. They watched as Brian fussed around trying to have everything packed like he wanted.

"Yeah," Paul said, lighting a cigarette. Paul knew exactly why the extra security was needed but he couldn't say. He had a very simple part in this whole mission, and he wanted it kept that way...no complications.

The bodyguards helped Neil and Mal pack the van with equipment and luggage in the van. The Beatles and Neil would ride with Brian in his sleek Zodiac Zephr today. "Come on, come on!" Brian scolded all of them as he tried to get them to get in the car to get underway. We cannot be late!"

To the band members' surprise, they only rode an hour when they pulled into a fenced parking lot with guards. "Out you go, boys," Brian announced. "We're boarding a plane here."

The flight was a brief one down to the southernmost tip of the U. K., but it certainly beat bumping along in the old van for hours. They were approaching a veritable castle, surrounded by miles of green fields and woods.

"What an amazing place!" exclaimed an awed Ringo as he gazed around.

"I'll have an estate just like it some day," John said smugly. "And you can all come for tea."

"Yeah, I'll bring the scones!" laughed George.

Paul was silently watching to locate guards and determine how many men were in place. It never hurt to be prepared, he thought.

132

"Now, lads, " Brian began, "our only chance to check out this new stage they've just built for you is today. Mal will put your luggage in your rooms. We'd better do our sound checks now. You've got your first performance in only two hours."

LAND'S END, CORNWALL, ENGLAND

During the soundcheck, George was the first to see Sandy approach Brian's table in the club area of the compound where they would be performing. He slid across the stage to Paul like they were discussing the chords they were playing. "Look up right in front of you and you'll see the bird you're supposed to marry next month. Long blonde hair, name's Sandy." When Paul looked up from his left-handed bass guitar[70] and arched his eyebrows at his new friend, George continued, "The two of you agreed not to have sex until after the wedding; just lots of hugs and kisses. She's a real innocent. She just got out of a convent and you met her six months ago at her estate in Germany."

"I hadn't counted on having to meet her yet," Paul whispered tensely.

John had now moved over to see what they were talking about. He continued to strum on his rhythm guitar as he added, "She rides horses and faints when she gets excited. She has a sister who is a model in London. Pretty birds..."

"Right," Paul replied, thinking of all the information Brian and the agency had supplied on her, none of which seemed to have prepared him for coming face to face with her. "Did they have any secret signals from stage?"

"He'd wave to her," George replied.

John had moved back to the drums. Their music continued as he asked Ringo, "Any stage signals Paul and Sandy had?"

Ringo puffed on his cigarette thoughtfully. "She'd blow a kiss, and he'd stomp his left foot, bending his to the side."[71]

133

Nodding to Ringo, he continued to play his guitar as he moved back to the other two band members so he could share what Ringo had just described.

Paul waved to Sandy as if just spotting her. She immediately blew a kiss, and he did the stomping motion John had described.

"Is she supposed to be here?" Paul asked, sounding a little anxious.

"I don't know if they had set it up or not. Paul always furnished her a copy of our schedule, and she'd just show up when possible. We'll try to keep you so busy that she can't get to you much," George assured him.

"Thanks, George. Deceiving the crowd is one thing, but it will be hard to fool her if we're alone together." Paul sounded worried.

Neil walked on stage then and asked them to move to their microphones for the necessary sound checks. After performing a number, the room erupted in applause and screams from the people who had collected to watch. The crowd surged forward as they left the stage. Neil, Mal, and Brian shepherded The Beatles back to the dressing rooms, allowing only Sandy to join them from the crowd.

The beautiful blonde came over to hug Paul. He returned the hug and kissed her lightly on the lips. "I missed you," he whispered looking into her eyes.

Sandy whispered " I missed you too."

Brian, catching frantic glances of the other three band members, put his hand on Sandy's shoulder in a fatherly fashion. "I'm sure you're very tired from your long flight here. Let's leave the boys to make their final preparations for tonight's performance, and I'll show you to your suite." Sandy's eyes looked longingly at Paul, but she smiled at Brian and thanked him for his help. After they were gone, Paul collapsed on a couch behind him. "Whew, mates, that was close! She is one gorgeous chick, though."

"We'll run interference for you as much as possible. We're going to need a lot of closed practice time during these three days of performing!" John assured him.

Paul was not the only one to see the beautiful Sandy for the first time that afternoon. The Van Heusens were sitting in on the practice session and recognized her from the photos in the Interpol file. "She's as pretty as her pictures," Geoff eyed Sandy's long legs appreciatively.

"Hey, you're a married man!" Tres protested, as she also looked the beauty over. "Geoff, she seems nervous. Look how her eyes dart all around the room like she's looking for someone. I'm afraid she already suspects something is 'up'."

They were very much aware that Sandy might cause complications for their mission if she perceived that "Paul" was an imposter. They needed him on stage so he could switch open a hidden door to the underside of the stage. If she exposed him as an impostor, the whole mission could be scrapped.

"Let's make friends with Miss Wellington and keep her away from Mr. McCartney as much as possible in the next three days," Geoff suggested.

Watching Sandy as she chatted with Brian Epstein and the others at their table, Tres recalled that her number one interest was horses. "Okay, let's go find some riding outfits, shall we?"

* * * * * * * *

Tres and Geoff's suite was perhaps the most elegant they had ever occupied. Fireplaces in every room, thick oriental rugs, fine oil paintings, and a brass king-sized bed graced with a mirrored ceiling greeted them as they settled. The exterior glass walls were adorned with huge curtains that could be drawn for privacy. As Geoff mixed drinks for them at the bar, Tres tried out the heart shaped Jacuzzi sunken in the outside corner of the bedroom. She allowed the hot rushing water to relax her. In spite of the luxurious image of this place, she knew Crown was watching with his hideous cameras hidden around the room. It made her skin crawl. She shivered in spite of the water's heat.

"Careful," Geoff cautioned, "it's full" as he handed her a glass and then slid into the bubbling churning water next to her.

"This is marvelous!" she breathed as she sipped her drink, "it's like a honeymoon suite."

Geoff with his face very close to hers, whispered, "Let's have a honeymoon then." Kissing passionately, the two managed to set their glasses down before stripping out of their bathing suits and becoming one under the foamy water.

Crown leaned forward in front of the monitor before him. He smiled hungrily, rubbing his hands together. "Why don't they get out of the damn water?" he fumed, "I can't see!" Remind me to have that damn pool drained tomorrow. It will have a malfunction of some kind!"

"Yes, sir," came his technician's reply.

* * * * * * * *

After receiving word by phone that the Beatles and the Van Heusens were on their way to Crown's estate, Wellington sat back to take a tea break, feeling very satisfied. He gazed at the pictures of his nieces on his desk. He hadn't seen either of them in a month. Smiling, he picked up the phone again and reached Candy.

"Hi, sweetie!" he greeted her.

"Da," she answered, "I'm glad you called. Guess what! I just found out I'm going to be featured in a fashion layout in Time magazine this month. Isn't that just fab?"

"Yes, sweetie, that's great. We haven't gotten together in so long. I want to find out all the wonderful things you've been doing. I was hoping you and your sister could make time to see me this weekend. I'd love to take you both to see the Blackpool lights."[72]

"Oh, I could go, but I know Sandy couldn't."

"Eh? What's your sister busy with?" Wellington asked.

"Well, I know she's got plans with Paul. She's flown to Paul's band's performance site. You know, I finally met his band mates recently, and they're really very nice."

"Good. Well, let's wait until Sandy comes back. Call me when you two are both available and we'll make plans. Take care, now, sweetie."

"I will, Da."

"Love you!"

"Love you too, Da!"

Wellington put down the phone and picked up the file on Crown. Tea break's over, back to work, he reminded himself. He wondered how things were going at Crown's estate. He hoped fervently that they were successful.

He took his last sip of tea as he looked in the folder and dropped his teacup and saucer with a bang. Hopkin's report on the deceased band member was the first item. It was Paul McCartney, his niece's fiancée! The 5" x 7" photo showed unmistakably the young man Sandy had introduced five months ago in London. There was no doubt.

How devastated Sandy would be when she found out her true love was dead! But how could she, he realized with a jolt, when he had been replaced by a double! Immediately, Wellington's mind spun to the conversation he had just finished with his other niece. Candy said Sandy was going to spend the weekend watching Paul's band play. Wellington felt rising panic overtaking him. Oh, God, he thought frantically, Sandy was going to the Crown Estate!! This meant Sandy would be around the replacement the agency had found for Paul! She might figure out the hoax and cause a scene or trigger violence from Crown's thugs. She would be in the middle of the mission he was directing! She could be in grave danger!

Wellington paced and swore trying to figure some way to keep Sandy from the certain danger that she faced. Eventually, worn out from his hysterics, he sat in his luxurious office high atop the commerce building and cried in despair. Even with all the power his position provided as the head of the Interpol London office, there was no way he could help his niece and prevent this potentially disastrous situation. He just had to hope it turned out well for his sweet Sandy. Even if she made it out of Crown's estate safely, he knew she had some huge emotional scars ahead of her when she found out about losing Paul, the love of her young life.

* * * * * * * *

The group assembled at the Crown stables was small due to the previous evening's late night partying. The few horse enthusiasts present included Sandy, Tres, and three teenaged boys. All were dressed in appropriate riding clothes...jodhpurs, coats, and boots. They stood under the covered area in front of the box stalls as they waited for the stable boys and groomsmen to get horses ready for them. Sandy had chosen a brown tweed coat with a black velvet collar and taupe riding pants. Her long flaxen hair was french-braided. She looked like the consummate professional horsewoman, Tres thought. In the bright morning light she was even more beautiful than she appeared last night in the smoky club atmosphere. She had smooth youthful skin without a line or blemish, and the blush of enthusiasm lit her face. Being nineteen had its advantages.

Tres casually observed the rest of the group around them. The teenage boys had bonded immediately, slapping each other's shoulders and laughing loudly at comments made in their clustered group. These wealthy young men were the pleasure-seeking heirs that would someday replace their elders at the family empires. The ones currently in control of family fortunes were nestled in their beds this morning nursing hangovers from the spirits these youths were luckily too young for yet. Tres found herself thinking of Sandy's boyfriend and wishing fervently that he could still be like those vibrant jovial boys around her. What a loss! Well, she told herself, she just had to put such thoughts out of her mind. There was no time for sentimentality now. She needed to concentrate on keeping this young girl busy so she wouldn't have a chance to realize that there was an impostor in her fiancée's place.

Sandy was standing at a box stall. She was stroking the neck of a huge bay through the top half of the stall door. "Whoa, boy," she whispered, her head close to his as he shied slightly nostrils flaring. The horse immediately calmed, nuzzling the blonde girl's shoulder. Tres stepped closer. This was her chance to make contact.

"He's beautiful, isn't he?" Tres observed.

The younger blonde startled slightly.

"Oh, I'm sorry. I didn't mean to scare you." Tres assured her, touching her on the shoulder.

"Oh, that's okay. I was just thinking about my fiancée... we're getting married next month. I guess I was just daydreaming." Sandy said.

"Geoff and I just finished that wedding deal, or rather 'ordeal', I should call it. But the married part after the ceremony is worth going through it. Hi, I'm Tres."

"I'm Sandy. It's a pleasure to meet you."

The two blue-eyed blondes smiled warmly at each other.

"You know, I think I know your fiancée. He's with the rock band that was playing last night. Paul is his name, isn't it? Are you having a large wedding?" Tres asked. The response Tres got from Sandy was totally unexpected. It was as if a door had been closed and locked. Sandy's face paled and she looked pained, almost frightened.

"Um, I, uh, excuse me, I think they're bringing the horses." And she turned quickly on her heel and walked briskly away to the approaching stable boy.

The rest of the morning was spent riding without further conversation. Sandy seemed to be concentrating on her jumping, and Tres couldn't find a casual way to approach her. Something was definitely wrong. Had she guessed so quickly that Paul was an impostor? Surely, she had not. They'd had such brief contact so far with him. If it wasn't that, was it that the question of a large wedding was painful? Maybe that was it. Perhaps she didn't have the money for a large wedding and she was insulted by her question. That might upset a perspective bride. One look at her wardrobe last night and today told a different story, however. Her clothes looked fitted to her by a tailor, and the gold jewelry items she wore were investment quality. No, Tres decided after much consideration, it couldn't be money. Maybe she and her Paul had disagreed in the past about the size of the wedding. That must be it.

Tres made sure she finished the last few jumps ahead of Sandy and was standing in the stable yard when Sandy trotted in her horse. "Sandy!" she called and waited to see if there would be any response. When she received eye contact, and Sandy rode her sorrel mare up to her, Tres continued, "Please excuse me if I offended you by asking about the size of your wedding. Could we have lunch together? We seem to have so much in common, and I'm a little bit lonely because Geoff has business meetings today."

Sandy swung off the mare, turned the reins over to the waiting stable boy, and smiled slightly. "Okay," she said. "Lunch sounds good."

The two women of similar height, build, and coloring looked like sisters as they strolled up the gravel road toward the dining hall. They chatted about 'girl stuff' as a guy would say...the texture of their hair and how much curl it would hold, their families, how they each learned to horseback ride. By the time they reached the dining room with its snowy white linens and silver, they found they had even more in common than they thought. Thank goodness she's more relaxed, thought Tres. Maybe I can get her to help us.

Over salads and tea, Tres learned a lot more about her new friend, but she still seemed tense about something. Tres finally decided she would have to bring it up to find out what was bothering her new friend.

"What did you need to talk to me about, Sandy?" Tres inquired casually.

Sandy looked embarrassed. She blushed and stared at her fork as she toyed with it. Finally she took a deep breath and met Tres' eyes.

"Look, I'm not supposed to tell that Paul is marrying me. The band's manager says it would hurt their record sales. They're just beginning to have some success. Could you please forget who he is?" The waiter brought their after-dinner coffee and Sandy stopped talking. After a brief pause, she continued, "When I told you I was marrying, I had no idea that you might have seen us together after the sound check last night."

Oh, that was the reason for her panic! She had inadvertently revealed a secret! Tres smiled reassuringly at the desperate-looking girl across from her. "Relax, Sandy, I understand. I'll keep it to myself. What a shame for you, though, not to be able to announce your good news. I guess that's how the music business works."

"Yes, it's not fun to have to hide our plans, but if it will help the Beatles find success with their fans, I'll do it." Sandy agreed.

"Do you think he's worth all the secrecy?" Tres said as she bent forward conspiratorially.

"Yes, I love him more than life," breathed Sandy heartily.

Tres sat back and studied the flawless beauty before her. She couldn't help but feel a twinge of guilt about using this naive young girl. But she couldn't know the truth, not yet. This mission was too important. If the warheads should reach their destination without being disarmed, the whole Western Hemisphere could be at the Russian's mercy.

"It must be really hard for you to find Paul's career is more important than your marriage, Sandy. Have you thought that it might be this way for a long time...as long as his band is together? And from what I heard and saw last night, it might be a really long time!"

"That's what my uncle says," sighed Sandy, pushing her bangs away from her eyes. "He keeps telling me to 're-think!' 'Re-think' he says. I am nineteen years old, old enough to make this decision!" she said adamantly as she tapped her forehead. "I've got to trust my own thoughts and feelings!"

"Is nineteen legal age in Germany?" Tres asked, taking a sip of her coffee.

"Oh, I may seem German because of my accent, but I am American. My uncle who is my guardian works for the government in Britain. I was raised in Germany."

At Tres' upraised eyebrows during another sip of coffee, Sandy related how she and her sister had been raised in a convent after their mother died, and how she had only recently chosen to come out into the world. That explains the air of innocence, thought Tres.

"My life has changed so much since I came away from the convent and I met Paul."

"Did you leave the convent for him?" Tres asked.

"Oh, no, I made my decision a few months before we met at my family's estate in Germany. But he is the best thing that has ever happened to me. I really love him. If it weren't for him, I'd be totally nuts!"

"Why?"

"You see this collar?" Sandy said, touching the lush black velvet near her neck. "My life seemed like this before—so soft, smooth, predictable, and since I left the convent, it's like this," she said, rubbing her hand on the rough tweed, "all rough, harsh, and confusing with too many options." Tres looked solemnly at the coarse material. With its nubs and multitude of shades crossing each other, it really did typify the struggle this poor girl must be feeling when faced with this world so new to her.

"What an interesting way to describe it," observed Tres, "do you ever like to write?"

"I keep a diary, but that's all; it's just for me."

"You might want to think about writing for other people some day. It would be a career compatible with traveling with a musician and his band." Tres and Sandy both laughed.

"I'll file that suggestion away for later," she said. "It's fun talking to you, Tres. You're making this weekend fun after all."

"Guy troubles?" Tres questioned.

Sandy blushed and looked at her twisting hands. "He seems so busy. He hardly has any time for me at all. I'm almost sorry I came."

Tres looked concerned about her new friend. "Maybe you ought to give him some space and wait for him back in London. He'll have more time when he's not performing."

Sandy looked thoughtful. She wiped a tear that had slid down her cheek. "I don't think I can just LEAVE him. He seems so intense with his music this weekend, and he obviously needs my support, even though he is too busy to be with me."

"Even though it hurts?" Tres suggested.

"Yes, right. I can't run off every time I feel neglected. We'll never have a marriage."

"Sandy, why don't you hang out with Geoff and me while Paul is busy? It will get better. You'll see. He's probably just very stressed about making a good performance here. This is a crucial time for them. After all, they've just released their first record, right?"[73]

"Yes, that's true. Okay, I'll do things with you and Geoff. You don't think he'll mind?"

"What? Oh, of course not. He likes to be around pretty ladies." Tres laughed.

That day after riding, Tres was really looking forward to a long soak in the Jacuzzi. She hurried ahead of Geoff to shower and, with a towel wrapped around her, she prepared to plop herself into the Jacuzzi's comforting mists. The tub was empty! A note from housekeeping was attached to the controls. 'Sorry, malfunction has occurred. We will fix as soon as possible. Accept our treat basket as apology.' she read. Next to the tub sat a heart shaped basket containing an assortment of fruits and goodies. Opening the cellophane, she was amazed to find all sorts of sex toys and edible creams among the items that spilled out over the floor. Hmmm..., thought Tres, Crown wants a show. Tres couldn't help but blush as she inspected their treats. She wondered if Geoff would be interested in any of them.

"Mmmm., goodies?" Geoff whispered as he kissed her neck from behind her. When she jumped slightly, he grabbed her shoulder and kissed her uplifted face. "I didn't mean to scare you!

Tres smiled mischievously. "I was just thinking..."

"Yes?..."

"About how to use some of this stuff..." she giggled as she spread the items around on the carpet in front of her."

"Ha!" Geoff laughed. "Lessons later! I've got business right now. Crown wants to see me in less than an hour. I need to shower and get going!"

"Okay, I'll take a nap then," Tres replied. "I'll rest up for tonight."

* * * * * * * *

Geoff was escorted into Crown's plush inner sanctum after only a few minutes of waiting in a small reception area. He immediately observed the glass outer wall with heavy curtains pulled back to reveal a gorgeous panorama of rolling green hills and the English coastline, with high cliffs and crashing waves.

"I see you're enjoying my vista," Crown observed as he strolled in behind Geoff.

Geoff, turning from the window, answered, "Quite impressive!"

The two men shook hands and their eyes told each other that each was very serious about the business they had to conduct.

During the next three hours, they discussed the capacity of the Van Heusen shipping line and the quantities Crown needed to ship. Haggling over the costs of shipping the illegal drugs took the longest, but Crown made it clear he had pictures and evidence that could end Geoff's inheritance. Geoff acknowledged that Crown had the upper hand this time, and a deal was struck. After signing the papers, the secretaries and assistants cleared out. Then the two men relaxed and had a drink on the balcony outside the glass wall of Crown's office. Geoff counted seven stories; it was a long way down. In fact, this was the tallest of the buildings in the compound. The neighboring roof was close by and on the same level as Crown's balcony. Its flat top was apparently used as a helicopter landing pad, he surmised, as he noted the lights marking its striped surface.

Euphoric at getting Van Heusen to comply to ship the drugs, Crown offered a tour of his administrative offices. Geoff jumped at the chance to find out more about the layout. You never knew when you'd need such information, he reasoned. As the two of them walked through the poshly decorated rooms, Geoff made mental notes about the exits, staircases, and air ducts. Geoff complimented Crown on his efficiently run organization.

"You've got a thing of beauty, too," Crown gushed, "your wife."

"Ah, yes. She is gorgeous and we do get along well. You're not married are you, Crown?"

"No, I just haven't found the right one yet."

"Such a pity. You have so much to share here with someone. I hope you find the right woman to marry. Tres and I are very close."

"She seems quite devoted to you. I wish to ask you a personal question if I may...?" When Geoff nodded, Crown smiled and leaned very close to Geoff to ask, "Was she a virgin when you married her? I've been waiting to find one, but I'm afraid my expectations are far too high."

Geoff looked surprised at Crown's revelation, but he quickly answered Crown's question, "Oh, yes, she was. It took a while to find her, but it has been worth it," he said encouragingly.

"I want the two of you to have a wonderful time here this weekend. Please make yourselves at home here on Crown Estate. It is a pleasure doing business with you."

"Thank you. And now I must find Tres and get dressed for dinner. We're looking forward to the concert this evening."

"Yes," Crown laughed, a little embarrassed. "My nieces had heard about this singing group from their visits to London. I believe they saw them perform at a place called the Cavern. Are you familiar with that establishment?"

Geoff stifled a laugh and the thought of the dank, dark, smelly Cavern being called an establishment. "Oh, yes, Tres and I love to go there!"

"Well, I think everyone enjoyed last night's music. I think they're pretty good." Crown boasted.

After a final handshake, Geoff stepped into the elevator feeling encouraged. He had gotten a good look at some areas Crown didn't mind him seeing in his complex. Now all they had to do was get into some areas not so easy to access.

* * * * * * * *

"I knew you'd be interested."

Crown looked sharply at the technician seated at the bank of monitors beside him.

"When did this occur?"

"Last night, or rather in the wee hours of this morning" the younger man pointed to a time stamp on the screen.

Crown grunted and switched off the monitor. He turned to stare piercingly at the man beside him.

"And did they go to separate rooms after this?"

"Yes, sir."

"And were the rooms watched to see that they didn't join each other later?

"Yes, sir, the whole time"

"I want her watched every minute to make sure." Crown insisted. He called over another guard and gave him urgent instructions. As the man hurried off to put Crown's plans into action, Crown turned back to the blank screen. "Play it again," he ordered.

With a swift flick of a switch, the monitor came to life again. Crown was spellbound as one of the young long-haired musicians he had hired chased a beautiful girl with long flaxen hair around the swimming pool. About fifteen others stood around with drinks laughing and talking.

"The band..." Crown murmured.

"And their entourage..." added the technician, enjoying the show almost as much as his employer.

The young man could be seen cornering the blonde against the building quite close the hidden camera, so the sound of their hushed voices were quite clear. As he playfully nuzzled her neck with kisses and pushed her against the building with his body, he whispered, "I caught you. Now at last you're going to be mine!"

"No, Paul, you promised to wait until we marry. Paul, what's gotten into you? You've had too much to drink!" the beauty was obviously surprised at his behavior.

146

Two of their longhaired friends then ran over to grab the man called "Paul" by the shoulders and pull him back.

When Paul protested to his mates, one of them said, "Now, Paul, she didn't wait nineteen years to lose her virginity at a swimming pool in front of everyone. Come on." In a loud voice, he called for help to another friend, still drinking by the pool. "Hey, Ringo, come help us throw this horny bloke in a cold shower!"

"See what you've done to me, Sandy! You've driven me bloody mad!" Paul laughed as the three men joined together to help carry the drunken man back to his bungalow.

The blonde Sandy laughed and yelled, "Good night, everyone!" and then disappeared into a neighboring bungalow. The others continued to party until the technician froze them in their places on the screen.

"Good," breathed Crown, "very good!" His silver gray eyes glittered with the tantalizing opportunity of obtaining a virgin. This house party had already been successful for him in business. And it still seemed to offer unexpected possibilities for him. Perhaps he could find some way to convince this virgin to stay.

Crown's fingers picked mindlessly at the red scar on his cheek. Damn, he fumed. It always seemed to bother him when he was excited. It was a permanent reminder of his struggle growing up on the rough dock area of London. He was only a lad of ten when his drunken parents sold him into the service of a gimp-legged Irishman named Harris who ran a whorehouse in London. They decided they'd rather have three quid than the pleasure of beating him daily.

Young Jason learned early to stay out of his new master's way as much as possible by busying himself with the mending and scrubbing of the establishment's bed linens. He discovered quickly the art of trading favors. The women gladly provided thrilling peepshows of assorted sex acts in return for Jason's help when escape was needed from an abusive john. Despite his adjustment to the life at the whorehouse, he dreaded the nights in bomb-ravaged London. The air raids and chaos that the German planes brought were not what bothered young Jason though. World War II

147

couldn't compete with the horror that Harris dealt with his groping pain-causing hands. Harris took great pleasure in beating Jason before forcing sex on him. After the first few terror-filled nights, the frightened boy would hide in the basement of the crumbling old house hoping to allude Harris' sexual advances.

Jason Crown rubbed his cheek trying to make the hideous memories flee. Whenever his scar became sensitive it took him right back to the place where the horrible life-changing event occurred. Crown could still hear the rustling creak of the wooden crates stacked around him as he hid in Harris' basement. As he crouched on the damp cement of the basement, he could smell the stench of rotting wood. The sound of old man Harris' awkward footsteps came back to him as he remembered the words that motivated him to change his attitude toward his life forever. "He's here somewhere, the little bastard! He's a good lay, he is! His ass is nice and tight!" Harris bragged to the hulk of a man with him. The men laughed heartily.

Caught up in his past, Crown sweated as he replayed the terrible scene in his mind. He was oblivious to the control room monitors around him. Once again he relived his horror at the prospect of becoming the ultimate victim, a whore. Heart racing, Crown gripped the back of the swivel chair in front of him imagining it to be the iron bar that had served as a weapon that fateful night. "Yes!" Crown whispered smugly as he fingered the hideous scar on his cheek. He was remembering the satisfying crunch as he pulverized the wretched men's skulls. The stranger had been caught by surprise and succumbed quickly, but that bastard Harris managed to slash Crown's cheek with a shard of glass before being overpowered. Crown smiled evilly. The disfigurement was a small price to pay for the freedom he needed, thought Jason Crown as he gazed around the luxurious control room with the state of the art equipment. The mutilated corpses had provided an additional benefit: enough money to escape and set up a smuggling ring, which he eventually parlayed into the vast fortune he now controlled. Jason Crown had become a survivor that night, boldly proclaiming with his murderous actions that he would never be a victim again. In illegal trading circles, Crown was known as a powerful and ruthless man who always got what he wanted. He stared at the monitor near him and focused his eyes on the blonde beauty who was targeted as his next acquisition. "You will be mine," he murmured.

* * * * * * * *

Sandy and Tres had quickly become close friends. They spent the next two days riding together through the beautiful countryside, laughing and talking. Sandy wished Paul could be with them, but he and the band stayed up almost all night performing in the smoky crowded club, and then slept most of the day.

Every day Geoff would meet them for a picnic lunch at noon. Tres and Sandy would arrive early and wait for Geoff under a huge oak tree near the tenth jump. Sitting in the shade was so pleasant after a morning's romp. They used it as a private time to share little secrets.

"Tres," Sandy ventured hesitantly.

Tres nodded encouragingly, expecting it to be a question about men or sex. Sandy was always so refreshingly candid and amazed by things others took for granted. "Yes?"

Sandy took a deep breath, bit her lip, and then blurted; "Have you ever felt like someone was watching you?" Her blue eyes were wide with fright and Tres noted the slight tremor that indicated that Sandy was genuinely frightened.

Tres covered Sandy's hand with hers to soothe her. "It's all right. There are a lot of strangers here, Sandy, and you're a beautiful girl! I guess some people just can't help but stare at perfection." Mentally, Tres smashed Geoff with a cream pie! That Bozo! His "innocent" staring the other night had scared the poor girl. Tres hugged Sandy gently and whispered, "Everything's okay, Sandy, you'll see. It's okay."

Sandy smiled at Tres as their eyes met again. "I'm sorry. I just panicked. I have felt like unseen eyes have watched me since I got to this place. I'm just being silly. I know." Tres smiled back. Geoff arrived then with a huge basket of goodies and they settled down to a feast.

Their picnics near the tenth jump provided more than wonderful food. Since Sandy had consented for Tres to confide in Geoff about her upcoming marriage to Paul, she could bounce ideas off them. They gave her lots of advice in making some wedding choices she had been putting off. "And you have helped me so much! You're almost the only people I can talk to about the wedding. I wish I could repay you in some way by helping you out." Sandy said and crunched into another bit of apple.

Tres and Geoff's eyes met, and Tres took a deep breath. This was exactly the opening they needed. "Actually, there is something you could do for us, Sandy."

Sandy looked at her with a mixture of surprise and eagerness, "Just ask..."

"Well, this is the last night of the house party, and we'd like for you to understand that we can't sit with you tonight at the club. We need to sit with some old friends. Tres took note of the immediate hurt in the younger girl's eyes. She hastened to add, "We don't mean to hurt your feelings. Forgive us for asking this of you, Sandy."

"Of course, I understand! I'm sure I can sit with Cynthia, Brian, and Neil. Could we meet in the morning at the stable or in the lobby to say good-bye?"

"Sandy, we'd love to, but we might leave late tonight. We've got to get back for business." Geoff said.

"Oh, well, then I guess I'll say good-bye now. It's been great getting to know you." Sandy looked so forlorn that Tres couldn't resist hugging her.

"Listen, let's exchange addresses and phone numbers, and maybe we can stay in contact after we leave." Tres suggested. "I'd love to hear all about your wedding!"

Sandy looked pleased.

* * * * * * * *

That evening, entering the darkened smoky nightclub, Sandy instinctively looked for Paul. She had seen him for

150

only a few minutes each day and he always seemed to be so busy even then. She missed the fun they always had before. No matter where they were playing, he always made time for her. I hope this is not what our life will be like together, she thought. She felt those eyes trained on her and glanced nervously around the crowded room. A chill swept through her, but she refused to go up to her room. Sandy was determined to find Paul.

She finally spotted him as he stepped out from behind the drum set, which as usual was up on a platform. He and his band were just getting ready to start their first set. Sandy managed to squeeze through the dense crowd to reach the table where Neil and Brian were sitting. She asked about Cynthia, but they said she wasn't feeling well and had stayed in the room. When the Beatles began to play, she was, as always, amazed at the group's dynamic sound. The crowd obviously agreed with her, clapping to the beat and singing along on some of the numbers.

Sandy glanced around nervously to find Geoff and Tres. They were sitting with the group of old friends they had told her about. They seemed to be having fun, toasting with their drinks and laughing as they listened to the music. Sandy wished she could be among them, but she had to understand and respect their request.

The evening seemed endless to Sandy. She wanted to see Paul so badly. She felt lonely even in this crowded club. Brian and Neil had their heads together, whispering, so she couldn't have a conversation with them. Sandy took another sip of her ginger ale as she saw Tres slipping discreetly away from the table. Sandy got up to follow her to the lady's room hoping to be able to share a few minutes of companionship. Then she noticed that Tres was heading toward the right side of the stage, the opposite side of the room from the lady's room. Sandy was curious to see where she was going. Tres went around the corner of the stage and down a long hallway. At the end of the hallway was a large wall mirror over a mahogany table with a flower arrangement. Sandy paused in her pursuit of Tres as she suddenly felt someone's eyes following her. An involuntary shudder

151

shook her momentarily before she followed Tres down the hallway.

Suddenly as if on cue, the section of the wall with the mirror swung around leaving an opening, which Tres promptly entered. Sandy watched her friend enter the dark doorway and wondered where it would lead her. Then she heard footsteps coming up behind her! Who could that be? Was it the person who had been watching her? Would they hurt her? Maybe, she thought frantically, if I go into the doorway too, I can hide until they leave. Inside the passageway it was very dark and she felt a rising panic, but she concentrated on thinking about Tres somewhere ahead of her. She crept along until she reached an opening illuminated by a soft glowing light. Peering around into the room, Sandy was amazed to see a number of huge wooden crates. Each one encased a silver cylindrical object. Tres was kneeling beside one of them with several small tools.

Sandy was just about to ask Tres what she was doing when she was grabbed from behind. One forceful arm trapped her hands behind her back and the other covered her mouth. The man whispered "Quiet and I'll let you go," but Sandy didn't have a chance to respond by nodding. Geoff lifted her limp body and carried it into the room where Tres was disarming the warheads.

"My God, Geoff, did you snap her neck?" Sandy whispered accusingly.

"No, she fainted. She'll be fine."

Geoff pulled out his set of tools and began helping Tres with the task.

* * * * * * * * *

Sandy awoke in the dimly lit room under the stage to see her two new friends on their knees busily turning screws on these large silver cylinders. Sandy opened her mouth to shout to her friends her surprise, but no sound came out. A strip of cloth was tied around her head gagging her mouth. She sat and watched in shock. Then she noticed that her hands were completely free, and she immediately ripped the gag from her mouth. Tres glanced her way and put her finger to her lips to let her know she had to be quiet.

Sandy crawled over to Tres and whispered in her ear as she worked, "What are you doing?"

"Something very dangerous. Shush!" Geoff answered in a voice that was barely audible.

Sandy obediently sat in silence. She listened to the concert going on over their heads. She realized then that they were under the stage where the Beatles were performing. She felt chilled as Paul sang 'Besame Mucho,' one of her favorites. At last Geoff and Tres hid their tools in the packing material of the crates and motioned for Sandy to follow them out of the room.

"What is going on?" Sandy questioned them.

Tres shushed her; the three were halfway down the hallway to the hidden door they had used. The hidden door began to open. Someone was coming! Geoff and Tres grabbed Sandy and headed to the other end of the hall. Lifting Tres up, Geoff held her in the air as she quickly and deftly opened a grate to an air vent. Quickly each of them crawled in. Three men walked down the hall right under their hiding place.

Sandy, very frightened, reached for her engagement locket that Paul had given her. It always comforted her to touch it because it made her feel close to him. It wasn't there! Sandy frantically felt under her blouse to see if it had moved, but it wasn't there!

"I've lost my locket!" she whispered as she continued to frantically search her clothes.

"Shh!" Geoff hastened to warn her as he gave her a frowning glance. In the dark cramped air tunnel he could barely see her panicked look, but the importance of the locket didn't register with him.

"I've got to find Paul's locket!" Sandy hissed as she released the clasp on the grate and hastily jumped down from their shared hiding place. She ran toward the room where the silver spheres were stored. "I must have dropped it under the stage!"

"Oh, no," Tres whispered in desperation as her shocked gaze met Geoff's. She too jumped down and began to chase Sandy. She had just caught up to Sandy to bring her back to their hiding place when the three men stepped back around the corner.

"I tell you, she's here!" a deep familiar voice insisted. All three men stopped walking as the man in the waiter's uniform boomed out an excited, "See? There she is! I told you I saw her come in here!" Sandy stared in amazement at the maniac that often stalked her in her nightmares. Colin Dodd was pointing at her with a meaningful leer.

"Stop!" the two guards ordered sternly as they drew their pistols. Sandy burst into tears, and the women clung together. Slowly the men advanced to them. Sandy crumpled to the floor in a dead faint.

Above in the air vent, Geoffrey remained motionless. His freedom was their only hope.

* * * * * * * *

Geoff kicked himself for being frozen by surprise when Sandy impulsively darted out of the air vent to retrieve her locket. What a stupid but predictable reaction! He should have realized the importance of that engagement jewelry to Sandy and anticipated that a teenager would act without thinking of the consequences. Although he wanted badly to pull a weapon and stop the whole mess right there, he had none on purpose. If they were caught, it was best to imitate two adventuresome guests who wandered into the wrong place by accident.

However, everything had changed when Sandy had followed Tres into the secret area under the stage. Now he had to invent a way to get them out of their dilemma. This might be difficult, he reasoned, as he had no diagrams of the layout of this building and no idea where Crown's men would take them. His only strategy would be to follow the air ducts, which should connect all parts of the building. Feeling something digging into his knee as he crouched in the air duct, he lifted a sparkling gold chain and locket and stashed it into his pocket. This must be the lost locket that had cost Sandy and Tres their freedom he pondered grimly.

He spent the next long, grueling hours in an exhaustive search to locate Sandy and Tres. He just hoped he could finesse their release in a way that wouldn't abort the mission. As Geoff crawled in the air conditioning ducts carefully peering through the grates into each room, he finally spotted a battered and bleeding Tres through one of the vents. He recognized the room! It was one that adjoined Crown's opulent office. Geoff lay very still patiently waiting to discover who else might be in this room. He was so tempted to wait until she was left alone and then spirit her away through the air ducts he had just traveled in. Biting his lip, he lay quietly, torn between saving Tres immediately or playing out the scenario in a way that would throw suspicion off the tampering of the missiles. The excitement that had always seemed to be enticing in this spy game was suddenly unfulfilling to Geoff. He'd gladly be bored the rest of his life if Tres could just be safely with him!

As he watched, one of the two men questioning Tres slapped her already bleeding face. The sound of her moans reverberated through the vent. Geoff closed his eyes and clenched his fists in a desperate effort to hold onto his self-control.

* * * * * * * *

When Sandy woke up, she was on the floor in some sort of office. Colin Dodd was sitting in a leather swivel chair staring at her. He reminded Sandy of a vulture patiently waiting for his meal. Two men in matching polo-necked shirts sat about six feet away, and they had guns trained at her. Sandy put her hands up and said meekly, "Please don't hurt me."

"We won't, as long as you're more forthcoming with the truth than your friend," said a stocky red-haired man wearing all black who glared down at her. "Who are you?" Sandy asked in surprise.

"That's not the question, my pet; the question is 'who are you and what were you doing in a restricted area?' You

had no business there.'" His tone was impatient and forceful.

"Uh, uh..." Sandy stammered. "I was just curious to see
what was in there."

"Come on, you can do better than that!" he insisted,
pacing the floor in front of her.

"No, that's it. I saw the door open, you know, the one
with the mirror and table, and I just came in! I'm very sorry
if I intruded. I won't do it again." Sandy was visibly shaken.
"I promise!" She had never been confronted by anyone with
such a cruel demeanor, and she was deeply frightened.

"Miss Wellington, we all know that your boyfriend in
the band triggered the release of that door that you 'just
came in'. We saw him 'accidentally' bump the wall tile that
triggered the secret door. Maybe you and he are robbers.
Now tell me the truth, and you won't look like this!" As he
spoke, the troll of a man grew even angrier. His face had
turned a bright red and he was clenching his fists in a threatening manner. He signaled one of the gunmen who nodded
through the cracked door near him.

Suddenly two guards came in and someone was shoved
to the floor beside her with a thud. Sandy looked next to
her and promptly screamed. Tres had been beaten so badly
her features were distorted. Her honey blonde hair was mat-
ted with blood, and her body was a mass of bruises and cuts.

"Tres, oh my God!" Sandy gasped.

"Now, Miss Wellington, you see we mean business. Tell
us what you know." his face was very close to hers.

"I...I...I...She...she...she..." Sandy stammered, looking
from the red-haired man to Tres and back.

"Yes?" The horrible red-haired man's face was even
closer to hers. He held a gun under her chin, "speak up!"
The man continued to stare into her face challenging what
she had said.

The sound of a door opening nearby attracted the
prompt attention of all the men in the room. All heads immediately turned to see a swarthy dark-haired man, stepping into view from around a bookcase. He surveyed the
scene with his hands on his hips and a questioning look on
his face. His slight gesture was all it took for the red-haired

troll to join him near the bookcase. A heated but muffled discussion swiftly followed, and Sandy was amazed to see a shadow of fear cross the shorter man's face. After the pudgy red-haired man exited, the tall dark haired man glided across the carpet to sit next to her. He was a handsome man, but looked very cruel, somehow. Sandy thought it might be the long scar down one cheek that made him look mean. He was dressed in a dark suit that looked very expensive. She thought immediately that he could be a pirate in one of those romance novels her sister hid under their covers to read after the nuns had gone to bed.

"Miss Wellington, I am Jason Crown. I apologize for my security man's rudeness. We certainly want you to be comfortable here in any situation." His words startled her with their kindness in comparison to her earlier treatment. "Now tell me why you were in a restricted area."

Sandy's face crumpled as she finally gave into the tears she had been holding back. "I didn't know where the hallway went. A door just opened and I went inside," she managed to sputter. Crown handed her his handkerchief, and she wiped her tears as she tried to catch her breath. "Please let us go! We didn't mean to wander into a place we shouldn't be...we were just exploring!"

"Now, Miss Wellington, " are you telling me the truth?" Crown bent down to look into her eyes as he held her chin up with his hand.

"I swear it," Sandy said emphatically, but the man continued staring at her sternly.

"I swear to God on this. Please believe me," Sandy begged. "I have just left a convent in Germany after deciding not to take final vows. I would not blaspheme God's name!" Crown pondered her words. So that's why she has remained a virgin so long, he thought excitedly. Well, that makes sense. He watched Sandy's reaction to the questions intently. The girl was sincere in her innocence, he felt sure. The tears in those big blue eyes were genuine. He glanced at the bleeding woman beside Sandy. Mentally, he recalled Geoff Van Heusen's reluctance to ship the drugs and his hesitancy to bring his wife here for the weekend. No, he decided swiftly, neither of these women fit the profile of an agent trying to sabotage those weapons under the stage. The situation wasn't as it originally seemed when he was notified that intruders were in the secure area. The Russians would never even have to know of this little breach of security, and it might be the opportunity he was looking to make his claim on this gorgeous virgin. The elation that he felt at being close to this beautiful creature, Sandy, made Crown feel a little heady which skewed his usual instincts in these matters. Sandy watched as the man silently assessed the look on her face, and sat back, apparently satisfied

"You don't need to be afraid now," he said. "We will not hurt you. Come with me. May I call you Sandy?" He took her hand and pulled her up so she was standing.

"How do you know my name?"

"It's my business," he smiled, nice white even teeth, but there wasn't joy in his smile, only a cold confidence. This was a man used to getting his way.

The sound of a fist slamming on the nearby desk caught everyone's attention. "No!" Dodd said emphatically as he arose. "No! Hey! The security guy with the red hair said I could have her when he finished with her. I'm the one that told him she had gone in there!"

Jason Crown turned coolly to inspect the angry man in the waiter uniform who clearly didn't know who he dealing with. He searched his excellent memory for the name of his employee. "Mr., uh, Dodd, is it?" Crown also glanced at the frightened girl who had slipped behind him to get further away from this ruffian who was obviously lusting for her.

Dodd nodded defiantly; clearly pleased that his intervention had kept this man from leaving with the girl he had stalked for so long. This had started out as a revenge move on Paul for taking his place in the band at the Jacaranda, but he had become obsessed with Sandy when she had rejected him in that hotel room in London. "This girl is mine!" Dodd insisted again.

"Mr. Dodd, I believe that you don't know I'm Mr. Crown, your employer. Now I strongly advise you to go back to waiting tables in the club. Your presence is not needed here."

"But..." Dodd started to protest. Then Crown's slight nod toward the door caused one of the security guards to move close by Dodd's side. Recognizing defeat, Dodd sullenly followed the guard's outstretched arm to leave.

Sandy sighed with relief and Crown couldn't help but smile slightly. Seeing him as her protector would help him win her trust. Now that the danger from Colin Dodd was past, Sandy felt bolder.

"What about Tres? Will you take care of her?" Sandy put her hands on her hips and met Crown's eyes steadily.

"Oh, we will, you can be assured." Crown turned to the two men who had dragged her into the room. "Please call the nurse and have first aid administered to Mrs. Van Heusen. Make sure she is comfortable."

"I want to stay with Tres," Sandy stated. She stood over Tres unmoving.

"No, no, now you come with me. She'll be fine. You'll see her in a few minutes," Crown comforted her as he took her arm and led her down a hall to a sitting room resplendent with velvet chairs, a flame-stitched couch, a coffee table, and a bar. A bank of TV monitors lined two of the walls.

"Now, just sit down and make yourself comfortable, Sandy." Crown said as he walked behind the bar and began pouring red wine into crystal glasses.

"Who are you?" Sandy asked bluntly. She shifted uncomfortably in the overstuffed burgundy leather chair and looked like she might leap up and run any minute.

"Well, call me Jason. I've been your host this week."

"All this is yours? The whole compound?" Sandy looked incredulously around the room and then at the tall handsome man who had sat across from her.

"So have you enjoyed your visit in my estate?" Crown took a sip of wine.

Sandy still looked uneasy. "Well, uh, yes, until tonight."

"I know. I know. This whole incident was unforgivable. It is so hard to get good people. Bob will be my security man no longer, I assure you. But was the rest of the week fun? I see you have a penchant for horseback riding. I do a bit of that myself," he said as he refilled the wine in her glass. As he sipped his, he looked amused at her surprise.

"I stay informed about all my guests. You really do like the outdoors, don't you, Sandy?"

"Well, yes, I do." Sandy looked uneasy that this man knew so much about her.

"Tell me which jump was most challenging on our course here."

"The twelfth, I think," she considered it for a moment. Although her heart was still racing, she managed to convey a calm exterior. "Yes, it had the water trough as well as the fence-type barrier. My horse would also shy at the hedge that was close by, so that one was difficult."

"The outdoors suits you, Sandy, not the stale, dank, smoky night club environment. You would thrive if you could always live like you did this week instead of choosing to stay up all night and sleep all day like those performers out there." He nodded toward the area behind him. "If you marry that long-haired singer, you'll be doomed to live his lifestyle. You will be unhappy."

"I love Paul!" Sandy said indignantly.

"You may love him now, but you'll come to resent him when you never see him, or he sleeps with all the groupies that even now crowd around him. You know, I have this whole compound that would be at your disposal if you would consider staying here with me. Arabians, thorough-breds, any type of horses you could dream of would be yours."

"You can't be serious!" Sandy exclaimed.

"Oh, I am, and I want you to think about it seriously. I think you're wonderful and I'd love to have your companionship here."

"We've only just met. You're mad!" Sandy accused.

"Am I, Sandy?" Crown leaned forward and looked Sandy in the eyes. "Has Paul spent very much time with you this week?"

"Well, uh, uh...no," Sandy stammered, "but he was busy!"

"Yes, and with his profession, he will always be busy. He'll never have time for you. You'll always be sitting in the stale air of some nightclub or other waiting for him to get off stage just to say 'hello' for fifteen minutes before another set starts."

Sandy frowned and looked down at her wineglass. As she traced the shimmering glass edge with her finger, she had to admit to herself that she was unhappy with her relationship with Paul this weekend. He seemed so distant. He didn't want to be alone with her at all, and he was too absorbed with the band. She didn't seem to matter at all. Sandy looked up and smiled slightly. "You're very observant, Jason. I do love Paul, but this week has been disappointing to me."

"Listen to me, Sandy..." Crown began but his words were interrupted by a sharp knock on the gray steel door behind him. Turning toward the door, he called "Enter!" and one of the men who had been left with Tres opened the door and glanced at both of them.

"Uh, someone wishes to speak to you, Mr. Crown," the man's eyes glanced nervously back and forth between Crown and Sandy. He nodded slightly to a red door on the other side of the room. Crown promptly rose and walked toward the red door.

"Stay here, Sandy and think about what I said," Crown advised. "I'll be right back."

Both doors closed, and Sandy sat quietly mulling over the amazing events of the last two hours. What an adventure she had had this evening! Poor Tres had been beaten, but thank goodness Jason Crown arrived when he did to put an end to the nightmare! He seemed to do the right things to appear kind, but there was something about him she strongly distrusted. And yet, he was right about the way Paul was treating her. Paul did not act like himself. If she didn't know better she'd think that he was a different person from the one she fell in love with. Sandy sat there another five minutes and then decided that she should just thank Jason for his kindness and be on her way. Glancing at her watch, she noticed that The Beatles' second set should be ending soon. She could see Paul in a few minutes if she hurried.

When she entered the red door where Crown had gone, she could hear him angrily reply to someone on the other end of the telephone. "The bombs beneath the stage are safe! No! No security was breached! And that's that!" He angrily slammed the red phone down and banged his fist on the table. "Damn Russians!" Crown punched three numbers on a white phone and ordered the person on the other end to locate Bob Chapman and slit his throat. "Tell him it's for informing on me to the Russians!" he fairly shouted into the phone. Sandy shrunk back in fear from the obviously irate man, jarring a vase on the end table beside her. Immediately, Jason Crown swung around to stare incredulously at the shaking girl. Sandy instinctively grabbed the table and doorknob on either side of her as she felt the lightheadedness that plagued her whenever she became stressed. Somehow she stayed conscious to see Crown race across the room and hold her up.

"Sandy, it's okay. Here, sit down." he said soothingly. Once she was seated and had had some water, Crown sat beside her and chided her, "I warned you to stay where you were. Now that you've overheard that conversation, you no longer have a choice about staying or leaving. I would have preferred that you **chose** to stay here with me." His eyes glinted sharply with determination. "But now you **have** to stay."

"No!" Sandy exclaimed immediately.

"Sandy, I don't think you understand. Choices are over for you, but if you agree to cooperate, I'll send your band friends on their way with no harm done."

"You don't mean that you would hurt Paul and his friends? Oh, my God!" Sandy gasped as the realization began to sink in. Jason Crown meant business!

"Yes, Sandy, I would. This is my compound, and my word is law here. One signal from me and your precious Paul will never play guitar or sing again. Sandy, think, if you do love him, let him go. I will treat you well, and you'll have whatever you desire"

"Except freedom." Sandy drew in her breath. "Jason, I thought you were kind. Why did you save Tres from that red-headed brute and me from that awful Dodd man if you're this evil?"

"I'm a survivor, Sandy. Tres and you were innocent in your wandering so there was no need for force. But now you've heard my phone conversation and stumbled onto my secrets, I cannot allow you to leave. If I did, the Russians would kill you anyway. Believe this or not, but I do care for you. I need you. For the first time in my life, I truly feel something special that I thought I would never feel. Keeping you here is the only way to protect you."

Sandy's thoughts raced. This was crazy! But he definitely had the upper hand, and she felt so helpless. Tears spilled down Sandy's face. She covered her face with her hands and tried to imagine any way out of this situation, but she could think of no other solution. She didn't want to see Paul, John, Cynthia, George, and Ringo beaten like Tres had been. After about ten minutes of silence, Sandy finally uncovered her face and wiped her tears away. "What do you want me to do?" she said resignedly.

"Copy this and sign it. My men will make sure he gets it," he said as he handed her a sheet of paper. He had written a letter to Paul while she had been in shock over the ultimatum.

Sandy held the letter in her hand and wept bitterly. She had gotten herself into this mess and there was no way out now. If she didn't go along with this madman, Paul and all of his friends would be in serious danger. He was right. There was no choice.

Sandy sighed. She started writing.

Dear Paul,

I'm writing this last letter to you as I leave. Please don't try to find me. It would only be too painful to see you again. I love you and always will. But I can't live your lifestyle. I can't be like Cynthia and the others who sit and wait and adore while being kept prisoner by your demanding schedule. I need my own life back, my horses and the clean air.

Please think of me fondly. I love you and wish you success in this wild career of yours. You and your band have a true gift for what you do. I'll watch you and share your triumphs from afar.

Love always,
Sandy

It was done. She had copied the letter he had given her. But while the letter she had just written was forced upon her, its contents rang true, and she knew that Paul would recognize that. She wondered how this man could know so much about her when they had never met before. He was right about her need for her lifestyle instead of Paul's. She knew that Paul thrived on performing. He would never give up the noisy clubs filled with music to live her type of life.

Sandy was very sad. Paul was the one true love of her life, and while they were very different people, there could never be another who gave her such excitement and desire.

* * * * * * * * *

Sandy's note was waiting on Paul's suitcase when he came into his bedroom. "Hey, mates, let's play some cards," he yelled back to the others as he rummaged around in his bag for a deck. Stopping momentarily to pick up the fluttering piece of paper, he read it and handed it to John who had followed him into the room.

"Hey, George, look at this," John said as he handed it to George. George read it quickly and handed it to Ringo. Amazed glances were exchanged. "I guess we don't have to worry about Sandy any more," John said matter-of-factly.

Mal burst through the suite door, calling, "Okay, lads, we've got to go right away!" When he saw the living room was empty, he began opening the bedroom doors until he finally found them sitting on the bed looking moody.

"Hey, you lads don't lag about. There's been some sort of disturbance and explosion or something, they say, in the building where you performed tonight." He paused briefly to catch his breath. "Brian sent me up here to get you. The management is most anxious for us to leave the complex tonight. I think they fear an attempt to harm you. We need to go straight away—get whatever you can carry. There will be a helicopter waiting on the roof. Brian says he'll have someone pack the rest of your things for you later, and it'll be sent to you."

All four men immediately began to scatter in all directions to gather their belongings. "Are there security people to take us to the helicopter?" Paul asked.

"Yes, they're waiting outside the door to the suite now." Mal said.

"Mal, find Cynthia and send her in here," John requested urgently.

"Okay. You blokes hurry now!" he urged as he rushed out of the suite.

A few minutes later, the blonde slipped through the door. John immediately stopped packing and took her aside. "Cyn, do you know anything about Sandy leaving?"

"No, when did she leave? I've been resting all evening as I wasn't feeling well." George, trying to move his suits from the closet to the case on the bed, brushed against Cynthia, and she immediately stepped out of his way.

"Ta," George murmured and continued to pack.

"I don't know, Cyn, but she left poor Paul a note saying that they're through, and we're worried about where she went. We just want to know that she's okay." John said.

John kissed her lightly on the lips. "I'm awfully glad you're here. We've got to board a helicopter in a few minutes. They'll pack our things and ship them later. Come on with us. I want you to ride with me." John reached down to rub her swollen abdomen and they smiled at each other.[74]

* * * * * * * *

As the small but somber group hurried with the guards to the helicopter on the roof, silver gray eyes watched intently. "Your friends leave you so easily" Crown whispered to the sobbing blonde next to him at the glass wall. "You know their music is really what they live for." As Crown reached out to touch his companion's silky blonde hair, his hand received a slap. "Ha! Ha!" he chortled, "such spirit, you'll fit right in here."

Sandy cowered in front of the glass wall in Crown's office. What could she do to get out of this mess, she thought wildly. She was caught and she knew it.

Suddenly a calm feeling came over her. She tuned out the room with the gun-carrying men and the frightening threats of this maniac. She was suddenly back on the afternoon when she met Paul. He was rubbing her hurting head under the oak trees at her uncle's estate. She heard his words vaguely. What was he saying? Both of them were laughing. He was telling her about Brer Rabbit and the Tarbaby since she had never heard it before.

Sandy breathed deeply and opened her eyes. She realized what this vision meant. Paul was telling her how to get away from this horrible man! A children's fable. It was daring, but if it worked...then again, if it didn't, she couldn't be any worse off than she was right now.

Summoning all the courage she could, Sandy sighed deeply and audibly, catching Crown's attention just as she hoped. "What is it, Sandy, are you tired? You're not going to faint again, are you?"

"N-n-n-n-no," Sandy stuttered wide-eyed. "I'm just glad you aren't making me go out there on the balcony and wave good-bye to them." She feigned her relief, but Crown took it as genuine. Although he cared for this girl in a way he hadn't experienced before, he yearned for power over her. He would not be satisfied until she accepted that he possessed her.

"Well, my dear, you know that Paul won't believe this unless he actually sees you waving to him. Come, let's go out together and bid them farewell!" He grabbed Sandy's shoulders and guided her ahead of him through a French door onto the balcony. She glanced frantically around as though to grab onto something. "Look, you've got to accept this situation. You're going to be here with me. The sooner you accept it, Sandy, the easier it will be on you."

Tres, who had been bandaged up and was sitting in Crown's office, managed to pull herself up into a standing position so she could see what was happening between Crown and Sandy on the balcony. She watched in dismay through the glass wall as the drama unfolded. She would be able to report later the young girl's bravery.

Sandy gritted her teeth and grabbed the railing of the balcony and bowed her head. It would take all the courage she could muster to do what she knew she must. She had noted the adjoining building's roof, which held the helicopter, was about five feet from the balcony's edge. She began to pray the simple prayer the nuns had taught her not so long ago in Germany: "Our Father who Art in Heaven, hallowed be thy name"...Sandy's eyes betrayed her thoughts as her gaze swung irresistibly to her destination only a few strides away. Brownie, her favorite bay mare could easily make that, she thought. And she would do it.

Crown watched as she positioned herself as close to the end of the balcony as she could get in an effort to get closer to her love on the helicopter. He tried one more time to get Sandy to accept the situation. He wanted desperately for her to look at him like he had seen her gaze at the McCartney youth. "Take a last look and wave good-bye!" he urged her. To his surprise, she didn't burst out crying like he thought she would.

Instead, she turned her head, swirling her waist-length golden hair as she said defiantly, "I wouldn't let Paul make love to me before we married, and he was my life. I'll die before you ever touch me!" And then she was airborne, swinging lithely over the railing in a frantic scramble to reach the nearby rooftop. Crown made an effort to tackle her, but Sandy was too fast. Her years of horseback riding had toned her muscles to near perfection. His brief grasp on the heel of one of her boots was enough to throw her off balance, however.

For one frightening but hopeful second, it looked like she'd make it. She hung to the ledge and finished the prayer she had begun on the balcony. But Sandy couldn't hold on. Her scream during her long fall to the ground from the seventh floor was covered by the sound of whirling helicopter blades as the Beatles' craft was airborne. Tucked tightly inside the helicopter by their security guards, Paul and his friends never saw the horrendous drama that was taking place.

When Sandy plummeted to her death, still filled with love for Paul, her death unwittingly completed the process, which ultimately reunited them. After her fall, Sandy became aware of a bright light beckoning her. She stared into the bright light to see a familiar figure walking toward her. As he got closer, she saw it was Paul waiting there with open arms for her. Filled with delight, Sandy ran to join him.

"Hello, love, I've been waiting for you..." he whispered as he put his arms around her and kissed her gently. Together they walked further into the tunnel that led to the white light.

Crown gazed down at the rumpled shape surrounded by a pool of blood far below and uttered, "Oh, what a waste!" He shook his head, as though to shake loose the image of the beautiful frantic girl falling to her death. Feeling cheated of his prize, he ran his hand through his thick black hair. He felt a sense of loss that he had never felt before. For the first time in his life, he knew that **he** needed another person, and he fell to his knees trying to deal with this realization. Vulnerability was not something that Jason Crown allowed himself since he had obtained his ugly facial scar. He fingered it absentmindedly as his survivor instinct emerged again. "It's that guitar player's fault! I'll make that McCartney pay some day for what he cost me!" he vowed in an ominous tone and then went inside his office to deal with his other intruder.

"Now you will tell me one last time, Mrs. Van Heusen, exactly what you were doing in that hallway where you were found?" Crown's voice was low and deadly. He was exasperated over the events of the last few hours, and in no mood to deal with the detailed cover-up that would be necessary. His eyes pierced hers in a solemn stare.

Tres sat up and tried to get her swollen mouth to move. "Like Sandy said, we were just exploring and that wall moved, so we came in to see what was in here." Tres shook her head and contorted her face and body to try to look as scared as possible. She realized the only hope for the success of the mission was for him to think she really had wandered into the area unwittingly.

"Please, please let me go. Sandy's death was an accident, but if you kill me, that will be murder. We really got in here by accident. We had no reason to come in except curiosity," she begged and began to cry. "I want my husband! Geoff!"

* * * * * * * *

'God, please help me help Tres...' Geoff prayed fervently as he slid stealthily back through the maze of air ducts. After emerging in an unoccupied room and straightening his clothes, he visited numerous areas of the compound asking for Tres. He had to appear like the concerned husband looking for his wandering wife. This was one time that Crown's cameras would be used for him instead of against him, Geoff decided vindictively.

"Crown...Crown...let me in!" Geoff ordered, knocking finally at the door of the plush office complex.

Inside Crown's glass-walled office where Tres sat in pain, Crown glared at her and then at the office door where Geoff was pounding. "Just a minute, Mr. Van Heusen," he called through the door to Geoff. He then snarled to one of his two henchmen, "Carry her back into the other room and then go get me an update on the condition of the merchandise." Since Chapman had already informed the Russians of the security breach, he decided he'd better have irreproachable proof that there had been no tampering of the bombs.

Tres' head was throbbing as she felt herself being lifted and carried into the adjoining room. When she saw the man who carried her dash out of back door of the office, she had the thought that she would never see Geoff again. Hovering on the edge of unconsciousness, Tres was vaguely aware of what Crown was saying to the man who had now returned. "You're sure. No sign of any tampering. Everything is fine. Hmmm..." Tres felt extremely light like she was floating...she was flying above a field and down below she could hear Geoff's voice. No, no, I can't let myself black out, she thought as she struggled to stay in reality.

Geoff faced Crown indignantly as he entered the office. "Where is my wife?" Crown's oily smile disgusted him. Crown stood his ground and met Geoff's gaze coolly.

Crown countered Geoff's question with another question, "Why would I know?"

169

"With all the cameras you have in this place, you know where everyone is!" Geoff answered calmly. Geoff made an effort to maintain a non-threatening stance. His fists wanted to reach out and strike the S.O.B. in front of him, but he forced his hands into his pockets.

"Why isn't she with you?" Crown probed. Geoff despised the casual way Crown flicked lint off his jacket as he tried to look unconcerned.

"She was, but she and her friend went to find the ladies' room. I think they got lost." Geoff frowned at his business associate. "With all these people crowding in here for this concert tonight, I'm worried about her. There are too many dangerous types around these rock and roll bands..."

"Yes, quite. I see your concern. Well, I'll certainly get my staff to look at the tapes of the last hour. Do you think that will do it?"

"She's been gone about that long.".

"I'll let you know as soon as I get any word. Where will you be?"

"Our room. I'd like to carry out the shipping deal we've worked out. Don't let me down in this, Crown." Geoff admonished as he opened Crown's office door.

"Oh, I won't, I assure you, Geoff," the older man promised. After the mahogany door closed, he sighed with relief that the loose ends of this evening were being tied up neatly. The shipment of bombs was not compromised, so he would not have to suffer through any Russian reprisal. Chapman and his persistent disloyal actions had been eliminated, and the Van Heusen drug shipping deal, which was worth millions, was saved. Except for losing his virgin, fortune had smiled upon him this evening, Crown surmised.

* * * * * * * *

Tres returned to consciousness to see Crown standing over her again.

"Glad to have you back with us. Would you like to go back to your husband now," he asked softly.

170

"Uh...yes!" Tres managed to gasp. She made an effort to sit up, but Crown's hand on her shoulder held her down.

"Well, I accept your story that you didn't mean to come into the private areas. Now you must agree to what has happened this evening..." he leaned down so she could see his steely eyes very closely.

Tres nodded. "Uh-huh..."

"Your friend jumped from the railing because she was upset over her boyfriend leaving in the helicopter. Her death was an accident. Do you agree?"

Tres nodded. "Yes..."

"And you were beaten up by some thugs who tried to steal your purse." His face was so close to hers now that she could feel his hot breath on her cheek. Tres cringed involuntarily.

Crown smiled, apparently satisfied that a professional in espionage would not have the reactions he saw in this young woman.

"Do you agree" he asked.

Tres nodded once again. "Yes. Yes. There were two of them. They wanted money."

"Excellent. I'll have someone help you get back to your suite. It's a shame for a guest at my estate to have such a horrible experience." In spite of her training, Crown's smug smile gave her chills.

When Tres was finally delivered to Geoff in their suite, he had their bags packed. "Oh, honey, I'm so glad to have you back," Geoff whispered as he wrapped a blanket around her on the couch. "Let me get a bellboy up here for the luggage, and we'll go." Tres only nodded. She was drowsy from the pain medication the nurse had given her. "I've got a helicopter waiting. It will take less time to get you to London." Again Tres' response was a nod, but she smiled weakly with her eyes closed.

"Promise you'll hold my hand all the way there? I need you." she whispered.

Geoff bent to kiss her on the lips. "Yes, Tres, I won't leave you for a minute. I promise."

Tres nodded and was still. Geoff kissed her cheek and worried about what type of injuries she might have. He couldn't help but think about how he would usually be worried about the outcome of the mission. Priorities in life had really changed for both of them. She had needed achievements and he had needed excitement. Now what they both needed most was each other and the love they had. Geoff held her hand on the helicopter ride to London and remembered the lyrics to one of the Beatles' songs, "...and when I touch you, I feel happy inside..." Simple yet true, mused Geoff as he gently squeezed Tres' hand.

LONDON

The debriefing revealed that the beautiful girl who had died so bravely was the niece of Wellington, the temporary head of the bureau. He was crushed by her loss, but Tres was glad she could at least give Wellington the comfort that his niece died trying to stand up for her ideals.

There was still the unpleasant uncertainty that they might not have been successful in their mission. If they had not convinced Crown and his people that the warheads were untouched, the whole mission was in vain. The Russians would simply scrap the whole shipment and make up some more. The only way that they could breathe easy was if the disarmed warheads reached Cuba without detection of the tampering. Then when it would be too late to replace them, and they would have to back down when the American President Kennedy gave them an ultimatum.

"Time will tell," Wellington said philosophically as the debriefing ended, and Geoff and Tres left by ambulance to get Tres some medical care.

* * * * * * * * *

Sitting in Tres' hospital room, Geoff idly thumbed through a copy of Time magazine, when he suddenly stared. "Whoa!" he exclaimed. Incredibly, there was a full-page spread on a model who looked just like Sandy. Looking closely, Geoff examined the credits to find that her name was Candy Wellington. How ironic, thought Geoff, to see Sandy's twin in a magazine, looking so alive and robust when her sister had just recently plunged to her death. Damn Crown! His evil could ruin the lives of millions of people.

Geoff glanced at his watch. It was about time for Tres to be returning from her examination. When they had wheeled her off on the gurney, he had given her a gentle kiss. She seemed to be in great pain, so they had given her a generous dose of pain medication.

"I love you. See you soon!" he had whispered as he stroked her hair.

By now that painkiller had kicked in, and she probably didn't even know where she was, but he wished she were back here with him. He sat alone in the hospital room and thought about all that had happened on the Crown mission. Thank God Tres had not been taken as poor Sandy had been. The thought of losing Tres made him quake with fear. Startled out of his reverie by a nurse entering the room, Geoff was glad for the interruption.

"When will my wife be brought back in? Have you heard?"

The petite redhead looked genuinely confused. "Your wife? There's been no one assigned to this room today. I'm here readying it for a chap who's coming out of O. R. in a few minutes." She hung a plastic bottle on a rolling rack beside the bed as she spoke.

Geoff, stunned by her reply, stared open-mouthed at the young nurse.

"Yes, yes," he insisted, "She was taken from this room a few minutes ago, I mean about 45 minutes ago. Now, where **is** she?" he finally found the words he needed to say. The nurse just shook her head.

"You can try the entry desk. Maybe they moved her to another room."

Geoff hardly heard the last of her reply. He was dashing down the pale green hall, dodging slow moving patients and visitors to get to the registration desk. Out of breath and sweating, he jostled the waiting visitors drawing sharp cries of dismay. Grasping the edge of the counter with white knuckled fists, he demanded, "Where is my wife?"

"Sir, these people were here first" the prim looking lady reminded him firmly. The matron's warning didn't detour Geoff as he pounded on the desk.

"WHERE IS MY WIFE?" he howled.

"Mrs. Reed, please direct the gentleman this way." a distinguished-looking man suddenly loomed from a nearby doorway.

"Sit down, sit down, I'm Mr. Campbell," he waved Geoff toward a leather chair.

"I don't want to sit down! I WANT MY WIFE!" Geoff shouted, hands on his hips.

"Who is your wife?" the man smoothed his full moustache and placed his hand on his telephone.

"Tres, I mean, Alexandria Van Heusen," Geoff said firmly.

After dialing a few numbers and asking a few questions about Tres, he murmured "Hmmm," and hung up.

"No one by that name has checked into our hospital as a patient or a visitor."

"WHAT? I KNOW SHE'S HERE! I BROUGHT HER HERE MYSELF IN THE AMBULANCE!" Geoff's voice rose in volume to a full shout once again.

"I'm sorry, sir, but you need to leave now, " said the administrator crisply, standing up to indicate the end of the conversation. "Our records are correct. We don't have your wife here."

A few minutes later, Geoff was tossed unceremoniously into the brisk night air of London by the hospital security guards. Geoff shook his head in disbelief at this whole mess. He hoped fervently that he would wake up from this horrible nightmare to find Tres beside him in bed.

* * * * * * * *

"It will be a few minutes before Mr. Wellington can see you..." the plump middle-aged secretary began nervously. "Hmmm. He's on the phone..." She twirled a cinnamon colored curl with her fingers.

"Damn it! He **will** see me and **NOW!**" Geoff exploded as he brushed her aside to swing open the red double doors.

"No, No! You can't go in there! Mr. Wellington, I'm very sorry! He wouldn't wait!" Her voice sounded shrill like a small child tattling on a little friend.

As Geoff strode to tower over Wellington in his desk chair, he thought briefly that he had always liked Bea, until now.

"Uh, it's quite all right, Bea," Wellington nodded to Bea as he hung up the phone. "I was expecting Mr. Van Heusen."

"I'll bet you were, you bastard!" Geoff's face was a thunderous expression of the anger he felt inside, thought Wellington, as he swung around to face him. Youth was a perilous time, he decided, rich with emotions, but poor in the self-control it took to make effective decisions.

"Have a seat, Geoff," Wellington offered.

"Why does everyone want me to sit down? I don't want to sit down! I want Tres! It's that bloody simple. I want Tres!"

Wellington bobbed his head. "Yes, I know you do, but that's not what's best for you." He pulled an ivory pipe from a drawer and lit it. The puffing and wheezing of the smoke reminded Geoff of the warm fires he and Tres had enjoyed in the last few months.

"Who the **hell** are you to decide that, Wellington?"

"Look, Geoff, you knew when you signed on with us that Interpol would control who you worked with and where you served. You agreed to those terms. Now grow up! We're not choosing football teams on the playground here!" Wellington's gray eyes glittered cruelly back at Geoff.

"But we're married!"

"Ah, you're mistaken. Check legal records in the U. K., and you'll see; you've never been married. The older man puffed laboriously on his pipe.

"You can't do that!"

"Oh, yes. And if you're worried about your trust fund, don't. When you do marry, the time stipulated in your father's will starts. You'll find the right girl eventually."

"Where is she, Wellington?" Geoff demanded.

"That information is not available, Geoff, you know that." Wellington replied patiently.

"I can't believe this! I love Tres!" Geoff complained bitterly.

"You **think** you do, but think, Geoff. You two slept together. We can't have two agents sharing such intimacy. It would only endanger you both. Trust me. It's better this way."

Geoff sat in stunned silence. This was his worst nightmare...to have finally found the love of his life and then have her taken away. He wanted to crush Wellington's all-knowing skull, but the espionage training kicked in. He realized that violence wouldn't get him what he wanted.

"You're an S.O.B., Wellington, but I guess we'll both have to live with it." Geoff growled at the older man.

Wellington grinned, "That's it, mate, let it out. But you know I'm right. Now you take a little time off...a vacation will do you a world of good. Chase a few skirts, and you'll come back as good as new!"

Geoff nodded stiffly and left Wellington's plush office while he could still control himself enough not to rip him to shreds. His mind was numb as he sat in a nearby coffee shop. All he could think of was Tres. He could see her beautiful blue eyes...how they glittered with determination whenever she was helping to plan strategy.

So many memories came flooding back to him that he was overwhelmed. The booth around him became his haven with its shadowy depths. He gratefully slumped in the dark corner and gave into his grief. Bitter tears of remorse fell unashamedly onto his folded arms. How had he let this happen? Didn't he know what the agency's response would be after this mission? He should have seen this coming and resigned once he had gotten back from the Crown estate. Oh, God, where was Tres? Was she safe? Was she missing him? Did she share his agony? There was no telling what they had told her to get her to go along with this scheme.

Geoff sat with his head in his hands a long time. He had lived his whole life without having anyone close to him until Tres. His parents were always jetting around the world to some glitzy event. Maids and nannies couldn't supply the love he desperately needed. Now he realized now how precious Tres' love and intimacy was. That's all that mattered to him now...not the money, power, and excitement he had thought was so important.

A song came on the coffee shop radio that broke through his internal turmoil. The gentle sound of "P.S. I Love You,"[75] spoke to him. The Beatles...that was the group whose concert they attended the last evening Tres was with him. He remembered her shimmering blonde hair in the lights of the club and the softness of her hand when he held it at their table.

Suddenly, his mind cleared, and he straightened up with new resolve. He couldn't accept this. He had to get over this self-pity and get on with the matter at hand. There had to be a way to find her, to get her back into his life. Pulling out the ever-present notebook, Geoff began making a list of agents who owed him favors and could help him look for Tres. Snapping it shut with a satisfying smack, he left that booth ready to take on the world. He would find Tres he decided, or die trying.

* * * * * * * *

Back in his flat, Geoff poured himself another glass of whiskey as he slumped in his overstuffed chair. Time had passed since he had instigated the covert search for Tres, but there was no sign of her. He was losing hope. She **must** have been taken to a hospital as badly as she was hurt, Geoff thought. Still all the operatives he had put on alert were giving negative reports about any hospital patients of her description. Glaring at the television screen a few feet away, Geoff stretched out to hear the evening news. The commentator looked grim as he described how tensions had increased between the U. S. and Cuba. Backed by a satellite map of Cuba, he went on to say that Soviet-supplied missile installations were evident in Cuba, which could have triggered war. The presence of the the warheads had prompted a naval blockade by the United States. Today, October 28, the Russians had agreed to remove the weapons. The Cuban Missile Crisis was over.[76]

Geoff sighed and took another deep pull on his drink. Well, at least their mission had been successful. Maybe soon his own private mission would be too. He shook his head and covered his head with his arms as the tears began to fall again for Tres.

BOSTON, MASS.

Tres sat up in bed listening to the joyful shrieks of the neighborhood children playing outside her second story window. Sliding carefully out of bed, Tres watched them build a snowman, sled down the driveway, and toss snowballs at each other. Such simple carefree joy! She thought wistfully how Geoff and she had had so much fun in the snow in the Alps. Tres abruptly turned away from the window and pulled her fuzzy robe closer. Why do I always think of him in every instance? No matter what I'm doing, I can't escape him! "Ahhh!" she exhaled heavily as she sank onto an overstuffed chair, "Stay out of my mind, Geoff!" she warned an empty room.

It had been a long struggle to recovery. The blows she'd taken had resulted in a concussion. There had also been damage to her spine. Pinched nerves in her hip still bothered her. The doctors said it would take years for her body to resume the active life of karate and sports she had enjoyed before.

The physical problems that Tres endured didn't concern her family nearly as much as the emotional scars left from her encounter with Geoff. Tres was a listless shell of her former self, not the vibrant driven self-confident girl they knew. She rarely talked and especially not about Geoff and their break-up.

Tres shivered and pulled a blanket over her. She grabbed a fuzzy brown teddy bear from the shelf nearby to cuddle. Immediately she recalled the day Geoff bought a little white polar bear for a crying child in Heathrow airport.

"No! No! I won't think of you!" Tres yelled aloud as she propelled the stuffed animal across the room, crashing it into a framed picture. As soon as the heavy frame thudded to the floor, the bedroom door opened.

"Alexandria!" her Mom, Janis, cried as she swooped in. "Are you all right?" She saw the broken picture frame and then the tears on Tres' cheeks and realized that her daughter needed some company.

"Oh, honey," she whispered urgently as she went down on her knees and hugged her weeping daughter. "Shh! It's okay!"

"It's **not** okay!" Tres straightened out of her Mother's embrace. "It's **not** okay! He didn't love me! He used me! Geoff used me! I was just part of the big mission! He can go to **Hell**! And I want to **tell** him so!"

"Did he tell you he didn't love you, honey?"

"No."

"Then how do you **know**? Did he just say he didn't want to be married anymore when you two broke up?"

"No."

"Well, what **did** he say then?"

"He didn't say anything. He had someone else do it."

"You mean..."

An outraged Tres crossed her arms and fully shouted at her Mom. "Yes!"

Now, calm down, Alexandria. Now you took someone else's word that Geoff didn't want you?"

"Oh, Mom..." Tres lay back on the chair resignedly. "You just don't understand the agency."

"No, that may be true, but I do understand relationships. Now you and Geoff were very close. Your father and I would never just walk away from each other. Love is not that way."

"Well, he DID walk away, Mom. And that proves he doesn't love me!"

"But you still love him. I know that man you work for explained to your father and me that Geoff shouldn't see you...something about a psychological report, but I think you need to talk directly to Geoff, Alexandria. You owe him that."

"I owe him nothing! He's through with me. He's made that clear enough by not even trying to see me while I was recovering."

Alexandria's Mother bit her lip. Should she tell her daughter that right after she came to recuperate with them that Geoff had called? They had been warned to shield their daughter from Geoff. But if she had these strong emotions, she needed to work them out with him.

"Come on, honey, come downstairs and have some breakfast." urged her Mother.

"No," Tres shook her head. "I'll just go back to bed, Mom."

Janis sighed. The fire was gone from her daughter's eyes. That cold vacant look that had become a shroud for her old vibrant persona was back in place. All she wanted to do these days was sleep.

"I'll bring something up to you later. Dad and I love you."

With her Mother gone, Tres curled up on the bed and let the hot tears pour down to soak her pillow. She could think of nothing but how Geoff's face looked when she last saw him at the hospital. How could he stand there and smile so lovingly and lie to her about his commitment?

LONDON

The freezing drafts of Britain's harsh winter permeated Geoff's flat, but he didn't notice the cold as he slumped in his overstuffed chair with a glass of scotch in his hand.

Staying with the agency these last few months had been the hardest thing he'd ever done. Each time he saw Wellington he felt like spitting on the S.O.B. But at least his job gave him access to all the phone numbers and reports he needed to keep the search going. Geoff had called in all his favors. He had agents all over the world looking for Tres. Wherever Wellington had hidden her away was a secure place.

Geoff was vaguely aware of the BBC compere smoothly introducing his guests for the show..."playing a song from their latest LP release...John, Paul, George, and Ringo." As the beautiful harmonies of "There's A Place" began to fill the dirty flat, Geoff almost didn't hear the faint knock on the door. Two knocks, two more knocks, then three knocks. In his haste to get to the door in his inebriated state, Geoff tripped on fish and chip wrappers littering the floor. He fell to his knees and slid most of the way to the door.

"Yes?" he said when he finally managed to crawl to the door.

"It's Simon," came the reply.

"Simon says?" Geoff replied.

Silly greeting but effective, Geoff thought as he opened the door to admit Ian, a chap from the agency. After settling down with their drinks, Ian spilled his news, "They think they've found her, Geoff.

"Where?" The glint in Geoff's eyes returned as he leaned forward expectantly.

"No, they're not sure..."

"Where?" Geoff grabbed Ian's lapels and brought them face to face. "Tell me, damn it!"

"America...Boston...her parents' house...." Ian said quickly. He straightened his clothes after Geoff released him.

"Damn! Her Mother **swore** she wasn't there when I called."

"Well, maybe she wasn't at the time. Our fellow over there who's been watching the house says he's picked up on pharmacy supplies being delivered which would correspond with her injuries. She could have been transferred there recently from a hospital." At Geoff's contemptuous look, he said defensively, "Well, hell, Van Heusen, he HAS got his full-time job with the agency to do, after all! He's just doing this as a favor to you, Geoff. He must have missed the actual event of her arriving."

Geoff resignedly fell back against his chair. "Yeah, sorry. I'm just a bit anxious."

Ian looked around the disheveled flat distastefully. "Looks like you could use a maid, mate." He picked up a dishcloth near his boot and tossed it toward the kitchen area.

"Nothing matters without Tres," Geoff said dully. He took another deep drink of his liquor.

"Yeah, well, pull yourself together, mate. You've got to mount that white charger and get yourself over to America. If she's well enough to be home, she might be well enough soon for a mission. Wellington is no fool. He won't waste any time getting her lost in the field."

Geoff nodded and rose with Ian. "Thanks, Ian, I'll leave tonight." he promised before he saw his friend out the door.

BOSTON

Geoff slumped down in the front seat of the little gray rental car. Tres' dad was blowing the snow off the sidewalk. "Damn, don't they ever both leave home at the same time?"

Tres' mom pulled up in the family station wagon, apparently from a trip to the beauty parlor. Geoff watched through his binoculars as she paraded around her husband showing off her new beehive hairdo. This is getting me nowhere!, he thought in despair. Laying his head back, he stared up to begin counting the holes in the lining of the roof once again. That had become his little project to keep his mind busy during this stakeout. He had to find the right time to enter the house and find Tres. He knew she was there. He had flowers delivered in her name from her uncle and aunt who were missionaries in Africa. Her mom had received them graciously. (That ruse always worked to verify someone's presence.)

Picking up the binoculars and looking again, he was immediately interested in what he saw this time. Tres' dad was carrying a tuxedo in a clear plastic bag as he followed Tres' mom into the house.

Geoff's heart leaped to life. His head roared. If a tux had been rented, that meant they were going out! Or did it? Could they be having a party at home? Geoff looked down at his watch. What was the date? Of course! God, it was New Year's Eve! He hadn't even been aware of it because he was so consumed with thoughts of Tres. I'll just hope and pray, he thought, and wait!

* * * * * * * *

At 8:30 P.M. the door opened and Tres' parents emerged, dressed in their finery. As soon as their car left the drive, he donned a black turtleneck and black ski cap to begin the trek through the shadows to Tres' house. Entrance through the attic window on the back of the house was easily accomplished. A quick check of each of the ten rooms yielded no one, however.

Frustrated, Geoff stood on the front staircase and prayed for help. "God, please..." he began. Then he heard it. A tiny sound, then silence. Again, a little splash. Then silence.

The bath, I didn't check the bath, Geoff chided himself as he crept up the stairs. As he got closer to the bathroom in Tres' room, the sounds were more audible. There was no singing though. It might not be her! A cold fear gripped Geoff. She ALWAYS sang in the bath!

Taking a deep breath, he flung open the door. And there she was. Her blonde hair was swept up in a twist on the top of her head with feathery little tendrils cascading down around her angelic face. Water glistened on her ample breasts. The rosy nipples he loved to taste were peeping from billowy soapsuds.

There was a minute of silence as both absorbed the shock. Then Tres threw her bathing sponge at Geoff, which he dodged. Soapy water splattered across the black and white tile floor.

"Get out!" she screeched.

"No," Geoff said firmly as he stepped forward.

"Get out, I said. I don't want to see you!" Tres said through clenched teeth.

Geoff walked closer. He wanted to touch her. It had been **so** long. He stretched out his hand to help her out of the tub.

"No, get out! **Now!**" she yelled.

183

"Tres, there's something that I need to explain to you."

"No!"

"Tres, please! Please! I love you, Tres!

"You said that. You already said that a long time ago. You said it many times. It didn't mean anything then, and it doesn't now!"

Geoff went down on his knees beside the tub. He had to let her know he was sincere. Grasping her hands, he stared straight into her eyes, "Tres, please listen. I really need you. I have been looking for you since Wellington hid you from me."

Tres looked surprised. "Are you trying to claim you didn't abandon me?"

"No, I didn't abandon you! Think, Tres! Wellington wanted two agents who weren't intimately involved. He made the choice to separate us. I've had forty agents looking for you for the last two months." Geoff leaned forward to kiss her, but she turned her head away. He continued to try to convince her in a low voice. "Tres, whatever Wellington told you was a lie! I love you. I've searched for you constantly so we can spend the rest of our lives together. Please listen!"

Tres turned her back to him. "Could you please hand me a towel?"

"No." Geoff shook his head and grinned. "You're too beautiful to cover up." She noticed how his eyes dipped to gaze at her breasts. It made her tingle even though she didn't want it to.

"Get out! Get out now or I'll scream!" Tres warned.

"No! I'll never leave you!"

"You mean again? Get out" Tres screamed and tried to push Geoff out of the bathroom.

She wasn't strong enough to move him and she screamed in rage at her weakness.

Geoff was so absorbed in Tres' reaction that he didn't hear the quick footsteps coming up behind him. Grabbed from behind, Geoff acted instinctively. He came back with his elbow that doubled up his surprise attacker. A quick glimpse of sparse gray hair as he turned to throw his opponent kept him from completing the potentially lethal move.

"Dad!" Tres shrieked as Geoff froze and let the older man go.

"**You leave my daughter alone!**" Carl Feldon managed to gasp in spite of the blow he had just received. "**Get out of here like she said! Now!**" Although Tres' Dad knew Geoff could end his life in one blow, he persisted in trying to protect his daughter. The older man staggered to the nearby wall to steady himself. He clutched his abdomen and was obviously in pain.

Geoff backed slowly out of the bathroom. "I...I...I love your daughter, Mr. Feldon. I'll never stop loving her." He turned back to Tres who was clutching a towel around her wet body. "Just give me a chance. Just let me talk to you. Please!" he begged to Tres.

"**No! Leave!**" Tres insisted.

"You heard her, son. **Out!**" the older man ordered. He stood between Geoff and Tres in an instinctive effort to protect her. Near the door to the bedroom stood Tres' mother with tears streaming down her cheeks. Geoff walked by her with his head down.

"She needs time, Geoff," Mrs. Feldon sounded genuinely sorry for the rejection. She touched Geoff on the arm. "I'll talk to her. Maybe she'll let you come back soon and you two can talk it out." Geoff grabbed Tres' Mom and hugged her.

"Thank you for being so open-minded. I **do** love her. I've had people looking for her ever since she disappeared from the hospital. I came as **soon** as someone found her. **You** know I called about her here." Geoff said softly.

"Just give it time, Geoff. She just needs time," the gray-haired lady answered as she wiped the tears away.

The next two weeks, Geoff lived in the rental car. He watched the house constantly hoping that one day, Tres would relent and come out to see him. Since she didn't, he began to call the house twice a day to try to talk to her. Tres' Mom stood at the window in her daughter's room and held back the lacy curtains. "He's still out there, dear!"

Tres' Dad who sat in a nearby chair nodded. "Yeah, I wish he'd help me shovel the snow off the walk tomorrow instead of just sitting there watching." He puffed thoughtfully on his pipe.

"Well, he can just go away. He deserted me and I can never trust him again!" Tres mumbled as she turned over in bed to face the wall.

Tres' Mom gave a significant look to her husband and took a deep breath. She knew what she had to do. "Tres, we haven't been honest with you, and I'm sorry," she said softly.

Tres sat up and looked at her Mom in surprise. She had never known her Mom to lie to her before. She waited patiently. When nothing else was said for a few minutes, Tres asked "What is it Mom? What do you mean?"

Her Dad pulled his pipe from his mouth and spoke, "She means that I asked her not to tell you Geoff had called."

"Oh, he calls all the time! Every time I get to sleep he calls!" Tres wailed, covering her head with a pillow.

"No, dear, " her mother said, shaking her head at her daughter, "this was back when you first came home."

"What?" Tres sat up in bed looking from one parent to the other in amazement. "He did **what**? He called **then**?"

When both of them nodded, Tres gasped, "Mother!" She looked from her mom to her dad and back again incredulous that they would keep Geoff's call a secret.

"Honey, that nice man at the agency where you work said it would be best if Geoff and you didn't have any more contact. He said Geoff would try to reach you but not to tell you."

"What? Wellington did that?" the angry girl shrieked.

"I'm sorry!" Tres' mother whispered.

Tres' dad spoke up. "Now it's really my fault! I told your Mother we needed to follow that fellow's directions; that he knew better than we did about such things. I'm really sorry, baby"

"So all this time..." Tres began. She looked like she was deep in thought.

"Yes, he was looking for you," her mother said.

Tres slid beneath the pink flowered comforter. "I need to be alone." Tres' trembling voice was muffled under the covers. Her parents crept quietly down the stairs to give her the privacy she needed.

* * * * * * * *

A few days later, Mr. and Mrs. Feldon were shoveling the sidewalk next to the street where Geoff's car was parked. "Honey, let's go out tonight!" Tres' Dad called to her Mom. "I hear there's a good movie that starts at 9:00!" Geoff made a mental note to write them a letter one day advising them not to publicly announce their plans. Unscrupulous people would take that as an invitation to enter the house. He absentmindedly stared at the ceiling as he lay flat on the seat to avoid being seen.

"Yes, dear, 9:00 it is, then, Tres' Mom said very clearly. Almost a stage whisper thought Geoff. "I guess Tres will be taking her bath then, won't she?" her Mom continued.

"You're right. 9:00 is what time she usually takes her bath, right before the show she likes to watch on TV," Tres' Dad announced.

Geoff's face had a huge silly grin on it. "It's a date!" he whispered to himself.

That night at 8:50 P.M. Geoff watched intently as the Feldons' car pulled out of the driveway. His shadowy figure once again slithered across the darkened yard and up to the second story window. This time he knew exactly where to look for the girl that haunted his existence.

Once again, the soft lapping of the water led him to her bathroom. As he got closer, he heard the soft melody she was singing. Gently pushing open the door, Geoff feasted his eyes on a beautiful sight. Tres was submerged in piles of foamy bubbles. The water beaded on her full breasts, and Geoff longed to caress those rosy nipples to see them harden with desire. Her hair was pulled up into a ponytail with a baby blue satin ribbon. The curls tumbled down her neck looking so touchable.

She stopped her singing as soon as she saw him. "What are you doing here?" she challenged with a withering look that made him wonder momentarily why he had come.

187

"I'm here to talk. I have to tell you what happened." Geoff said solidly.

She said nothing so Geoff went down on his knees beside the tub. He looked directly into her green eyes and spoke from his heart. "I've looked for you ever since you disappeared. I've stayed in the agency just so I could keep the contacts to help me look for you. Wellington is clever. He was looking out for our performance in the field. But he doesn't know how much I love you. I would never give up. I called here. I've looked everywhere. And if you kick me out tonight again, I'll still be sitting in that car out there until I grow so old, they'll come and take me away. That will only be because I've lost my mental faculties. I won't leave you willingly." He stopped and continued to look directly into her eyes. "I mean this, Tres. I love you and I'll never stop."

Tres sighed. "My parents finally told me a few days ago that you did call when I first came home. I thought you really didn't want our marriage except for the mission's sake. That was what I was told." Tres sounded bitter.

Geoff reached out tentatively, wanting to touch her but not daring to. For a moment, time stood still, and they each struggled with the decision of whether to give their trust again. Since she didn't flinch, Geoff sensed that permission was granted for him to at last touch her again. When Geoff's fingers gently stroked her shoulder, Tres shivered. "You're cold, love," Geoff said as he stood up and pulled her out of the bath water. He looked into her eyes and could sense no resistance. "Let me warm you up," he whispered as he pulled her tightly against him and covered her mouth with his. He kissed her thoroughly, running his tongue sensuously over and under hers. His hands drifted hungrily down her slick back to cup her buttocks.

Tres didn't protest. In fact, she couldn't help responding. Her arms went around his neck as she kissed him passionately. Geoff continued to rain small kisses all around her mouth and down her neck as she gasped, "I love you, too, Geoff. I'm sorry I believed Wellington. I thought you pretended to love me to complete the mission. I have missed you so much."

"Let's go into your bedroom and let me show you how much I've missed you," Geoff whispered hoarsely. He guided her hand down to feel the hard bulge at his crotch.

"Only if I get to show you how much I missed you," Tres smiled up at him. They had needed other things in the past, but now both of them knew that they needed each other.

NEW YORK

Paul, John, George, and Ringo were crammed into the Ed Sullivan Theater elevator with their manager, their two road managers, and three Sullivan employees.[77] They all braced themselves for the onslaught of cameras and reporters that would inevitably be waiting on the other side of the silver sliding doors. "Ding" the bell rang as they reached the second floor. One of the Sullivan security men stepped out with arms spread, halting the mad dash of the waiting crowd. Paul sighed inwardly with relief, as there were no hysterically screaming girls in the crowd confronting them. They had only been here one day, and this was already getting to be a bit much. In England, they were popular and drew crowds, but these American girls...they couldn't go from one room to another without a mad scene. Only anxiously leering reporters now gleamed ravenously at them.

"Hold it, now, guys!" the stocky security man stated authoritatively. "The Beatles and Mr. Sullivan will see you for the rehearsal at 1:30 P. M. today in the ground floor auditorium. We ask that you give these boys some peace right now as we've got to get them to make-up and give them time to check out Studio 50's set-up.[78] You'll get your stories, just not right now."

The band stood smoking quietly while the security man spoke, trying to ignore the cosmic flashes of light that persisted throughout the man's speech.

The other two men with the Beatles began to gesture and gently escorted the horde of reporters into the elevator as the Beatles and their managers exited into the hallway. As the exchange was made, Paul suddenly saw her out of

189

the corner of his eye. There she was. This time he knew he was really seeing her. She wasn't a figment of his imagination. She was petite but slender, ash blonde hair to her waist, huge blue eyes, and she had a hauntingly sad expression. When he turned to take another step and glanced back, she was gone, just like the last time. Maybe, he thought, I'm going mad. Maybe seeing Sandy was a sign I've completely lost my mind, he mused.

I thought our relationship was through when she left me that note at the Crown estate gig, Paul thought with a sense of dread. He knew that if she had guessed that he was an imposter for her fiancée, the Beatles' dreams of success were finished. Yet, here she was following him, appearing and disappearing as though magically. I have to end this relationship permanently, Paul thought frantically. I've got to talk to her! No more of this sleuthing; it was just too spooky and was preoccupying his energies which should be spent on this American tour. They already had a number one hit in America.[79] This was the success that the group had struggled for five years to achieve. Yes, whatever he had to do to get rid of this girl, he would have to do it, he decided.

The make-up people had prodded and examined them, and it was time for the sound check, so they would ensure all the equipment worked properly for their performance. They were whisked down passageways quickly to the theater hall so they could avoid the press.

George had a hoarse throat, so Brian approved his return to the hotel to be cared for by his sister.[80] He'd be feeling better for tonight's show, the entire group hoped. With George missing, Neil, one of their road managers, offered to stand in for him.[81]

Paul was just warming up his bass guitar when he saw her again. Over in the wings, a petite blonde leaned in the shadows watching as he broke a guitar string. He'd only gotten out the first two letters "sh–" when John leaned close to his ear, "Just change the bloody string, Macca. If the press get hold of yer tongue, son, we've had it. Watch yer mouth!" John then ignored the face Paul made at him. He continued his rhythmical strumming as Paul began the arduous task of fixing his guitar, grumbling all the while. When he finally had the bass tuned, Paul glanced in the wings to see the girl again, but she was gone. He was positive it was Sandy, but he had to get his mind back on this performance, now a few hours away.

After the soundcheck and press conference, Paul, John, and Ringo were forged through a chanting mob into the black limousine for the ride back to the hotel. Girls climbed on the hood, hung onto the doors, and screamed from all directions. "Hey, look at that one!" John exclaimed. "She's got hold of the windshield wipers!" All three laughed and waved as two policemen dragged the girl from the hood of the car.

Paul held a small radio to his ear. "It's 4:30 Beatle time here in New York City," the announcer stated, "and it's thirty-five Beatle degrees."[82] Paul's eyes became wide. "Whoooo!" he yelled and shook his long dark locks side to side. All three laughed hysterically. It was incredible how wonderful stardom felt at that moment. This is where they had always hoped that they'd be yet it was wilder than their dreams.

"I think they like us here." Ringo stated calmly as girls clawed at his window. The scene as they left the car and entered the hotel was a nightmare. Mounted police as well as police on foot tried to hold back the enthusiastic crowd, but in the end, policemen had to hold hands and surround the three Beatles to push their way through the mob of hysterical girls. "Push Paul out first. He's the prettiest," quipped John.[83] Despite many pushes, pokes, and jabs, the three at last made it to their suite.

"Whew!" Ringo moaned as he loosened his tie and fell on a bed. "I'm hungry. Hey, ask Brian when we can eat!" he called to John in the living room.

John, hastily taking off his coat and tie, glanced around to look for Brian. He spotted him across the room with several men he didn't know. They all looked uptight in their smart suits, which always bothered John. He was the one who felt they were 'selling out' when they had agreed to make Brian happy and wear suits for performances.[84] So it was with great relish that he had an opportunity to embarrass their posh manager.

191

"Hey, Warden Epstein," he said as he nudged their friend and manager with his elbow. "Food! When do the prisoners get fed, sir?" He was on his knees, crumpling his blue corduroy hat as he begged. Brian and his visitors laughed heartily at John's piteous expression.

"All right! The lot of you can wait. I've got food coming in twenty minutes," he said, glancing at his watch.

John crawled on all fours to the bedroom door as the men continued to chuckle. "Feeding time here at the prison is in twenty years!" he yelled to Ringo, who was lying on the bed reading a book. "Help!" John screamed in mock terror as Paul lashed at him with an imaginary whip, and the two of them tumbled into Ringo's room. Paul pushed John's rear with one foot, and they both ended up on the floor giggling.

"You've got your hands full, Brian," commented one of the visiting men as he and the other men shook their heads at their dramatics.

"They are a silly lot sometimes, those four, but **so** talented," Brian said. The others nodded in agreement. As he spoke, the door slammed shut, and they could hear a pillow fight going on among the three young men.

"Feed us, warden!" they all howled repeatedly. Brian looked embarrassed. He shook his head at the other men.

"Being stuck in hotel rooms drives them nuts! But I hope they get used to it." Brian said solemnly.

* * * * * * * *

After dinner, the three band members and Neil sat smoking, reflecting on the wild day. "Hey, Paul, you looked distracted during our sound check," Neil observed. He had been right at Paul's elbow on stage in George's place. Neil had been with them their whole careers, and they often entrusted some private moments to him, so it didn't seem intrusive when he asked, "Are you nervous about tonight's show?"

"No!" Paul shook his head. "I thought I saw someone I knew there at the stage."

"Oh?" John raised his eyebrows. He always had to know what Paul was thinking.

"Yes, well, I've actually seen her several times lately." Paul said.

"Oh? A bird's on your mind? What a bloody surprise!" John teased.

"It's not just any bird. It's Sandy. I've been spotting her in odd places. It's like she's following me."

"Oh, no!" Ringo said as he exhaled smoke.

"I was afraid that wasn't finished. It was too easy." John stated as he crushed out his cigarette. He frowned and shook his head.

Neil nodded. "Yeah, it seems that she's changed her mind, that one has. She's a pretty lass though.."

The room was quiet for a few minutes as each man considered the possibilities. Finally Paul spoke, "I've got to talk to her, to break it off completely. She'll know I'm not Paul if she's around me much more."

"Maybe she'll just think that success has changed you. A lot has happened since you saw her last." Neil suggested.

"Yeah. I thought that Paul must have been daft to have never slept with her, but it's a good thing. If you fancy her, at least you won't have to try to imitate Paul's humping." John laughed and took a sip of his drink.

Paul looked thoughtful. "At least she'd be the only one to know beyond a shadow of a doubt that I was an impostor in that way, and it'd be bloody impossible to prove."

"I reckon you're right there, son," John snorted. "When we were in Hamburg with George, Pete Best, and Stu Sutcliffe, we all shared girls in one big fucking pile in our rooms at the Bambi Kino theatre.[85] Between the whores and the groupies that hung about our rooms, our dicks just about fell off! But Paul was never much of an orgy man," John grinned delightfully and then suddenly looked sad as he was thinking about the good times with his friend. He rose abruptly to stand by the window, arms crossed. As he appeared, back lit by the room light, a thousand girls screamed his name and surged over the wall of already battered policemen. The others looked at each other silently. They knew what John was thinking, how much he missed

193

his close friend whose little red car had wrecked after one of their characteristic disagreements.

"Let's check on George again," Ringo said suddenly as he and the others left the room.

Paul remained to put his hand on his new friend's shoulder. John didn't turn. He looked down at his hands as Paul spoke. "I can never replace Paul for you. I know that. You mates were much too close. I'm sorry you lost him."

The crowd below the lighted window caught sight of Paul then and roared its approval, overrunning once again the dedicated 'men in blue'. Both men ignored the fracas they were causing outside. They were silent for a few minutes as the squeals escalated to frenzy.[86] "I didn't mean to hurt him," John stated as he faced the window.

"I'm sure that wherever he is, Paul knows that, Johnny. The crash was an **accident**. It was just horrible timing for it to follow your argument".

The phone rang in the living room. "Hey, boys, get away from the window!" Brian shouted toward the bedroom. "The police are threatening to walk off the job if you don't." John and Paul shared an amused but chagrined glance at Brian's request. They were trapped by the very success that they had long craved. John was giggling, which was his usual response to grief,[87] but he wiped a tear from his eye discreetly as they both walked to the door to follow Ringo and Neil to George's room.

"Thank you, Paul, you're a good mate, too," John said in a low voice, "It's just that I wish Paul and Stu could be here to see this." They had caught up with Ringo and Neil hanging on the door jam of George's room, peering in. Ringo had heard the mention of their two deceased friends. "What? So they could be as bored as we are?" he responded.

"Ahhh!" John made a threatening noise and pushed Ringo as in a mock fight which thrust the other three into George's room where they all ended up laying in a pile on the floor.

"Shhhh!" George's older sister attempted to hush them, but it was too late. George was awakened. George was up on one elbow surveying the mass of bodies beside his bed.

"What? Intruders in me room?" George lifted up and hit those he could reach with an available pillow.

"A flogging!" Paul quipped in a falsetto voice, "Please don't cane me. I'm the innocent one!" Paul was trying to get up, when George's pillow caught him at just the right angle, knocking him back into Neil and Ringo who were also scrambling to get up. They bumped John and all fell again on the floor, giggling, a tangle of flailing arms and legs.

"You'll pay for this, lad!" John warned, leaping over toward the bed to grab George's pajama shirt and pull him down on the heap of laughing musicians.

"Stop!" shouted George's sister, hands on her cheeks. She lived in America and hadn't been around George and his friends for years, so she was shocked as well as amused at their outrageous behavior.[88]

"All right!" came an authoritative voice from the doorway. "That's enough, boys!" Brian's hands were on his hips and he tried to look his sternest. "Now the car will be here in thirty minutes for the final run-through for the Sullivan show. Get ready and quit this fooling about before someone gets hurt!"

Unabashed, the five men climbed to their knees and followed John's lead as they all bowed over and over to their manager, arms swaying over their heads in homage. "Oh, for pity's sake," the impeccably dressed man stated as he stomped his foot and turned to go back to the living room. "And you among them, Neil!" he sputtered in disgust to their road manager who was joining in on the prank. At that, the four Beatles each slapped Neil affectionately on the shoulder or back, and all five of them laughed.

"Now, George, are you sure you're well enough...?" the pretty blonde began.

"I'm fine, Sis, now quit acting like Mum and let me get dressed. As you go, be sure you get your ticket for the show tonight from Eppie. The security guards will give you a hard time again if you tell them you're my sister to get in. They say all the girls are claiming it now that you were successful last time."[89] George grinned at her.

George's sister laughed. "Take care. I'll see you tomorrow."

"Ta," George kissed his sister's cheek as she left.

The rest of the evening was a blur for the Beatles and their managers...the screaming fans, the crush of visitors with backstage passes, the clamoring press...Everyone wanted a piece of them. Their only release came when they got on stage. They truly enjoyed playing their music. Now that fame had come, it was the only time they were back in control. Even when the four young men were shepherded back to their hotel room at the Plaza, a number of people managed to penetrate the Beatles' security force. All four promptly filed into the bathroom following the concert to avoid the flood of people lounging in all the bedrooms and living room of their suite.[90]

"Who are these people?" Ringo sounded amazed nodding at the closed bathroom door.

"Oh, people who can't take 'no' for an answer... politicians, P. R. people, marketing people, hangers on," Paul answered as he bent to light his cigarette on a match John offered. George and Ringo both lit up also and all four sat back smoking silently, Ringo and Paul on the side of the bathtub, John on the toilet seat, and George on the sink.

"Let's give them time to thin out, and then we'll go change," John suggested. "With the crowd outside the hotel, we can't go anywhere, but we can party here."

"Is Mal getting us some good-looking birds?" Paul asked.

"He said he would. What about all these people?" George worried.

"We'll lock the bedroom doors! Take turns guardin' 'em if we have to!" Ringo suggested adamantly.

"How about you, John, plans with Cyn?" Paul asked sweetly. Even though he had attended John's wedding when he married Cynthia, he couldn't resist teasing John about his ineligibility for the groupies he so enjoyed.[91]

John promptly hit his friend's shoulder playfully but with enough force to knock him back into the bathtub where he was perched. "Ouch!" Paul complained and pretended to cry.

"The wife's probably going to be asleep soon. I never knew pregnant women got so tired all the time. Don't worry about me. I'll get mine tonight, though," and John laughed as he pulled the sprawled Paul back up onto the side of the tub.

"When we go back out there, I'll get Neil to make sure the liquor cabinet is stocked and we have plenty of food. Maybe some sandwiches." Paul always keeping the group on track began to plan.

"Don't forget cigarettes. Make sure we have plenty of those." George reminded.

"Yeah, and condoms. Don't forget those!" Ringo added. Everyone nodded emphatically.

Paul pulled out a small notebook from his suit jacket to jot down the various items they wanted.[92]

"Efficient Paul," observed John and then leaned forward to oink at his friend.

"Jealous John," Paul replied to John and returned the oinking noises in John's face.

Ringo shook his head at the two beside him and turned to his other friend. "How's the fever, George?"

"Much better, thank you. I feel a little tired, but I'm jazzed about our gig tonight. I may pass on the birds though. I don't know. It depends on how good-looking they are."

"Leaves that many more for us!" Paul winked at John. "But we'll tell you tomorrow all about what you missed," And all of them laughed. They were sharing their need to celebrate. After all, tonight's performance was before the largest television audience ever recorded in American history.[93] Success was a heady sensation.

* * * * * * * *

The next day, Paul awoke alone about noon. Neil and Mal had removed all the visiting groupies from the suite during the wee hours of the morning, making arrangements for transportation, and bribing members of the press with promises of exclusive interviews as needed.[94] Paul's first sensation when he moved was that of a horrible hangover. He stumbled out into the living room in his robe to find Brian,

Neil, and Mal calmly reading papers and watching television. "Aspirin," Paul whispered. Mal obligingly arose to bring him water and aspirin.

"Can you drink some juice?" he asked.

"Cup of tea, please," Paul again whispered and sank down on the couch covering his eyes, waiting for Mal to bring it to him. Mal had performed this service many times. It was part of his job and Neil's job to take care of them whether it was handling their luggage, settling disputes, fixing faulty equipment, or as in this case, being the nursemaid. Their recent huge jump in fame was going to intensify the number of unusual tasks they would be asked to do, Mal reasoned.

One by one, the others wandered in, all silent, like Paul, all hungover, except Cynthia. John's pretty blonde wife, usually quiet anyway, was the only one who helped herself from the buffet breakfast laid out on the bar in the suite.

After a half-hour of nourishing silence, Brian finally folded up the Wall Street Journal and spoke. "Boys, we've got a press conference this afternoon and a tour of Central Park. Try to pull yourselves together." Four sets of bloodshot eyes glared murderously his way.

"Be good lads," he droned on. Take a nap and a bath. You'll feel better...By the way, excellent reviews on your performance on the Sullivan Show last night."[95] He laid his paper on the coffee table between several pairs of legs resting there. "Did you realize no crime was reported for the ten minutes you played last night?"[96]

George's eyebrows arched and he pursed his lips. "Hey, we're crime-fighters!"

This brought the first smile of the morning to the lips of those who had partied too much last night.

* * * * * * * *

That afternoon, the struggle to get to and from Central Park was wild. Mounted and walking police held off thousands of fans who shared what was called 'Beatlemania'. The band had never experienced anything like this phenomenal on such a grand scale. It was thrilling, amazing, and very scary. Fans broke through barriers and could (and would) if given a chance, tear them literally apart. All of them knew the dangers, but Brian, Neil, and Mal constantly reminded them to stay together, stay within the police protection area, and move quickly from car to building.

When their stretch limo pulled up to the Plaza Hotel after their excursion in the park, which was actually a photo opportunity, Paul saw her again. She was standing at the edge of at the hotel away from the crowd of screaming girls surrounding their car.

When the police opened the door and each of the others exited, Paul sat transfixed watching her. The long flaxen hair was blowing in the stiff February breeze. She reached up to pull a strand of it away from her face. There was a sudden glint of gold near her neck, and then it was Paul's turn to get out of the limo. His eyes were still on the blonde beauty near the building. The whole crowd scene around him faded and all he saw was her. She was calling him. He could feel it. Ringo ahead of him stopped suddenly due to a delay in getting the group through the crowd. Knowing this was his one moment; Paul instinctively ducked under the linked arms of the policemen beside him and charged through the crowd to the astonishment of all around him. He dashed toward Sandy and followed her as she began to run down the side of the building. As soon as the fans recovered from their shock, they began the chase also.

Paul felt compelled to catch her. He had to talk to her; to end this mysterious stalking that made him so uneasy and distracted. Then Paul's mind returned to the reality of his situation. The screaming fans were getting closer. Where was she going? Ah, an unguarded back door to the hotel...the employee's entrance around the back. She was clever! He bounded up the steps two at a time behind her, chased her up the hall, around a corner, and then, she was gone. GONE! Paul could hear the frantic mob behind him. There were no policemen here ready to intercede. He was about to be ripped apart! Paul thought about something George had said recently in an interview. 'If their fans ever got hold of them, they'd die laughing.[97] He had thought that amusing once, but it didn't seem so right now!

"Sandy!" He yelled as he stood squarely in the middle of the long hallway. His voice echoed around. The fans had reached the stairs. "Sandy!" he tried again. I know she can hear me, Paul thought. She has to be in one of these rooms. "Sandy, let me in! Please! They'll kill me...Sandy!" he wailed.

Abruptly, a door opened a little ways up the hall, and he dove into it just as girls came pounding down the hall, screaming and crying.

Paul, panting from fear and exertion, leaned against the locked door staring at the nonchalant beauty whose body language told him she was annoyed.

"You could have been hurt," she scolded coldly.

Paul breathing heavily stumbled over to the bed and collapsed. "Why did you disappear? Why didn't you let me in sooner?" he wheezed.

"I didn't ask you to follow me,"

"Sandy, I needed to see you. We have to talk.." Paul said.

Both were silent as they continued to listen to the wails and screams coming from the other side of the door. They could hear the police arriving to remove the girls from the hallway.

"Come on, young ladies, these people in these rooms didn't come to stay here to be bothered with all this noise," a man's stern voice chided as the screaming subsided.

Neither spoke, but they stared suspiciously at each other. Finally, Paul decided he had to be the one to get this conversation started. There were some things he needed to know. "Why have you been following me?"

The question appeared to make her angry. The girl had her arms folded over her chest and she patted her foot. He could tell that she was trying hard to stay in control.

"I had to see you to face you with something." The tension increased between them as they silently stared at each other. When Sandy finally spoke again, her tone was coldly bitter. "It was so easy for you to leave a defenseless girl behind at Crown's Estate, wasn't it?" she accused.

Paul was shocked. She thought he had left her at the Crown compound? It hadn't happened that way at all. She should know that. Maybe she thought that he should have chased her down and begged her to come back to him. "Sandy, the letter you left me in my room...you said you never wanted to see me again, that you had left the estate and not to try to find you. I believed it..."

"Oh." was all she said.

He was now sitting on the side of the bed. She suddenly sat down beside him. As she did, Paul could see clearly the locket around her neck. He recognized it as the one that the real Paul had given Sandy as an engagement present. It reminded him of his mission in finding her, to let Sandy down easy, but more importantly to end the relationship permanently to safeguard his secret impersonation of Paul.

"They're probably missing you by now," she said.

"Yeah, we don't want Brian going mad. The mates will be out looking for me and we'll all get torn apart by that mob!"

"Call him," she suggested gesturing to the phone on the bedside table nearby.

She smiled as she heard the howl on the other end of the line as he held the receiver to his ear. "WHERE ARE YOU?" screamed Brian Epstein.

"I'm fine, Eppie. Relax, I'm fine. I'm in the hotel in another room. I'll call you when I need you to send some people over for me, okay?" Paul responded.

"NO! DO YOU HEAR ME? NOW WHERE ARE YOU?"

Paul hung up.[98]

They sat in embarrassed silence for a few moments, both staring down at the rug.

And then their eyes met, and both felt the undeniable attraction. The girl realized from the start that Paul did not know who he was dealing with. He had never been able to tell her apart from her twin. It wasn't right to have this need for intimacy with her sister's fiancée. Still, she reasoned, Sandy had died, and he thought the relationship had ended long ago. Obviously he didn't know of Sandy's death. If she

201

was honest with him that she was Candy, and he was still attracted to her, maybe it was okay.

Paul was numb over the strong desire he suddenly felt for this girl. The few times he had been around Sandy, she had never seemed this dynamic or spirited. He knew he couldn't divulge his true identity, but maybe she would be willing to begin a new relationship.

The space between them on the bed had miraculously disappeared. Paul found his arms around her as he tentatively kissed her cheek. It felt so natural to hold her close. She smelled like roses and her skin was so soft!

"Paul..."

He immediately stopped kissing her, waiting for her to protest.

"I know you think I'm Sandy, but I'm not. I'm Candy. I've been worried that you had hurt my sister. That's why I've been following you. I wanted the truth."

Paul looked deeply into Candy's eyes. "I loved your sister. I would never have hurt her."

"I know that now. And **she** left **you**...is that true, Paul?" Candy looked up into Paul's huge expressive eyes and became entranced with the beauty of this magnificent man. I should tell him that Sandy's dead, she chided herself, but she knew that his sensual mood would end with that news.

"Yes." Paul nodded. "It was a sudden decision on her part."

"Do you still want to kiss me, not my sister?" Candy wished with all her heart for his answer to be 'yes'. She wanted him desperately.

"Yes," Paul said. He grasped her face with both hands and kissed her deeply, enjoying the taste of her. "I know why you're named Candy..." and he kissed her again. Everything from there seemed to go in fast motion. It was an afternoon that both Paul and Candy would always remember.

* * * * * * * * *

The others had never seen Brian so frantic. In the hours following Paul's disappearance, he paced the floor, bit his nails, swore, drank wine, and muttered to himself. At one point, John, George, and Ringo locked themselves into the bathroom to plan strategy.

"I know it! I know it!" Brian fumed to Neil and Mal. "They're going to try to escape. They're going to try to go out THERE and they'll all be killed! Why did he do this? I'll have him chained to me if we ever get him back!"

Neil and Mal were worried too. They knew how dangerous a mob of fans could be. They looked at each other and at the bathroom door and pondered what to do.

The phone rang, and all three jumped to get it. Brian was faster. "No, it's not convenient. No, not now. Tomorrow! Yes, tomorrow. Call me tomorrow. Good-bye."

Neil's eyebrows were raised in anticipation. "LIFE magazine reporter," Brian explained briefly as he shook his head and rolled his eyes. Any other time he would have been thrilled to talk about a cover story, but right now Paul's survival not his promotion was foremost in his manager's mind. Looking more frustrated than ever, he paced around the couch. "Neil...Neil...go in there," he pointed at the bathroom door, "and tell them we just have to wait. Beg them. We can't let another one out of here!" Brian insisted, almost in tears.

"Right!" Neil answered and knocked on the bathroom door. "Could I come in, mates?" he asked. The door opened to admit him.

As the door closed, the phone rang again. Mal got there quicker this time as Brian had paced to the bar. "Uh-huh, here's Brian," Mal handed the receiver to Brian who jumped across the room in one bound to accept it.

"Paul! Where are you?" Brian began. "Stay right there, and I'll bring the police to get you straightaway." Brian wiped his forehead with his handkerchief in relief.

After Paul had told him the room number and the location of the room, he added, "Uh, Brian, bring me a shirt and some pants, will you? Mine are a little ragged looking. They sort of got ripped off me."

"I understand. Right. Oh, goodness, I hope there weren't any photographers there when the girls did that!" Brian's tone sounded extra pious.

Paul laughed. Dependable Brian, always thinking of their image.[99] Well, that was his job, thought Paul. "No, Brian, no photographers. We're safe there," he said into the phone with a smile. Paul decided to only share the details of today's adventure with his three mates, and well, maybe Neil and Mal. Let Brian think those 'horrid' girls overran him. Maybe he'd feel sorry for him.

After hanging up, Brian immediately began making the necessary phone calls as Mal knocked on the bathroom door to deliver the good news to the mates inside. Then, with Paul's fresh clothes in a duffel bag, Brian grabbed his coat and paused long enough to point his finger at the three remaining Beatles who had filed out of the toilet. "You stay here, boys, do you hear? I mean business!" he threatened. Ringo cocked his head to the side and frowned as though he didn't understand. George put his hands up as if he was being arrested, and John jumped forward trying to bite the finger Brian was waving at them. Brian shook his head mumbling to himself as he walked toward the door to the suite.

Watching their peculiar but likable manager walk out, George delivered the first line of their standing joke, "One day we're going to drive him NUTS!"

"HE ALREADY IS!" John and Ringo chorused gaily.

* * * * * * * * *

Meanwhile, Paul sat alone on the bed he and Candy had shared just a short while ago. He reread the following note that she had left him while he slept:

> *Dearest Paul,*
> *I think you're wonderful. I'm glad you loved my sister. I know she loved you.*
> *I enjoyed our experience together. It was "gear" as you say.*
> *Much success in your career! Hope we see each other again sometime.*
> *Love always,*
> *Candy*

Paul lit a cigarette and thought about the two sisters and his strong but very different feelings for them. They were both gorgeous, but with his career taking off, he wanted to stay unattached right now. He hoped he would somehow meet either or both of them again when he was ready to settle down.

SUSSEX, ENGLAND[100]

In the late 1970's, Tres and Geoff were on a horseback ride through the woods when they decided to leave their estate and trot on the road a while. As they approached a neighboring estate with its huge stone fences. Tres felt dizzy and needed to dismount. Concerned, Geoff glanced through a nearby wrought-iron gate, and spotted some people who might help them.

"Hey, could you help us? My wife may faint. Could you help please?" Geoff called through the gate. The huge black spidery wrought iron gate swung open and Geoff immediately recognized Paul McCartney, now a mature man.

Holding Tres up with one arm and grasping the two horses' reins with the other hand, Geoff attempted to enter the doorway.

"Here, let me help," Paul said grabbing the reins. "Come in."

Geoff lifted the barely conscious Tres up and took her inside the door that a pretty blonde woman opened for them.

While lying on the couch in their huge den, Tres began to get more color and eventually could sit up. While Tres had rested, everyone introduced themselves, and Geoff told them how they were neighbors to the west.

"You're used to people knowing you, but do you know us?" Geoff asked.

Paul and his wife, Linda,[101] looked baffled.

"No, I don't believe so. Have you been to our concerts? Maybe we saw you there."

Geoff smiled. "Do you remember a three-day gig at Crown estate in 1962?" Paul and his wife both looked blank. Paul obviously thought he was a daft fan, thought Geoff.

"Remember when you opened the door for us, Paul." Geoff said simply.

The color drained from Paul's face. A guarded frown crossed his handsome face and he gave a significant look to his wife. She looked frightened and backed away from Geoff slightly.

"Linda, you need to go check on the children. Tell them I'll be back out in a few minutes and we'll open Stella's[102] birthday presents then." He looked and sounded distracted as he nervously ran his hands through his long brown hair. "Paul, are you sure...?" Linda moved closer to a white control panel set into the wall like she might need to punch a button or two.

"It's all right, love, go ahead." McCartney nodded at the door. Linda glanced from Geoff to Tres and then silently took her cue and closed the double doors behind her.

Tres spoke, "Relax, Paul, we're completely out of that life now. We are your neighbors by accident, and I really did feel faint today on our ride. Since this coincidence has occurred, however, I wanted to tell you something no one else could." Tres said softly.

Paul looked very interested. This man who had become a rock star legend[103] leaned forward in his chair, "Yes?"

"The reason you never saw Sandy again was that she died the night you left Crown's estate."

Paul drew in his breath sharply.

"She followed us into secure areas Crown didn't want us in and was captured. She saw you boarding the helicopter that night. Rather than let Crown have her, she tried to jump to the roof where you were and fell to her death. Sandy really loved Paul. And I'm sure they were reunited by her death." Tres had tears in her eyes when she finished recounting the story.

"I'm glad you told me. I always wondered what had happened to her. I didn't know if I broke her heart by avoiding her at the Crown estate, and that's why she never contacted me again, I met her twin sister later, but she never hinted that Sandy had died."

"This coincidence today convinced me that you were meant to know..." Tres smiled.

"Thank you." Paul sat looking down at his hands for a few moments. "I have struggled with what to do with myself for years. Replacing someone else has been difficult. I'm really natured a lot differently from the other three chaps I was asked to throw in with. While they have accepted me in the past, it's really hard not to give in to the businessman tendencies I have.[104] The group's had some real problems, as I'm sure you've read in the news.[105] Paul laughed and stroked the light beard he was sporting. I do love my wife and my children and living in the country. This is really my life now, not the old Paul's."

"We're glad you've found a way to make things work out for you, Paul. You have a tremendous amount of talent that is your own. You may have replaced someone else at one point in time, but your musical growth has been your own." Tres said.

"Yes, and you kept a lot of people from being disappointed by doing what you've done." Geoff added, "The Beatles have been and still are very important in many people's memories. Without you, that magic would have never happened for them."

Paul looked genuinely moved. "Thank you. I'm glad I've been able to share my talent. I'm very lucky to be paid for doing something I love."[106]

"I feel better now, " Tres said as she reclined on the couch. She slowly sat up. Paul and Geoff both looked concerned as she tried to stand.

"If you need to stay longer, feel free," Paul offered.

"No. I think I'd better go home," Tres said and immediately grabbed a chair to support herself.

Geoff caught her and carried her back to the couch. "I'll go home and get the car. Watch her until I get back, please" he said dashing out the door to mount his horse.

Paul sat and watched the lifeless form on the couch as he heard the two horses gallop off. This woman knew Sandy, he thought. She was there when she died. That seemed so long ago, but he could still remember Sandy's beauty and innocence. He prayed fervently that Sandy and Paul were reunited that evening at Crown's Estate. He sensed that there was real love there which is indeed rare.

When Linda walked in a few minutes later, Paul stood and gave her a stirring kiss, which delighted her but also surprised her. "Love you," her murmured into her hair as they hugged.[107] He felt so grateful that he had found Linda, the great love of his life.

Tres revived a few minutes later to find both Paul and Linda sitting at her side.

"Where's Geoff?" she whispered.

"He's gone to get your car. Are you all right?" Linda asked.

Tres blushed. "He doesn't know it yet, but I think Geoff's going to be a father."

Paul clapped his hands, and he and Linda grinned. "We're so happy for you. Why don't you tell him? He's worried out of his mind about you." Paul urged.

Tres shook her head. "I'm not sure yet, but I'll go have a test tomorrow. We've hoped for years to have a child, and I want to be sure it's true when I give him the news."

Geoff charged into the room just then. And the three of them helped Tres to the green Jaguar parked outside.

"Take care," Linda said, "Let us know..."

"Okay," agreed Tres. "We're just over there if you'd ever like to visit us." She indicated the direction of their estate.

Geoff and Tres waved at the throng of children in birthday hats that suddenly swarmed around Paul and Linda as they drove down the circular drive and through the wrought iron gates.

* * * * * * * *

The next night snuggling in bed with Tres, Geoff remembered the love he saw when all those children were hanging onto Paul. He smiled at the thought of becoming a daddy.

"Tres," he sounded concerned for her in her pregnant condition, "is there anything you need?" Then he thought of her nightly request for a kiss. "Oh, I know. You need a kiss before you can go to sleep."

Tres turned and smiled at him. She whispered simply, "Love is all I need."

Geoff gave her the kiss as a bonus.

FOOTNOTES

[1]This refers to the first flight for the Beatles to any gig. Brian Epstein, their new manager arranged this. Before, they had either gone by train or van/ferry. George was unwell on this trip and flew over the next day with Brian Epstein.
Lewisohn, Mark. The Complete Beatles Chronicles. New York: Harmony Books. 1992, p. 56.

[2]The Star Club was a much nicer venue with better pay than the other places they had played in Hamburg. Sometimes they played with Gene Vincent or Little Richard who were passing through.
Greenwald, Ted. The Long and Winding Road: An Intimate Guide to the Beatles. New York: Friedman/Fairfax publishers. 1995, p. 96.

[3]The Beatles were scruffily dressed in black leathers until Brian Epstein, their new manager insisted upon cleaning up their image by wearing suits in public appearances.
Hertsgaard, Mark. A Day in the Life: The Music and Artistry of the Beatles. New York: Bantam Doubleday Dell Publishing Group, Inc. 1995, pp. 64, 65.

[4]George had a following which included a group called the "exis" who were very fashionable. They were German art students.
Harry, Bill. The Ultimate Beatles Encyclopedia. New York: Hyperion. 1992, p. 293.

[5]This is poetic license. The drummer during this trip to Hamburg was Pete Best, handsome but reportedly moody and quiet. Much later, June 6, George Martin their new producer showed dissatisfaction with Best. The other members of the Beatles agreed, thus having Brian Epstein, their manager, fire him. They then recruited Richard "Ringo" Starkey, who had played with many bands and whose nature suited the Beatles more.
Hertsgaard, Mark. A Day in the Life: The Music and Art-

istry of the Beatles. New York: Bantam Doubleday Dell Publishing Group, Inc. 1995, pp. 45, 46.
Lewisohn, Mark. The Complete Beatles Chronicles, New York: Harmony Books. 1992, pp. 58, 59.

[6]Stu was the Beatle's first bass player. He was convinced by John Lennon, his close mate to purchase a bass guitar with money earned from the sale of one of his paintings. He never learned to play very well, often turning his back to the audience and camera to hide his lack of ability. He fell in love with a German photographer and left the group to pursue his art. He eventually died of a brain hemorrhage right before the Beatles' 3rd trip to Hamburg.

Greenwald, Ted. The Long and Winding Road: An Intimate Guide to the Beatles. New York: Friedman/Fairfax. 1995, p. 31.

Ms. Kirchherr adds that John Lennon was very protective of her following Stu's death and she will always remember his kindness.

Interview, Astrid Kirchherr, Aug. 9, 1997, Hyatt Regency O'Hare Hotel, Chicago, Ill.

[7]Astrid Kirchherr stated that animosity between Paul and Stu grew from Paul's growing interest in perfecting the group's musical ability while Stu had little musical ability.

Interview, Astrid Kirchherr, Aug. 9, 1997, Hyatt Regency O'Hare Hotel, Chicago, Ill.

[8]John and Paul were "on exactly the same wavelength, with the kind of deep mutual recognition that can sustrain a friendship for many years."

Miles, Barry. Paul McCartney: Many Years From Now. London: Secker & Warburg. 1997, pp. 30, 31.

Paul's deep complex and close relationship with John is revealed in his speech inducting John posthumously into the Rock 'n' Roll Hall of Fame (Jan. 19, 1994). One of his statements was "The joy for me, after all our business shit that we'd gone through, was that we were actually getting back together and communicating once again...That was great for me, because it gave me something to hold on to."

"Access All Areas," Club Sandwich #69, published by The Paul McCartney Fun Club, Westcliff, Essex, UK, p. 8.

[9]To most Englishmen of that era, Hamburg was an city of breathtaking wickedness. The area they were to work in was the legendary cabaret district, a "sex-soaked" part of town.
Norman, Philip. Shout!: The Beatles in Their Generation. New York: Warner Books. 1981, p. 82.
Hertsgaard, Mark. A Day in the Life: The Music and Artistry of the Beatles. New York: Bantam Doubleday Dell Publishing Co., Inc. 1995, p. 22.

[10]Actually, Ringo played in Hamburg in another band when the Beatles were there.
Harry, Bill. The Ultimate Beatles Encyclopedia. New York: Hyperion. 1992, p.623.

[11]This notorious area featured a "bizarre mixture" of pubs, tea shops, clubs, cinemas, and dance halls. The Beatles and other singing groups worked very long hours for low pay in subhuman living conditions.
Harry, Bill. The Ultimate Beatles Encyclopedia. New York: Hyperion. 1992, pp.618-620.

[12]Pete Best, who was a member of the group at the time the Beatles played in Hamburg, said that they would swap partners during the orgies they had with their female fans.
Best, Pete. Beatle!: The Pete Best Story. London: Plexus. 1985, pp. 53a-56.
Hertsgaard, Mark. A Day in the Life: The Music and Artistry of the Beatles. New York: Bantam Doubleday Dell Publishing Co., Inc. 1995. pp. 43, 44.

[13]Paul and the other Beatles wanted desperately to be famous and practiced looking famous in photographs well before they were working steadily.
McCartney, Michael. Remember. New York: Henry Holt and Co. 1992, pp. 28, 76-77.

[14]Neil Aspinall was originally a close friend of Pete Best, the drummer who was asked to leave the group. He also was John Lennon's school pal. He became one of the most trusted and loyal members of the Beatles' organization and is currently employed by Apple Corps.
Harry, Bill. The Ultimate Beatles Encyclopedia. New York: Hyperion. 1992, p. 50.

[15]George Martin, their producer, had great influence on The Beatles' music, offering suggestions, arranging their increasingly complex scores, and playing instruments in their songs.
Harry, Bill. The Ultimate Beatles Encyclopedia. New York: Hyperion. 1992, pp. 437-440.

[16]The Beatles often played during lunchtime in the cellar-like atmosphere of the Cavern club. It is a place they are most often associated with since they played regularly there for a time and drew large crowds there.
Lewisohn, Mark. The Complete Beatles Chronicles. New York: Harmony Books. 1992, pp. 30-31, 67.

[17]Cynthia Powell, a shy reserved girl was drawn to John in spite of his roughness. She changed her looks to suit him and helped keep their marriage secret.
Norman, Philip. Shout!: The Beatles in Their Generation. New York: Warner Books. 1981, pp. 57-58.

[18]Cynthia and John married when John found out she was pregnant and they were often separated during their marriage due to his career. John has admitted in numerous interviews that he frequently had affairs.
Rolling Stone magazine, Jan. 7/Feb. 4, 1971, excerpts taken from Greenwald, Ted. The Long and Winding Road: An Intimate Guide to the Beatles. New York: Friedman/Fairfax. 1995, p. 17.
Red Mole magazine, Mar. 8-22, 1971, excerpts taken from Greenwald, Ted. The Long and Winding Road: An Intimate Guide to the Beatles. New York: Friedman/Fairfax. 1995, p. 17.

[19]Mal Evans, a former bouncer at the Cavern club in Liverpool, was hired as their roadie but actually became the Beatles' companion, friend, and even musical protege at times (when sound effects were needed on albums). He often provided security and procured girls for them following performances.
Harry, Bill. The Ultimate Beatles Encyclopedia. New York: Hyperion. 1992, pp.232, 233.

[20]George Martin is quoted as saying, "John absolutely screamed it. God alone knows what he did to his larynx each time he performed it, because he made a sound rather like tearing flesh."
Vol. 2, The Beatles video Anthology. Capitol Records, Inc. Hollywood, California.

[21]Brian Epstein, their manager was often called "Eppie" by the Beatles.
Harry, Bill. The Ultimate Beatles Encyclopedia. New York: Hyperion. 1992, pp. 224-229.

[22]The word 'grotty' was introduced internationally in A Hard Day's Night, the first Beatles film. Alun Owen, the screenwriter, said it was a Liverpool term abbreviated from grotesque, i. e. "Grotty Jean" a folk figure from Liverpool. Alun Owen speaking in the film You Can't Do That: The Making of A Hard Day's Night.

[23]On the opening night of the Casbah Club, George Harrison and three others calling themselves the Les Stewart Quartet were scheduled to play, but when a quarrel developed, they broke up. George introduced the Quarrymen (Paul and John plus him) to Mrs. Best, the owner of the club, and they played at the opening along with the drummer, Ken from the other group.
Fulpen, H. V. The Beatles: An Illustrated Diary. London: Plexus Publishing Limited. 1983, p. 12.

[24]The term "pie" was a slang term used among the Beatles for a woman's genital area. In the song, Penny Lane which was issued as a single on 17 February 1967. Paul's

comments about this song include the following: 'And we put in a joke or two: "Four of fish and finger pie.: The women would never dare say that, except to themselves. Most people wouldn't hear it, but "finger pie" is just a nice little joke for the Liverpool lads who like a bit of smut.' In 1997, Paul issued an album called Flaming Pie in which the title song has lyrics which support this definition.
Harry, Bill. The Ultimate Beatles Encyclopedia. New York. Hyperion. 1992, p. 515.

[25]George Harrison's sister, Louise, lived in America when the Beatles appeared on the Ed Sullivan show. George grew up in a poor but loving family.
Harry, Bill. The Ultimate Beatles Encyclopedia. New York. Hyperion. 1992, p. 527.

[26]Brian Sommerville worked with the Beatles for 10 months providing the needed air of authority to deal with theatre managers, police, and the press. He arranged the publicity deal with British European Airways which enabled the Beatles to have unlimited air travel between London and Paris in return for their carrying the Beatles carry-on bags.
Harry, Bill. The Ultimate Beatles Encyclopedia. New York. Hyperion. 1992, p. 527.

[27]An occasional nickname for Paul was Macca as John calls him in the Let It Be video. Paul states in his 1989 World Tour program that his nickname among the Beatles was "Macca." George's was "Hazza" and John's was "Lennie."
The McCartney World Tour program, London. EMAP METRO. 1989, p. 9.

[28]In Great Britain, sandwiches are also known as sarnies and butties. A yolk butty would have egg as its filling with butter spread on the bread.
Observation by the author, London. May and Nov., 1997.

[29]The Beatles and their road managers were often trapped in hotel rooms and dressing rooms with little else

to do but to play cards. Alun Owen, the writer who stayed with them on tour to try to capture their lifestyle in the screenplay for A Hard Day's Night stated that they were confined like "prisoners of their success. There's a price to pay for that kind of success."
Hertsgaard, Mark. A Day in the Life: The Music and Artistry of the Beatles. New York: Bantam Doubleday Dell Publishing Group, Inc. 1995, p. 81.

[30]Since Cynthia Powell met John in art school, she changed her hair and clothes to look more like his dream girl, Brigette Bardot, put aside her own career plans, and lived the lifestyle John wanted for them.
Robertson, John. Lennon. London: Omnibus Press, 1995, pp. 8, 12, 16.
Guiliano, Geoffrey, The Lost Beatle Interviews. New York: Penguin Books U. S. A. 1994, p. 302, 303.

[31]When the Beatles played in Germany, fans would literally wait in their sleeping quarters to have sex with them.
Hertsgaard, Mark. A Day in the Life: The Music and Artistry of the Beatles. New York: Bantam Doubleday Dell Publishing Group, Inc. 1995, pp. 43, 44.
Best, Pete. Beatle!: The Pete Best Story. London: Plexus. 1985, pp. 53-56.

[34]Paul McCartney used to play the guitar to block out unpleasantness and escape the world. It became a sanctuary to comfort him after his mother's death.
McCartney, Michael. Remember. New York: Henry Holt and Co., 1992, p. 27.

[33]At the beginning of their residency in London, John, Paul, George and Ringo shared rented living space at Green St. on Park Lane. John moved out to live with Cynthia and Paul moved out to live with his girlfriend's family, the Ashers of Wimpole Street. The Saddle Room mentioned in this passage was an actual pub that Ringo and George used to visit.
Vol. 2, The Beatles video Anthology. Capitol Records, Inc. Hollywood, California.

[34]Paul introduced George to John's skiffle group. George played the song, "Raunchy" for them late one night on the top of a bus to gain admittance to the group.
Vol. 1, The Beatles video Anthology. Capitol Records, Inc. Hollywood, California.

[35]This reference is to the freakish style of dress and demeanor of some British youth at this time in history. Greasy flaps of hair were combed back on the sides of the head and shirts and socks were bright colors. For a more complete description, including destructive behavior, see the following book:
Norman, Philip. Shout!: The Beatles in Their Generation. New York: Warner Books. 1981, pp.31, 32.

[36]This word refers to the way that John used to raise the spirits of the early Beatles when they would become discouraged with their careers. They had a repeated choral conversation in which they would agree that they were going to "the toppermost of the poppermost!"
Vol. 1, The Beatles video Anthology. Capitol Records, Inc. Hollywood, California.

[37]Maggie Mae was a product of Liverpool gossip.
Harry, Bill. The Ultimate Beatle Encyclopedia. New York: Hyperion. 1992, p. 422.

[38]Lewisohn, Mark. The Complete Beatles Chronicles. New York: Harmony Books. 1992, pp.57, 88, 89.

[39]Ringo was quoted as saying about touring, "...it was like 24 hours a day with no break...it never stopped..."
Greenwald, Ted. The Long and Winding Road: An Intimate Guide to the Beatles. New York: Friedman/Fairfax. 1995, p.29.

[40]The meaning of this word in the British sense is drunk.
George Harrison relates this in Vol. 7, The Beatles' video Anthology. Capitol Records, Inc. Hollywood, California.

[41]This fictional character is a reference to the close relationship the Beatles had with the Rolling Stones. George Harrison first recommended them to Dick Rowe of Decca Records when they were playing rhythm and blues in pubs.
Norman, Philip. Shout!: The Beatles in Their Generation. New York: Warner Books. 1981, p. 277.

[42]Interview, Walter Shenson, Aug. 1, 1997, N.C. Museum of Art, Raleigh, N. C.
Interview, Astrid Kirshher, Aug. 9, 1997, Hyatt Regency O'Hare Hotel, Chicago, Ill.

[43]Michael McCartney, Paul's brother, relates Paul and he would buy their Dad a costly Havana cigar for Christmas when they could afford it. The boys enjoyed the wonderful smell created when their Dad would let the cigar burn through lavender he would put on the ashtray.
McCartney, Michael. Remember. New York: Henry Holt and Co., 1992, p.25.

[44]Paul's blue Mercedes, license 900 MPL, routinely has a sprig of lavender on the dashboard. Observation of the author (May 1997 and Nov. 1997) and interviews with fans.

41 John shared his sexual exploits with his friend, Pete Shotton, who played with him in the first band that John organized.
Shotton, Pete and Nicholas Schaffner. John Lennon In My Life. New York. Stein and Day. 1983, p. 94.

[45]Rory Storms' real name was Alan Caldwell. He was a blonde likeable youth who stammered when he talked but strangely not when he sang. He was the leader of the group called the Hurricanes and often did acrobatic feats to thrill the crowds.
Norman, Philip. Shout!: The Beatles in Their Generation. New York: Warner Books. 1981, p. 67.

[46]There are documented cases of John Lennon's violence.
Greenwald, Ted. The Long and Winding Road: An Intimate

Guide to the Beatles. New York: Friedman/Fairfax. 1995, p. 29.
Hertsgaard, Mark. A Day in the Life: The Music and Artistry of the Beatles. New York: Bantam, Doubleday, Dell Publishing Group, Inc. 1995, p. 242.
Miles, Barry. Paul McCartney: Many Years From Now. London: Secker & Warbug. 1997, p. 587, 588.

[47]Paul's father was a cotton salesman.
Burrows, Terry. The Complete Illustrated Story: The Beatles. Italy: Carlton Books Limited. 1996, pp. 16, 17.
Harry, Bill. The Ultimate Beatles Encyclopedia. New York. Hyperion. 1992, pp. 446, 447

[48]This refers to the adult pleasures and dangers the group faced in their German gigs.
Norman, Philip. Shout!: The Beatles in Their Generation. New York: Warner Books. 1991, pp. 90-93.

[49]Neil Aspinall, the Beatles' longest-surviving and current employee, was often sent on errands as well as serving as a body guard, driver, and numerous other functions.
Guiliano, Geoffrey, The Lost Beatle Interviews. New York: Penguin Books U. S. A. 1994, p. 206.
Harry, Bill. The Ultimate Beatles Encyclopedia. New York: Hyperion. 1992, p. 51.
Norman, Philip. Shout!: The Beatles in Their Generation. New York: Warner Books. 1991, p. 276.

[50]This reference is to Brian Epstein's homosexuality, which was illegal as well as considered immoral.
Hertsgaard, Mark. A Day in the Life: The Music and Artistry of the Beatles. New York: Bantam, Doubleday, Dell Publishing Group, Inc. 1995, p. 63. .

[51]Marchbank, Pearce. With The Beatles: The Historic Photographs of Dezo Hoffman. London, England: Omnibus Press. 1982, p. 16.

[52]Bennahum, The Beatles In Their Own words: The Beatles...After The Breakup. London, England. Omnibus Press. 1991, p. 116."Beatle fan magazine", Vol. 1, no. 3 from 1979 press conference with George Harrison.

[53]Paul actually had a car accident on Nov. 9, 1966, which resulted in widespread rumors that he had been killed. Fulpen, II. V. The Beatles: An Illustrated Diary. London. Plexus Publishing Limited. 1983, p. 108, 156-161.

[54]Harry, Bill. The Ultimate Beatles Encyclopedia. New York: Hyperion. 1992, p. 229.

[55]Usually there was an engineer in the studio if they were recording. Geoff Emerick and Norman Smith are two of the engineers they worked with. Some engineers did not want to work with the Beatles because they took too much control of the recording sessions.
Southall, Brian/Peter Vince/Allan Rouse. Abbey Road. London: Omnibus Press. 1997, p. 67, 68, 78, 79.
Taylor, Derek. It Was Twenty Years Ago Today. New York: Simon & Schuster, Inc. 1987, p. 21.

[56]Paul's brother, Michael McCartney is a musician and a photographer. More information about him is available about him in the following book:
Harry, Bill. The Ultimate Beatles Encyclopedia. New York. Hyperion. 1992, pp. 450-452.

[57]The Beatles spent many long hours traveling in a van going from one small town to another for their gigs, often eating, sleeping, and writing songs as they went along.
Marchbank, Pearce. With The Beatles: The Historic Photographs of Dezo Hoffman. London: Omnibus Press. 1982, p. 50
Vol. 2, The Beatles video Anthology. Capitol Records, Inc. Hollywood, California.

[58]John's mother, Julia, was hit by a car driven by an off-duty policeman as she was leaving his aunt Mimi's house, where John stayed. The tragedy affected John deeply.

Harry, Bill. The Ultimate Beatles Encyclopedia. New York: Hyperion. 1992, p. 383.

[59]Brian Epstein had a clipped upper-class accent, was immaculately groomed, wore well-tailored clothes, and had a stiff and formal demeanor. While this description seems to be the opposite of all that John Lennon was, John had been reared with his Aunt Mimi, who had similar characteristics.
Shotton, Pete and Nicholas Schaffner. John Lennon In My Life. New York: Stein and Day. 1983, p. 69.

[60]Strawberry Field(s), a charity home, was a real place in the neighborhood where John Lennon grew up. He attended parties and enjoyed himself there, often sharing his experiences with Paul McCartney as an adult.
Dowlding, William J. Beatlesongs. New York: Simon & Schuster, Inc. 1989, p. 149.

[61]When Ringo became ill and couldn't travel with the group on part of their 1964 world tour, George Harrison was rigidly opposed to touring with a stand-in drummer. George Martin and Brian Epstein convinced him to accept Jimmy Nicol as Ringo's replacement.
Harry, Bill. The Ultimate Beatles Encyclopedia. New York. Hyperion. 1992, p. 484.

[62]The Beatles achieved numerous awards early in their career.
Lewisohn, Mark. The Complete Beatles Chronicle. New York. Harmony Books. 1992, p. 59.

[63]The Grapes was a pub where The Beatles and other Liverpool musicians spent their time having a pint or two. However, this segment of the novel is set in London, so the use of the name The Grapes is a symbolic tribute. Of course the name of the pub they went to in London would have been different.
Shotton, Pete and Nicholas Schaffner. John Lennon In My Life. New York. Stein and Day. 1983, p. 71.

[64]During their touring days, the Beatles rarely had a day off, having 2 or even sometimes 3 commitments in a day.
Lewisohn, Mark. The Complete Beatles Chronicle. New York. Harmony Books. 1992.

[65]George Martin is quoted as saying of the Beatles' special aura, "...the minute the four of them are there, that is when the inexplicable charismatic thing happens, the special magic no one has been able to explain...you'll be aware of this inexplicable presence. It was brotherhood...they had an empathy and a kind of mind-reading business, an almost kinetic energy, such that when they were together they seemed to become another dimension."
Hertsgaard, Mark. A Day in the Life: The Music and Artistry of the Beatles. New York: Bantam, Doubleday, Dell Publishing Co., Inc. 1995, pp. 140-146.

[66]This name was chosen in the story because one of the rumors during the "Paul is dead." era centered around another man named Billy, a William Campbell who had won a Paul look-alike contest. Also, Billy Martin was the name used by Paul McCartney to book studio time following the break-up of the Beatles.
Fulpen, H. V. The Beatles: An Illustrated Diary. London: Plexus Publishing Limited. 1983, p. 158
Lewisohn, Mark. The Complete Beatles Chronicles. New York: Harmony Books. 1992, p. 345.

[67]George was befriended and helped into the group by Paul, who was slightly older. George and Paul became buddies because they rode the same bus to school, which was driven by George's father. They also learned to play the guitar together, using the same book.
Harry, Bill. The Ultimate Beatles Encyclopedia. New York: Hyperion. 1992, p.292.
Hertsgaard, Mark. A Day in the Life: The Music and Artistry of the Beatles. New York: Bantam, Doubleday, Dell Publishing Co., Inc. 1995, p. 20.

Norman, Philip. Shout!: The Beatles in Their Generation. New York: Warner Books. 1991, p. 51.

[68]In Britain, to slag is to argue or strongly disagree.

[69]This passage relates to the theory presented on radio station WKNR-FM on Oct. 12, 1969 that Paul McCartney had died in a car accident in 1966. 'Proof' was presented on the show and large numbers of other fans began pursuing clues that they thought were hidden on record album covers, words and sounds on albums, and images in films. Fulpen, H. V. The Beatles: An Illustrated Diary. London: Plexus Publishing Limited. 1983, pp. 156-161.

[70]Sources have differing opinions about whether Paul McCartney is left-handed all the time or is really right-handed but played the guitar with his left hand. Burrows, Terry. The Beatles: The Complete Illustrated Story. Italy: Carlton Books Limited. 1996, p. 17. Harry, Bill. The Ultimate Beatles Encyclopedia. New York: Hyperion. 1992, p. 453.

[71]This is a motion that Paul McCartney made in the video of "Hello, Good-bye". This video was shown on the Ed Sullivan show but was banned by the BBC because it was lip-synched which went against the British musicians' union. Dowlding, William J. Beatlesongs. New York: Simon & Schuster. 1989, pp.189, 190. "Hello, Good-bye" video. Nov. 10, 1967. Saville Theatre. London. Director: Paul McCartney.

[72]Busloads of people would take tours to see the Blackpool lights in Britain which gave Paul McCartney the inspiration for The Magical Mystery Tour film. Vol. 7, The Beatles video Anthology. Capitol Records, Inc. Hollywood, California.

[73]On Oct. 4, 1961, The Beatles issued their debut single, "Love Me Do." Lewisohn, Mark. The Complete Beatles Chronicle. New York: Harmony Books, 1992, p. 183.

[74]John and Cynthia's child was named Julian and inspired the song "Hey, Jude" by Paul McCartney.
Turner, Steve. A Hard Day's Write: The Stories Behind Every Beatles' Song. New York. HarperCollins Publishers, Inc. 1994, p. 147.

[75]This song, written in 1961 by Paul, was supposedly a message to his girlfriend, Dot. It became number 1 in America almost two years later.
Turner, Steve. A Hard Day's Write: The Stories Behind Every Beatles' Song. New York: HarperCollins Publishers, Inc. 1994, p. 24.

[76]This is a historical reference to the Cuban missile crisis in which President John F. Kennedy forced the Russians to remove missiles from Cuba on October 28, 1962 after much tense negotiation

.

[77]The time and place for the Ed Sullivan rehearsal is correct in this passage.
Lewisohn, Mark. The Complete Beatles Chronicle. New York: Harmony Books, 1992, p. 144.

[78]The Beatles played live in afternoon rehearsal for the first Sullivan show before a studio full of screaming girls.
Vol. 3, The Beatles video Anthology. Capitol Records, Inc. Hollywood, California.

[79]"I Want To Hold Your Hand" was #1 in the U. S. charts when the Beatles arrived in America.
The Editors of LIFE. From Yesterday to Today: The Beatles. Boston: Bullfinch Press. 1996, p. 50.

[80]Louise Harrison, who lived in the mid-western U. S., came to New York to see George play on the Ed Sullivan show. After the doctor examined George, who had an upper respiratory infection, he suggested that since Louise was there she might be the logical one to stay and look after him.

Interview, Louise Harrison, Aug. 9, 1997, Hyatt Regency
O'Hare hotel, Chicago, Ill.

[81]George Harrison was unwell, missed a rehearsal, and
stayed back at the Plaza hotel on Feb. 9 with his sister at-
tending him. He was present for the Feb. 8 rehearsal at 1:30.
Lewisohn, Mark. The Complete Beatles Chronicle. New
York: Harmony Books. 1992, p. 144.
Norman, Philip. Shout!: The Beatles in Their Generation.
New York: Warner Books. 1991, p. 224.
Robertson, John. Lennon. London: Omnibus Press, 1995,
p. 27.

[82]Disc jockeys in New York really did read the temperature in "Beatle" degrees and tell the time in "Beatle" minutes during the Beatles' first visit to America. Paul
McCartney is seen excitedly holding a radio to his ear to
hear the group's music and the deejays using the Beatles
name to describe time and temperature in Vol. 3, The
Beatles video Anthology. Capitol Records, Inc. Hollywood,
California.

[83]This is a direct quote from Victor Spinetti in the film,
The Making of A Hard Day's Night. The police protection
that is described here is very similar to the type that was
needed when the Beatles came to America. Spinetti makes
the point that the Beatles were completely relaxed in the
middle of all this madness or as he described it in the "eye"
of the Beatlemania hurricane.

[84]The Beatles' image was changed considerably by
their new manager, Brian Epstein, much to the chagrin of
John Lennon.
Norman, Philip. Shout!: The Beatles in Their Generation.
New York: Warner. 1991, p. 147.

[85]Several sources mention orgies that the Beatles took
part in when they were in Germany.
Giuliano, Geoffrey. Blackbird. New York: Penguin. 1992, p.
38.

[86]There were at least 100 New York city policemen plus a squad of mounted police trying to control the hysterical crowds of fans surrounding The Plaza Hotel, a usually sedate establishment where the Beatles were staying. The Plaza had issued a statement denying prior knowledge of who the Beatles were before they arrived and stating that they would not have accommodated them if they had known they were a rock and roll group.
Harry, Bill. The Ultimate Beatles Encyclopedia. New York: Hyperion. 1992, p. 527.

[87]John has stated that he didn't know how to respond publicly to death, especially as a youth, and had fits of hysterical laughter with much guilt afterwards.
Davies, Hunter. The Beatles, The Authorized Biography. New York: Dell Publishing. 1968, p. 17.

[88]George's sister had immigrated to Benton, Illinois in 1954.
Lewisohn, Mark. The Complete Beatles Chronicle. New York: Harmony Books. 1992, p. 122.

[89]One of the favorite ruses for fans to get past the policemen guarding the group was to claim to be a relative. Cynthia (John's wife), Julia Baird (John's sister), and Louise (George's sister) as well as others were turned away when trying to reach them.
Guiliano, Geoffrey, The Lost Beatle Interviews. New York: Penguin Books U. S. A. 1994, p. 320.

[90]This scenario is a reference to George Harrison's statement in Vol. 4, The Beatles video Anthology that the only privacy they could find was in the bathroom. (Capitol Records, Inc. Hollywood, California)

[91]After the Beatles returned from Hamburg and began to tour England, the U. S. and other places, the group still had orgies, details of one are given in this reference.
Hertsgaard, Mark. A Day in the Life: The Music and Artistry of the Beatles. New York: Bantam, Doubleday, Dell Publishing Co., Inc. 1995, pp. 92, 93.

[92]Paul is seen as the organizer, motivator, planner for the group, especially in the later years, often with the disapproval of the other band members.
Hertsgaard, Mark. A Day in the Life: The Music and Artistry of the Beatles. New York: Bantam, Doubleday, Dell Publishing Co., Inc. 1995, pp. 266, 267.

[93]Paul takes a "hands-on" approach on his projects. He likes for his music and performance to be "right."
Interview, Geoff Baker, May 17, 1997, Slurping Toad pub, London, England.
This passage is a reflection of Ed Sullivan and Paul McCartney's comments in Vol. 3, The Beatles video Anthology. Capitol Records, Inc. Hollywood, California.

[94]Many sources allege that press members knew the excesses of drink, drugs, and sex that the Beatles had but kept the secrets to ensure their access to the stars and their favors.
Greenwald, Ted. The Long and Winding Road: An Intimate Guide to the Beatles. New York: Friedman/Fairfax. 1995, p. 17.

[95]The Beatles' first appearance on The Ed Sullivan Show (Feb. 9, 1964) was rated as the #4 most memorable television moment in TV Guide: Special Issue, June 29-July 5, 1996, Vol. 44, no. 26, #2257, p. 64.

[96]Burrows, Terry. The Beatles: The Complete Illustrated Story. Italy: Carlton Books Limited. 1996, p. 81.

[97]This is an actual response by George Harrison in an interview when asked what they would do if their fans broke through the police barricades.
Harry, Bill. The Ultimate Beatles Encyclopedia. New York: Hyperion. 1992, p. 345.

[98]Paul was the member of the Beatles who could most annoy/tease Brian Epstein. It is reported that he often took great delight in "pushing his buttons."

Norman, Philip. Shout!: The Beatles in Their Generation. New York: Warner. 1991, p. 298.

[99]Brian Epstein transformed the Beatles from a group of leather-clad, swearing, unkempt rockers to clean, well-mannered, suited performers on stage. He gave them very specific instructions about what they could and could not do to effect a positive image.
Norman, Philip. Shout!: The Beatles in Their Generation. New York: Warner. 1991, p. 147.

[100]Paul and Linda McCartney purchased an estate in Sussex and moved there to keep their daughter Heather (Linda's first child, by a previous marriage) from mixing with a rough crowd in London when she was an adolescent.
Harry, Bill. The Ultimate Beatles Encyclopedia. New York: Hyperion. 1992, p. 446.

[101]Linda Eastman McCartney was the daughter of a wealthy show-business attorney. She grew up in Scarsdale, N.Y. Like Paul, she lost her mother early in her life (Her Mom died in a plane crash when Linda was 18). She met her husband Paul through her rock photography. She and her young daughter, Heather, came to live with him in his St. John's Woods home. They now have two daughters and a son in addition to Heather. Paul adopted Heather shortly after their marriage.
Greenwald, Ted. The Long and Winding Road: An Intimate Guide to the Beatles. New York: Friedman/Fairfax. 1995, p. 32.
Miles, Barry. Paul McCartney: Many Years From Now. London: Secker & Warburg. 1997, p. 506, 507.

[102]Stella McCartney is the second biological child of Paul and Linda McCartney (the third for Linda). Paul thought of the name 'Wings' for his new band while waiting for her to be born (Sept. 3, 1971). Note that this date would not agree with the story. Stella is now a head fashion designer for the Chloe of Paris.
Harry, Bill. The Ultimate Beatles Encyclopedia. New York:

Hyperion. 1992, p. 457.
"The Daily Mail." Thurs., Oct. 16, 1997, p. 40, 41.

[103]"Paul McCartney has sold more records throughout
the world than any other artist."
Harry, Bill. The Ultimate Beatles Encyclopedia. New York:
Hyperion. 1992, p. 457.
"The Guinness Book of Records" presented Paul McCartney "with a rhodium disc to commemorate becoming the
most successful composer of all time; the holder of the largest number of gold discs and the world's most successful recording artist."
Southall, Brian/Peter Vince/Allan Rouse. Abbey Road. London: Omnibus Press. 1997, p. 113.
George Martin praised Paul McCartney's skill as a com-
poser following The London Symphony Orchestra's performance of Standing Stone, a symphonic poem that
McCartney created by using a computer program.
Interview, George Martin, Oct. 14, 1997, Royal Albert Hall,
London, England.

[104]Paul had a troublesome relationship with Brian Ep-
stein because he had the most developed sense of business
and managerial ambitions.
Miles, Barry. Paul McCartney: Many Years From Now. Lon-
don: Secker & Warburg. 1997, pp. 477-480.
Hertsgaard, Mark. A Day in the Life: The Music and Art-
istry of the Beatles. New York: Bantam, Doubleday, Dell
Publishing Co., Inc. 1995, p. 68.
Norman, Philip. Shout!: The Beatles in Their Generation.
New York: Warner. 1991, p. 298.

[105]Paul wanted Apple Corp. to be run more like a business, with financial reports and less money just being
wasted. The Beatles had about two years of turmoil before
they finally broke up. John Lennon likened it to a divorce,
but it was especially painful and nasty because of the extensive media coverage.
Hertsgaard, Mark. A Day in the Life: The Music and

Artistry of the Beatles. New York: Bantam, Doubleday, Dell Publishing Co., Inc. 1995, pp. 250-288.

[106]Paul talked about how he loves all kinds of music and how he feels there should be no barriers between musical styles. He stated that he feels lucky to be paid for doing something he loves.
McCartney, Paul. "Standing Stone press conference." Royal Albert Hall, London. Oct. 14, 1997.

[107]Paul and Linda McCartney celebrated their 28th wedding anniversary on March 12, 1997. They were married at Marylebone Register Office with no other Beatles present.
Norman, Philip. Shout!: The Beatles in Their Generation. New York: Warner. 1991, pp.364, 365.
Linda McCartney stated in an article she wrote for the "Liverpool Echo" (Mar. 10, 1997); "He's not afraid to be a family man and in fact he's done a lot through his music and his ordinary values to promote the family thing of being kind to your kids and giving time to them."
Linda McCartney made her first public appearance in eighteen months (due to cancer) to cheer on her husband at the world premier of his Standing Stone symphony at the Royal Albert Hall, Oct. 14, 1997. She was accompanied by three of their four children. Linda loved the performance, said she was glad to be able to attend, and stressed that she wanted to send her love to my readers.
Interview, Linda McCartney, Oct. 14, 1997, Royal Albert Hall, London, England.